GILDED DREAMS

MEGAN STEER

Star & Wheel
Press

Library of Congress Control Number: 2019915858

Lines from "*Ombra ma fui*" from *Serse* by George Frideric Handel, 1738.

Cover Design: Megan Steer

Cover Images: author's own photographs and images from bigstockphoto.com

Star & Wheel Press

PO Box 168

Berwyn, Pennsylvania

19312-0168

www.MeganSteer.com

DEDICATION

For Paul: do not fade.

EPIGRAPH

*I mean by a picture a beautiful romantic dream of something that
never was, never will be- in a light better than any light that ever
shone- in a land no one can define, or remember, only desire.*
-Edward Burne-Jones

CHAPTER 1

ay 1892, New York City
The butler would not allow me past the entranceway, but I was certain Gabrielle was home. I spied a narrow alley to the side of her house where I could hide, and wait; she would have to come out, eventually. It had been an unusually cool spring, and I pulled my thin shawl tightly around my shoulders. Dusk would arrive in a few hours, and I prayed I would not have to wait that long.

Her house stood at the end of a long block of townhouses, each more elegant than the last. It was the largest construction, looming above its neighbors with five stories of gray stone culminating in a mansard roof and tower overlooking Fifth Avenue. Cast iron balconies decorated the windows on the second floor, and two life-size stone lions stood guard at the front door. A row of rose bushes marked the perimeter of the house, and gas lamps lined the walkway.

Pulling my shawl over my head, I crouched down and leaned against the brick wall. It had been a long, exhausting day, and I closed my eyes, allowing them to rest for a moment.

I don't know how much time passed, but I awoke to the sound of horses' hooves. Cautiously, I leaned around the alley wall and saw a sleek black carriage with gold accents standing in front of the house. A footman opened the door to the carriage, and I left my hiding place.

A statuesque woman in her late twenties appeared between the stone lions: it was Gabrielle. Her figure was still the hourglass ideal, with her dark copper hair swept up loosely in the current fashion. She was resplendent in a gown of watered silk, the color of pale peonies, and she wore a large, cream-colored hat accented with tea roses. Accompanying her was a young woman dressed in similar colors, albeit in a plainer style. She whispered something in Gabrielle's ear that caused her to laugh; I would have known that laugh anywhere. It was both husky and musical, and was one of my most treasured sounds from childhood. Together they descended the stairs as they made their way to the carriage, the butler leading the way.

"Gabrielle!" I called out as I stepped into her line of vision.

The butler was swiftly upon me and grabbed my arm, digging his rough fingers into my flesh. "I told you already that you are not welcome here. Now leave!"

"Gabrielle, it's me! Ava!" I called out again, despite the man who was trying to remove me from my spot on the sidewalk.

Gabrielle's head shot up, and she looked in my direction. "Forrest, who do you have there?" she said, as she walked towards us.

The man stepped in front of me in an attempt to block her view. "I'm sorry, Miss Lyons. This girl came to the door earlier asking for you, and I told her to leave." He glared at me over his shoulder.

Gabrielle ignored his words and pushed past him. Stopping short in front of me, her bright gaze swept over my tattered dress and filthy shoes, at last landing on my face. Her bemused expression changed to one of shock.

"Ava? Is it really you?" She studied my face for a moment, and then pulled me into her embrace before I could answer. "I can't believe you're here."

Like a child, I longed to bury my face into her neck, but feared I would dirty her beautiful dress. I could feel emotion rising in my throat and fought to stay composed. Gabrielle pulled away and rested her hands on my cheeks. "Something has happened. Are you all right?"

My eyes filled with tears, and I found it a challenge to keep my voice steady. "Father is dead, and I need help. I didn't know where else to turn."

Gabrielle's eyes filled with tears, too. "Of course. Let's get you inside, and you can tell me the whole story." She wrapped her arm around me again and began to lead me towards the entrance to her house.

"Gabrielle, your appointment!" called out the young woman in the plainer dress.

"Ah, yes. Monsieur Marcel," Gabrielle said. "Rebecca, take the carriage and go in my place. You know my taste and can pick out fabrics at least as well as I can, if not better."

The young woman named Rebecca all but squealed with excitement. "Of course, Gabrielle. Thank you," she said.

Gabrielle tightened her arm around my shoulders and led me through the front door.

❦

In my fatigue, Gabrielle's surroundings seemed a swirling torrent of opulence. I was aware of high ceilings, gilding, plush carpets, marble, and electric light. She arranged a bath for me and a change of clothes. Her cook, Mrs. Kreisler, brought me a delicious meal, and in between her staff members' attendance, I told her fragments of what had happened since we'd last seen one another.

When Gabrielle and I were finally alone in her private chambers, I sat beside her on a divan and gazed into the fire that burned in front of us. "Everyone's gone now," I said.

"Not everyone." I felt her hand slip over to hold mine.

I smiled at her sadly, and resumed staring into the fire.

"Where is your brother?" she asked. "Surely he would help you; your family was always much closer than mine."

"Rees is alive, but he is not the person I thought I knew." I looked down into my lap and traced my index finger along the floral pattern of the wrapper she had given me to wear. "My father loved me but didn't believe I needed any kind of inheritance."

Gabrielle cocked her head to the side. "That doesn't sound like the man I remember. How long ago did I last see you? Was it after your mother's funeral?"

"Yes, five years ago. After she died everything changed. It was small things at first: my father had one too many drinks now and then. Soon he spent every night at the tavern, and then afternoons, too. Then he and Rees started gambling, and Mother's jewelry began disappearing when we didn't have enough money for food. It was a very bad time." I shook my head, as though that motion would somehow cast off the memories. "I left school when Mother became sick to take care of her. Afterwards, it didn't make sense to me to return for such a short amount of time, so I worked at the cannery."

"Oh, Ava," Gabrielle said. "I remember that awful place."

"It felt like a monster that needed to be constantly fed. At least we were canning fruit, so the smell wasn't terrible. Although I still can't abide the scent of cling peaches," I said, attempting something like a joke. "I lasted there six months, until my father became sick, too, and I had to quit to take care of him."

"Why didn't you write and tell me things were so bad?" Gabrielle said, her voice cracking. "I would have helped!"

"I know you would have. I kept thinking that eventually things would get better. But that didn't happen," I said, as fresh tears filled my eyes.

"What happened after your father died?"

"Father was certain that I would soon marry, and that my husband would take care of me," I said. "What little he had, he left to my brother, and Rees let me know in no uncertain terms that he would not be sharing his inheritance with me ... that I was to find my own way in the world."

"That's appalling. What did he expect you to do? Where did he expect you to go?"

"Do you remember Otis Fleet?" I said. In my peripheral vision I saw Gabrielle nod. "He asked me to marry him, and became quite insistent."

"Oh, no, no, no," Gabrielle said with a shudder.

"I turned him down, of course, but my brother ordered me to marry him. In fact, he conspired with Otis against me and tried to entrap me. I'm almost certain Otis paid him a bride price; Rees wouldn't have cared what happened to me unless there was money involved," I said. The memory of all that had transpired felt like a strange nightmare that belonged to someone else. "I didn't know what to do, but I had your address hidden in my prayer book. So, I left with nothing but the clothes on my back, and used all the money I had to get to the city and find you."

"Do I need to worry about Rees or Otis Fleet showing up at my door?" she asked.

"No!" I said. "They don't know where I went. Mrs. Maubry, the baker's wife, helped me to escape. She knew I was coming to Manhattan, but didn't know where."

"I remember Mrs. Maubry. She was always very kind. I'll see that she is compensated for helping you—without telling her where you are, of course."

Gabrielle reached over and tucked a loose tendril of hair behind my ear. "I remember your beautiful hair, so dark and shiny. When you were a little girl, you were like my doll: delicate and fine-boned. You were what I imagined a fairy would look like," she said while she searched my face. "You still are."

She cupped my cheek in her hand. "I told you once, long ago, that I would always help you, and I meant it. You can stay here with me as long as you wish. I will help you in whatever way you need."

I looked at Gabrielle's pale face in the golden light of the fire, her green eyes filled with concern. She was easily the most beautiful woman I had ever seen, and had the biggest heart of anyone I had ever known. And yet now that I was seated in front of her, I found it difficult to put into words the one question I had come so far to ask.

She saw my hesitation. "What is it, love? You know you can ask me anything. I hope you know you can ask me anything."

I cleared my throat. "I want you to teach me to do what you do. I want to be your protégée."

Gabrielle leaned back without breaking eye contact. "And what is it exactly that you think I do?"

My cheeks flushed, and I looked down at my hands. "I'm not sure what to call your profession, exactly." I waited, hoping she would interject and save me, but she remained silent with a tight smile on her lips. "I know men pay money to be with you," I said. Unable to meet her gaze, I looked around the luxurious room surrounding us. "And they pay you very well."

Gabrielle laughed softly and crossed her legs. "Tell me,

back in Langley Falls, what did they say about my profession?"

"Gabrielle, they said many things. You know there was a lot of ignorance."

"Undoubtedly. But I want to know specifically what they said, so that I know what you think it is that I do."

I did not answer.

"Ava, I assure you, there is nothing that you can say that I haven't heard before," she said, as she rose from the sofa. "What did your brother say I was? A 'whore'?"

"Yes."

Gabrielle paced in front of the fire. "And your father, what did he say? Did he agree with your brother?"

I shook my head. "My father said you were not a whore, but rather a mistress. Rees said they were the same thing."

She laughed and walked back to where I was sitting. "Your father was far closer than your brother, but neither was correct. I am a courtesan."

"How does that differ from a mistress?" I asked.

"Freedom and money," she said and resumed her place next to me. "A mistress is a kept woman, at the financial mercy of one man. A courtesan has a select group of benefactors, of whom she is loyal to all, and faithful to none."

Gabrielle saw the look of confusion on my face and continued. "A courtesan has a very unique position in society. To the men who are my benefactors, I am companion, lover, and confidante. I must be well read, well versed in the arts, and provide an environment that is both serene, and stimulating," she said. "Most of all, I must retain my autonomy: I may feel affection for all, but never love. Is that how you wish to lead your life?"

I nodded. "Very much so."

"Why, Ava? Don't you wish to marry and have children?"

"With whom? Otis Fleet?"

7

"Of course not Otis Fleet! He was a repulsive, vulgar little boy, and I can't imagine that he grew any better with age."

Her description was apt. "I don't have any money, or any family anymore, and therefore, no prospects," I said.

Gabrielle slid towards me on the divan and wrapped her arms around me. "You're so very young. How old are you now? Twenty?"

"Yes."

"You've been through a hideous time and can't see things clearly," she said, brushing her fingers through my hair as I rested on her shoulder. "You'll stay with me as long as you wish, and when you're ready, I will make arrangements to introduce you to the most eligible bachelors in the city. We will find you a suitable husband—that is undoubtedly what your mother would have wanted."

I sat up and turned to her. "No, that's not what I want. I want the kind of life you have. I remember when you came back and visited us when my mother died. You spoke of a life that I didn't think was possible for a woman: with travel, and adventures. That's the life I want! I don't want to be at the mercy of a husband, or brother, or anyone."

"Yes, there are aspects of my life that are glamorous, with all the things you speak of, but I assure you, it is also one of hard work," she said. "I don't know that you'll have the stamina for it. More importantly, I'm protective of you, and I don't want you following in my path."

"I don't mind hard work," I said. "You should know that. We come from the same place and I'm not a child anymore."

"The hard work I speak of is very different from anything you know. It is a life of being stared at, and scrutinized, constantly," she said. "I have far more freedom than most women, yes, but even I am not completely free. Except when I am alone in my own chamber at the end of the day, I must always be available for one of my gentlemen. To be a courtesan also means to live on the fringes of polite society. Do you have the strength for that?"

I lifted my chin and looked directly into her eyes. "Yes."

Her expression changed to one of sadness. "Then this brings me to my next concern: what do you know of intimate relations? Are you a virgin?"

I blushed and looked down at my hands. "I don't think I'm a virgin."

"You don't know?"

"Well, it was all over so quickly, and it was dark. It was against the woodshed behind the house," I said.

I could tell Gabrielle was trying to suppress laughter. "And who was the lucky boy?"

"Lincoln Hanley. Do you remember him?"

She thought for a moment. "A little tow-headed boy, wasn't he? Why, yes! I imagine he turned into a handsome young man."

"He did," I said, "I mean, he is."

"And did you enjoy being intimate with Lincoln? Its brevity notwithstanding."

I felt self-conscious and embarrassed by such personal questions. "Yes."

"What about it did you enjoy?"

"Gabrielle!" I said. "I don't think I can answer that."

"Why ever not? It's a simple question, and one you should be able to answer if you're going to be a courtesan."

"I liked ... being with him," I said. "I don't know why you're asking me these questions."

"My love, I'm trying to ascertain your motives, as money alone is not reason enough to sustain you in the kind of life I lead," Gabrielle said. She leaned forward again and began smoothing the curls that framed my face. "There are many options for young women today that are far less taxing than being a courtesan. For example, neither one of us had a true formal education. We could look into that for you."

She searched my face, hoping to see interest, but found none. "You said you liked being with Lincoln. Specifically, what did you like?" she asked once more.

"I liked the way he looked at me. The way it made me feel."

"You liked being desired."

I nodded my head. "I'd rather be stared at and scrutinized than ignored."

"That is something we share in common," she said, and caressed the back of my head. Gabrielle was silent as she stared into the fire. "In the past, other young women have asked me to teach them, but I've always said no."

I studied her profile and hoped this turn of thought would be in my favor.

"But you are different, and if I were to pass on my knowledge to anyone, it would be you," she said. "So, it seems that you are to begin your education in becoming a courtesan."

I nearly leapt with joy. "Really?"

"Yes, but I say this with reservation. You will begin tomorrow, and I promise, it will be arduous, and not what you expect."

"I understand."

"You are to do all that I tell you to do, for everything has a purpose," she said. "And if it appears that this life is not what you choose after all, I will stand by my initial offer to find a suitable young man for you, or help you to find another profession."

"Thank you, Gabrielle. You'll never know how grateful I am," I said, and leaned over to kiss her cheek.

Visions of my impending poverty and despair vanished. I would be a courtesan.

CHAPTER 2

The following weeks were a blur of lessons in manners, comportment, world events, history, dance, and the French language. I was expected to read at least one newspaper daily, as well as a popular novel weekly (my knowledge of both was tested). Gabrielle also created a list of dictates by which a courtesan should conduct herself, all written out in her flowing hand.

A courtesan is at ease in every social situation, and puts all others at ease, as well.

She is both interested and interesting.

She maintains an air of mystery.

She avoids cloying perfumes.

She glides when she moves and never stomps.

The list was extensive and covered everything from the frivolous (*She avoids novelty hats*) to the serious (*She saves half of everything earned*). I learned it all by heart.

Gabrielle took me to her personal dressmaker, Monsieur Marcel, who made a new wardrobe for me, and to her aesthetician, Mrs. Plumley, who created a strict regimen of lotions and potions to which I was to adhere. I was plucked, buffed, coiffed and a lightly scented cloud of rose attar accompanied me wherever I went.

Most mornings started at six thirty and were spent with one of my assorted teachers. Gabrielle would arise around eleven a.m. and then join me for a late lunch, either at home or in one of the city's fashionable restaurants. A visit to a museum or a stroll through Central Park would often follow. Evenings I spent with her in her chamber before she went out, where she quizzed me about all that I was learning.

Her nights usually began at eight, when she would leave on the arm of one of her benefactors, or she would have one of her legendary parties at home, which I was never allowed to attend.

Life followed this pattern all through the spring and summer: lessons during the day, outings in the afternoon, discussions in her bedroom in the evening. When I had a rare moment to myself, I explored my new surroundings.

Gabrielle's house was a maze of hallways and hidden rooms. She had a taste for exotic marble, dark woods and gilding. She was a master of presentation and loved everything on a grand scale. At first glance, a visitor would think they were in the home of one of New York's titans of industry, but on closer inspection, they soon noticed that all the paintings and sculptures were slightly too suggestive to be in good taste. It was a brilliant sleight of hand: her environment was elegant enough to make her wealthy patrons feel at home, but contained just enough hedonism to remind them that this was not their day-to-day life. They had entered a dream world.

I was allowed to enter the formal rooms on the ground floor during the day, but at night, when Gabrielle was entertaining, they were off limits to all who were not actively participating in her party or serving her guests.

During those times, I moved through the house using the

servants' staircase off of the kitchen. Beyond the drawing room there was a further suite of rooms, each catering to different tastes, fantasies or desires that her guests might harbor. They too had their own separate staircase that connected to Gabrielle's bedroom upstairs. I had not seen any of these rooms, but was told of their existence, and watched Gabrielle disappear through a small door in her chamber when she said goodbye to me as she started her night.

Many nights I lingered in the servant's stairwell, listening to the raucous laughter coming from her party, and filled with longing. And many times, I asked Gabrielle when I would be allowed to attend.

"Be patient, my love. Your time is coming," she always said, before kissing me on the cheek as she swept out the door.

Though I was not supposed to enter the ground floor on nights Gabrielle entertained, I learned soon after my arrival that if I was quick and discreet, I could slip into the library near the grand staircase without being detected. This became my lone rebellion when the walls of my bedroom felt like they were closing in on me.

One night in September I headed down to the library to find a new novel to read. I made my selections and was about to return to my room when I heard the voices of a man and woman outside the entranceway. Gathering up my skirts, I ducked under a Chippendale desk and hid, praying the couple would not enter the room.

"Why do you want to go into the library? None of the fun is in there, I assure you," said a familiar female voice.

Rebecca, I thought, as my pulse raced. When I was first introduced to Gabrielle's assistant, I had assumed we would become fast friends: we were near in age, and both adored Gabrielle. I couldn't have been more wrong. Rebecca clearly resented my living in the house. She was polite, but icy, when Gabrielle was present, and showed me open disdain when she wasn't. If she found me hiding, I could only imagine the tongue lashing I would receive from her—and the glee with which she would report my wrongdoing to Gabrielle.

A deep male voice chuckled. "It's the whisky Gabrielle keeps by the fireplace that I'm interested in."

Their footsteps became louder and I frantically searched the room from my vantage point for a better hiding place.

"We have the same whisky back at the party," Rebecca replied. "Besides, we don't want to miss the fire dancers."

I didn't hear the man's muffled response, but their footsteps became faint and then there was silence. I continued to sit frozen far longer than I needed to, wanting to make sure they were truly gone. The grandfather clock struck midnight and startled me from my stasis. I crawled out from under the desk and swept up my stack of books. Rushing out the doorway, I looked over my shoulder towards the entrance to the private wing but failed to notice what was right in front of me.

"Where are you racing to? Are you late for a test?"

I slammed into something solid that knocked me to my knees, scattering my books onto the marble floor with a loud crash. Pain seared through my legs and I looked up in shock to the outline of a man, his face in shadow.

"I'm sorry," I stammered. "I didn't see you standing there."

"Clearly," he said. His voice was that of the man I'd heard moments earlier. "Are you injured? Let me help you up."

I accepted his hands and struggled to get back on my feet. His sleeves were rolled up to the elbow and I stared at the seemingly perfect form of his forearms. He was dressed in what had been formal attire; the jacket was discarded, and he wore his white shirt unbuttoned at the neck, hinting at a broad chest. Our fingers touched and I felt a heat surge through my body from that simple action. *Who was this man?* I looked up into his face, but in the dim lighting of the foyer it was hard to make out the exact details of him. I saw wavy hair, dark eyes, and full lips that were a contrast to the leanness of the rest of his face. A scar ran the length of his left cheek, but rather than mar what could only be described as a strikingly handsome countenance, it added mystery.

"Have we met? You seem familiar, but I don't believe I have ever seen you here before," he said, seeming to study me as intently as I did him.

His words snapped me out of my reverie. "I'm no one. And you don't see me now."

He grinned. "Don't I?"

"No, you don't," I said, and took the book he held out to me. "I am a figment of your imagination."

"I had no idea I had such a gift for visions. Or perhaps I unknowingly drank absinthe earlier tonight," he said.

I smiled. "What you do in your free time is not my concern."

His booming laugh echoed off the marble walls.

Soft footsteps sounded from behind us, coming from the entrance to the private wing. "Declan! Where are you?" Rebecca's voice bellowed.

I looked up into the man's face again. "Please," I said, "you never saw me, and I wasn't here." Before he had a chance to answer, I grabbed the last book from his hand and hobbled past him to the safety of the servants' stairwell.

The next morning it was announced that Gabrielle would be entertaining a very special gentleman for lunch and my attendance was required.

I wore a lilac day dress decorated with clusters of violets. My hair was swept up in a mother-of-pearl comb carved with swans: a gift from Gabrielle to symbolize my new life.

Gabrielle appeared in cobalt blue silk and looked me over with an approving eye. "You look perfect, Ava."

"Who is joining us today? Is it one of your benefactors?" I felt a flush of excitement. I had yet to meet any of her gentlemen: they'd all been voices in the night, and figures seen at a distance.

She finished affixing a sapphire drop in her left earlobe. "Not exactly. He is one of my dearest friends."

Janie, the head maid in Gabrielle's staff, appeared in the doorway. "Miss Lyons, Mr. Aldridge has arrived."

"Thank you, Janie," she said, studying her reflection in the full-length mirror. "We will be right down."

We made our way downstairs to the solarium. I trailed behind Gabrielle as we entered the room. A tall man stood facing out the windows to the garden beyond. It was a bright, early autumn day, and the sun filtered through the leaves and gave his thick, wavy brown hair a golden sheen. He wore a deep blue suit with silver-gray pinstripes that covered broad shoulders that whittled down to narrow, muscular hips.

"Is it really you, or does the ghost of Declan Aldridge stand before me?" Gabrielle called out.

The man looked over his shoulder with a wide smile. "How could I possibly stay away from you?" he said, and strolled towards her with an intentionally slow gait.

My breath caught in my throat: he was the man from the night before.

Gabrielle laughed and propelled herself into his arms. "You certainly took your time returning!"

They embraced one another and continued the teasing jokes of old friends. She turned from him, but kept his hand locked tightly in her own. "Come, Declan. I want to introduce you to someone very dear to me," she said. "Please meet Ava, my protégée."

Declan let go of Gabrielle's hand. His eyes swept over me but betrayed no knowledge of ever having met me before. For a moment I wondered if perhaps he truly had been intoxicated when I barreled into him and had no recollection of our meeting.

"Ava, how delighted I am to meet you," he said, and bowed without offering his hand, as one did when meeting a lady for the first time. "You are a *vision*."

"Likewise," I said. At the sound of my voice he raised his head. Our eyes locked for a moment and I felt a warmth flood through all the veins in my body. My face grew hot, and I knew my cheeks were undoubtedly flushed. I glanced away from him in an effort to gain composure.

"Come, you two," Gabrielle said. "Mrs. Kreisler has created a magnificent menu for us this afternoon."

We sat down at the table and commenced what was an extraordinary meal. It began with *consommé à l'Adélina* and continued for four more courses.

Declan did much of the talking as Gabrielle peppered him with questions about his life over the last five months. I learned that his family was in shipping, and real estate, and he was a world traveler. He was a marvelous storyteller, and I envied his adventures in far-flung cities, the likes of which I'd only ever dreamed of visiting.

"I am most curious to hear how you two know one another," Declan said, as the dessert plates were cleared away.

I looked to Gabrielle, not knowing what to say or how to answer. In the time I'd been in her home, she had introduced me as her "cousin," even going so far as to give me her own last name. But with Declan, she had introduced me truthfully: as her protégée.

Gabrielle smiled at me, and reached over to take my hand.

"We may speak honestly with Declan. He knows all my secrets."

She turned away from me to face him. "We grew up together in Langley Falls. Our mothers were the best of friends, more like sisters really. Ava is one of the few people who knew Maggie Lionel before she became Gabrielle Lyons."

Declan's eyes widened in surprise. "You've told me so little of your early life."

Gabrielle shrugged. "There is very little of it I wish to remember. Ava is the exception."

"How did you come to be Gabrielle's protégée, Ava?" he said.

She nodded to me with encouragement. "Well," I began, "both of my parents had passed, and I found myself in an unfortunate situation concerning my brother."

He tilted his head, listening.

"Gabrielle was something of a legend in our village," I said, and smiled at her. "She visited my family after my mother's funeral and told me that if I ever needed help in any way, she would be there for me."

"It was the least I could do," Gabrielle said. "You see, Ava's mother, Clementine, came from an affluent background, but she made the unfortunate choice of falling in love with her father's stable hand. Her family disowned her, and she and Ava's father married and moved to our little backwater. But that was my mother's great luck, for the two of them became fast friends. Auntie Clementine taught my mother all that she could. She taught her to read, and gave her books. She in turn taught me. I don't think I would have the life I do now without their friendship."

"What an extraordinary story," Declan said. "And how brave of your mother, Ava, to give up the life she'd known to be with your father."

Gabrielle nodded, and gestured to her surroundings. "This type of environment is what should have been Ava's birthright. I'm just correcting a wrong."

I had a flash of an image from early childhood when my mother took me to visit her own parents. I remembered a grand house, so unlike our own, and meeting an older woman who seemed unfriendly, but looked strangely familiar. We sat in a formal room while my mother spoke to this woman, until at last something was said that made my mother's eyes fill with tears. Seeing her upset caused me to start bawling, and I was quickly banished to the kitchen where the cook, a very kindly creature, dandled me on her knee and gave me treats.

When at last we left the house, I remembered looking down at the gravel beneath my feet, and how much I enjoyed kicking it as we walked. At some point, my mother stopped and knelt down, taking my face in her hands.

"Never forget, Ava, this is the life you are supposed to lead. Always hold your head high," she said.

I didn't understand the meaning of her words at the time, but I memorized them anyway. It was the only time I visited my grandparents.

My eyes filled with tears at the memory, and I looked over to Gabrielle. She had turned her face away from us to look out at the garden, but her expression was a cipher. Her chair sat at an angle, so that the late afternoon sunlight caught in her hair and transformed it into a halo of fire. She looked like a goddess in a painting I had seen on one of our recent museum visits.

"Pardon me, Ava," Declan said, breaking the silence. "But your eyes are the most unusual color I have ever seen." I blushed under the scrutiny of his gaze.

"What would you call that color?" he said to Gabrielle.

"Amber."

"Ah, yes, you're right: amber."

"A few years ago, I knew a Russian count who kept a pied-à-terre near Central Park. He was creating his own version of the czars' famous Amber Room, but on a far smaller scale. More like an amber closet, really," she said. "You can imagine how I longed to see it."

He nodded, bemused. "Of course."

"One evening, he invited me in to see the room, and it was as beautiful as I'd imagined—a glowing jewel of a place. But as I looked around, all I could think of was Ava's eyes, staring at me from every direction!" she said with a laugh that showed pearl-like teeth.

Declan laughed, too. "I can't decide if that would be a glorious sight to behold or a terrifying one."

"Both!" she said, and pinched my arm playfully.

I laughed along with them, realizing how much I enjoyed being the center of their attention. Declan possessed a quality similar to Gabrielle; a warmth, or radiance. It seemed as though colors were brighter in his presence.

Watching their interaction, I became curious as to their relationship. The easy familiarity they shared with one another reminded me of siblings, but Gabrielle had referred to him as a "dear friend." They looked to be similar in age, and I wondered if they had ever been romantically involved. They would certainly have made a striking couple, and I felt a confusing jealousy around this thought.

"Declan," I said, "how do you and Gabrielle know one another?"

"You haven't told her the story?" he asked Gabrielle.

"I only learned of your arrival in the city yesterday—I hadn't the time!" she said. "Rebecca told me you stopped by the party last night, but I didn't see you."

Declan caught my eye. "Ah, then. You should tell the story of how we met as you'll tell the tale far better than I."

Gabrielle took a demure sip of tea, and began. "As you

know, Ava, I left home at seventeen. My mother had died, and my step-father was ... not a topic suitable for lunch. I realized I had no reason to stay, save perhaps you." She reached over and caressed my cheek. The warmth of her palm was startling.

"I don't want this story to take all night to tell, so I will simply say that I left home and made my way to France. Specifically, to Paris."

She had never mentioned Paris to me before. I opened my mouth to ask more, but Gabrielle raised her fingers to silence me.

"I will tell you that tale another time," she said, and resumed her story. "In Paris, I soon found work as an artist's model, as well as a waitress at a higher end *brasserie*."

She raised her eyebrows briefly, and I understood the underlying meaning of "brasserie." I blushed and looked down at my hands for a moment. When I looked up again a dreamy expression had come over her face.

"One day, a tall, elegant man named Albert Aldridge walked into the brasserie during my shift and asked for me by name." She giggled with a delight that reminded me of a little girl.

"Albert had seen a painting that I had modeled for, and was so taken with it that he agreed to buy the painting on the condition that the artist introduce him to me." Gabrielle smiled and shook her head. "It was adoration at first sight for me. He was the kindest, gentlest man I had ever known."

"Uncle Albert was loved by everyone who ever met him ... save perhaps my Aunt Agatha," Declan said to me with a smirk.

Gabrielle ignored his comment. "Albert was very kind, yes, but also a great sophisticate and shrewd businessman. He personally knew the famous courtesans of Paris, the *demi-mondaines*, and saw something in me that I did not see in myself. He sensed that Manhattan would welcome a courtesan to rival the Parisians, and felt that I was the woman to assume that role."

"Our cultures are so very different in this regard," Declan interjected. "My uncle was visionary in his idea, if not outright brazen."

Gabrielle nodded. "Yes, that was my concern when he first suggested I come back to New York with him. In Paris, courtesans were tolerated as a fact of life, if not completely welcomed. I feared that in New York it would be another matter, that I would be openly scorned. Or worse, harassed by the Society for the Suppression of Vice."

I thought of the afternoons when Gabrielle and I dined at one of the more fashionable ladies' tearooms, and the way the other women would whisper about her, or outright glare when they thought no one was looking. I always found it unsettling, but Gabrielle pretended not to notice. She would sit up straighter, and make her smile brighter, until it seemed as though she was the main source of light in the room, and everyone else was in darkness.

"But you came anyway?" I said.

"Yes, darling," she said. "I think I would have followed Albert to Timbuktu, to be very honest. I always felt so safe with him, and he just made *anything* seem possible. He bought this house for me, and made necessary introductions, and my new life began."

Gabrielle smiled at her memory, but a sadness entered her eyes. "Albert was not to be mine for very long, though. He died just over two years ago from heart trouble. But not a day goes by that I don't think of him."

Declan rested his hand on Gabrielle's. "He loved you so, you brought a new vivacity to him," he said, and then turned to me. "Before he died, Albert made me promise to always look out for her, and make sure she wanted for nothing."

Gabrielle rested her hand on Declan's cheek. "And you have. I have never known a finer friend."

Some unspoken message passed between them as they gazed into each other's eyes, and I felt that I had suddenly become a voyeur. Quietly I reached for my tea, and in doing so caused the porcelain cup to scrape against the saucer. The sound roused Gabrielle, and she turned back to the table.

"But enough of these shadows. Albert would not approve of us dwelling on the past like this. 'Life is meant to be lived to the fullest!' was his favorite saying," she said. "So, you see, darling, Declan is to be trusted."

Declan searched my face for a moment, lingering on my mouth before he returned his focus to Gabrielle. "Forgive me, then, for asking this: what exactly does being your protégée entail, Gabrielle? Isn't that Rebecca's position?"

Gabrielle shook her head. "No, Rebecca is my assistant. Although she could easily become a courtesan of her own accord, she says she wants to remain as my employee. Ava is something different: to her I am teaching all that I know, so that she may go out on her own eventually."

"And are you enjoying your studies thus far, Ava?" Declan said as his lips curled to the side in a sardonic grin.

"You don't have to answer that, Ava!" Gabrielle said, and rolled her eyes. "You're incorrigible, Declan."

We all laughed, and soon our conversation drew to a natural closure. As we saw Declan out, Gabrielle hugged him, and then quickly withdrew, but held him at arm's length.

"Do not stay away so long this time," she said. "The city is far less interesting without you in it."

"You needn't worry about that," he said. Then taking my hand, he bowed and raised his eyes until they caught mine. "I intend to see much of you both."

Later that evening I sat in Gabrielle's chamber as she readied herself for the night ahead. Rebecca had left to repair the beading on Gabrielle's gown, but not before glaring at me as I took my seat on the divan.

"Declan was very taken with you," Gabrielle said. "I could tell."

My heart beat faster with these words. I felt an instant attraction to him in a way I had never experienced before. He seemed almost familiar to me. "He is a very charming man," I said in an attempt to sound nonchalant.

She chuckled. "That is an understatement. Declan has the soul of an artist but was born into a family where those sensibilities are not honored—other than by my late Albert, of course. Declan is forever battling his loyalty to them with his loyalty to himself. I think that kind of conflict can be quite compelling to a certain type of young woman. Over the years, you would not believe the scores of girls who have all but thrown themselves at him."

"How did he obtain the scar on his face?" I asked.

"I don't remember the specifics, as it happened before I met him, but I know the incident occurred in Paris, and that it involved a young woman. As you can imagine, it is not a memory he relishes."

I nodded. "And he's never been married?"

"No. Although there have been countless opportunities. I asked him once why he did not marry, and he said simply, 'There are far too many possibilities in this world for me to narrow it down to one.'"

This kind of frank speech shocked me. I had overheard my brother and his friends speaking before, yes, but I knew their words were not meant for my ears, that they didn't know I was listening. That a man would speak this openly to a woman he was not involved with seemed scandalous.

My thoughts must have shown on my face, because Gabrielle turned from her dressing table and studied me.

"You are shocked? Ah, yes, I can see that you are. I suppose I would have been, too, at one time, but that was so long ago," she said, and resumed brushing her hair. "Now, I appreciate his honesty. He said that if he were to marry, he would undoubtedly be unfaithful to his spouse, so it was far better to remain unmarried."

I could see his reasoning. "Were you and he ever involved romantically?"

"Oh, my, no! Perhaps if I had not been with Albert, I might have been tempted, once. But to me, Declan is a family member."

I felt a mild relief, but much of what Gabrielle spoke about at lunch had left me unsettled.

"One thought nags at me, Gabrielle," I said. "You told me from the beginning that I must guard my heart if I want to be a courtesan. That I can't fall in love with my benefactors."

She stopped brushing her hair. "That is true. If you don't fall in love it will make your life that much easier."

"But you were in love with Albert, and he clearly was in love with you. How could he stand to know that you were intimate with other men? And were you comfortable being involved with a married man?" In my fantasy of what Gabrielle's life entailed, it was populated with wealthy widowers and bachelors like Declan. In being a courtesan, I had not entertained the notion that I might become involved with men who had wives waiting for them at home.

Gabrielle looked down at her brush, and stroked her hand across its bristles. "You are so very young. At moments I wonder if I was too hasty in helping you on this path."

I felt my stomach drop at her words, and instantly wished I had kept my questions to myself. "I have displeased you?" I asked, softly.

"No, you haven't. I am just struck by your innocence at times, and that worries me. There are many kinds of marriages, Ava. Albert was already legally wed to his wife when I met him, but it was a marriage of convenience for both. Agatha knew of my existence, and as long as Albert was discreet, and kept her in the lifestyle to which she was accustomed, there was no issue between them. I knew his heart belonged to me, just as mine did to him. When you are certain you possess another's heart, does it truly matter with whom they share their body?"

"I don't know," I said. "I don't think I would like that."

Gabrielle arched her eyebrow. "As I said to you the night you appeared at my front door, the path of the courtesan is not suitable for everyone."

I sensed that this conversation had become a test, and I had not passed.

She turned back to her reflection in the mirror. "All right, darling. I need to finish getting ready."

I was dismissed. "Goodnight, Gabrielle," I said, and left the room.

True to his word, Declan became a frequent visitor. He often accompanied us to our afternoon museum visits, lunches at Delmonico's, and promenades through Central Park. I still felt butterflies catapulting around my stomach every time he spoke to me, and at night when I lay in bed, I thought about him more than I cared to admit. I knew he enjoyed my company, but I sensed that he viewed me as a novelty, or as Gabrielle's favored pet.

Declan's reputation as a rake was well known in New York society, but the Aldridge family possessed such wealth and social standing that his libertine leanings were overlooked.

When the three of us went out, I was acutely aware of the gravitational pull Gabrielle and he seemed to have on the attention of passersby (and on more than one occasion our outings were documented in the scandal sheets). Consequently, I often felt like I was in the shadow of an eclipse. I tried to tell myself that their affection for me was enough; that I didn't need to share their spotlight. But some days it all became too much, and I yearned to be seen for myself and not as their accessory.

It was on one of those days that I rebelled. It was a glorious day in mid-October. The sky was bright blue and sunny, and the temperature was cool, but not yet cold. The leaves were just beginning to turn, and the scent of damp earth and woodsmoke filled the air.

Taking advantage of the magnificent weather, the three of us decided to go for a Sunday drive through the park. It appeared that most of Manhattan had the same idea. The carriage's top was folded back, and we made our way slowly along, enjoying the scenery and watching the people as we passed.

I had not thought it possible, but Gabrielle seemed to have grown even lovelier in the autumn light. All around us the gilded trees echoed back the hues of her hair, and her skin glowed as though lit from within. Declan said something droll, causing her to throw back her head in laughter. I stared at her smooth, ivory throat, and felt a bitter resentment. I averted my eyes, just as something purple fluttered by my peripheral vision. I turned and saw a handsome boy, probably only a few years younger than me, flying a kite in the shape of a wide-winged bird. He was helping a younger boy, who looked like a miniature version of himself, maneuver their fantastical creature. I smiled, appreciating their uncomplicated joy.

At that moment a bell clanged. Beyond the boys, I saw an

older man ringing a large silver bell to bring attention to his cart.

"The ice cream man is here! This will be his last weekend, undoubtedly. Come, let's stop and have some. It will be nice to walk," Gabrielle said. Her cheeks were flushed, and her eyes sparkled. She wrapped her fingers around my upper arm, and squeezed. "Darling, won't this be fun?"

Declan motioned to the driver to stop the carriage, and we all descended.

Gabrielle clearly had purchased ice cream from the man before, and he beamed when he saw her. He also blushed as she spoke to him, and I could tell he was so focused on the beauty of her face that he didn't hear a word she said. I had grown used to Gabrielle's effect on people, particularly men, and I knew this simple transaction of purchasing ice cream would undoubtedly take longer than it should. I turned to look around me.

The park was bustling with children playing and young couples walking hand in hand. Every aspect of New York society was present, from the Knickerbocker families to the newly arrived immigrants. All coexisted in this oasis of green in the middle of the city. I took in my surroundings with wonder.

At that moment, the handsome young man with the kite looked up, and our eyes met. He gave me a wide smile and lifted his hand in a tentative wave. Without thinking, I smiled back and gave my own tentative wave in return. He laughed and then looked up at the kite. I watched it diving in the wind, and suddenly wished that I could join him.

Behind me I heard Gabrielle's lilting voice debate the merits of each flavor with Declan. I didn't look back, but put one foot in front of the other and kept going until I'd reached the two boys with the kite. The older one looked surprised as I approached, but delighted. He had dark, curly hair and a crooked smile. The younger boy, who was definitely his brother, suddenly saw me standing there and looked at me with wide eyes. He said something in what I thought was Italian. The older brother responded, and then turned to me and held out the stick attached to the string that guided their kite's movement.

"You want to try?" he said, with a thick accent.

I nodded enthusiastically. We both smiled at our awkwardness as he passed me the stick. It felt foreign in my hands, and I couldn't remember the last time I'd flown a kite. As soon as I took over, the kite dipped and stopped dancing in the wind the way it had for him. I moved my arms trying to get it back. The older boy saw my struggle, and reached over to help me. I felt the heat radiating from his body as he stood close and noticed the bronze sheen of his skin on the back of his hand. He gazed down at me in the way most men looked at Gabrielle. And then the wind picked up again, and I felt the stick almost wrenched from my fingers. We laughed as we battled to keep it from escaping.

"Ava, it's time to go," said a cool male voice.

Declan stood behind me, an ice cream cornet in each hand. His expression was neutral, but just for a second, I saw him glance from me to my handsome friend and fury passed over his eyes. Farther on the path Gabrielle stood as though she was a statue. Even at a distance I could tell from her posture that she was angry.

"Thank you," I said in a soft voice, as I handed the stick back to the boy. He started to say something in return, but glanced at Declan and stopped. He smiled and nodded.

Declan wordlessly handed me a cornet and we walked back to Gabrielle in silence.

She noticed me briefly as I approached, and then brushed a leaf from the skirt of her dress. "Declan," she said, without looking up. "Will you please bring the carriage around? It's getting late."

Declan left to alert the driver.

Slowly, I licked the ice cream, and kept my focus on the pavement before me.

"What on earth were you thinking in running off to fly kites with those boys?" Gabrielle said.

Her voice was low, so as not to draw the attention of any passersby. I opened my mouth to respond, but Gabrielle continued.

"Ava, if you wish to follow in my path, then you must conduct yourself properly when in public."

Shame, and anger, filled me. The blackberry ice cream didn't taste as sweet.

"All I did was fly a kite!" I said. "You're behaving as though I just ran through the streets in nothing but my chemise."

"You behaved commonly, Ava," she said. "And if you are to be a courtesan, then you cannot be common. You must be impeccable."

The carriage pulled up, and Declan stepped down. He guided Gabrielle in, and then turned to me. The ice cream had begun melting. I had no intention of eating it, and no place to put it. He saw the violet mess slowly snaking down to my wrist.

"I've lost my appetite," I said. Declan took the cornet and discarded it in a receptacle I had not seen. He handed me his handkerchief to clean myself, and then helped me into the carriage.

The ride home took place in complete silence. Occasionally Gabrielle would catch my eye, but I quickly averted my glance and stared at the passing scenery. I felt Declan watching me, too. I looked at him briefly; he studied my face with a combination of concern, and some other emotion that

I couldn't discern.

As we pulled up to Gabrielle's house, she indicated for me to get out first. I said goodbye to Declan, and actually felt relief when Forrest's rough hands helped me to the ground. I stood by the carriage, waiting for Gabrielle to alight. She and Declan said something to one another, but I couldn't make out their words. Forrest helped her descend, and I followed her into the house. Once inside she gave orders to Rebecca to draw her bath. Sensing something was amiss, Rebecca smirked at me before she walked away.

"Please join me in the drawing room, Ava. I'd like to speak with you."

Before I could respond she turned and glided away from me. My stomach was in knots as I followed.

Gabrielle stood by the fireplace, her figure silhouetted against the large bow window behind her. "Ava, I know you feel I'm being harsh, but please remember that I am helping you to cultivate an image," she said. "As I told you, and as I'm sure you've observed, I am scrutinized and held to a much higher standard than most women, so my manners and overall presentation must be faultless."

She ran her hand along the ledge of the marble mantle. "In Paris, the famous courtesans never would have deigned to be seen doing something as common as having ice cream in the park. They knew the importance of keeping themselves scarce," she said. "But we are not in Paris, and I have been more lenient with you."

"I don't understand," I said.

She ignored my comment. "What do we hold most dear? What do we value?" she said, and picked up a small jade bottle. "That which is scarce. That which is rare."

"Gabrielle, I don't understand what being scarce or rare has to do with eating ice cream and flying kites."

"Exactly," she said, and stared at me with a ferocity I had

never seen before. "To be a courtesan at the level that I am, at the level that I want you to be, means to be rare. Men must prove their worth to be with me. To be selected by me is an extraordinary achievement. I will never be found wandering the park and keeping company with strange men. I expect the same discernment from you."

I lowered my eyes and stared at the floor. "I'm sorry, Gabrielle," I said. "I wasn't thinking." It had been an impulsive moment, and felt so innocent at the time. Now I regretted my actions.

Gabrielle replaced the jade bottle on the mantle and stepped towards me. "I know you weren't," she said, and rested her hands on my shoulders. "I see a great future for you; please don't let me down again."

"I won't," I said. And I meant it.

CHAPTER 3

Halloween approached, along with Gabrielle's annual fancy dress party. Since the incident in Central Park, I had put renewed fervor into my studies and made sure that in public my demeanor was indeed "impeccable." So, it came as an upsetting shock when she told me, yet again, that she would not allow me to attend.

"But, why, Gabrielle?" I said. "It's been six months! What do I need to do to prove to you I'm ready? I can tell a salad fork from a fish fork. My dance instructor says I waltz magnificently. I speak enough French now that Monsieur Marcel understands me, and I can converse at length on the work of the Renaissance masters, should anyone care to listen."

Gabrielle heard the desperation in my voice, but remained unmoved. "Are you finished?" she asked and arched her elegant brow.

My shoulders slumped, but I nodded yes.

"I know this must be frustrating for you, darling, but I told you not to question my methods. Everything has a reason."

I cringed at the sound of those words. I'd heard them so many times they felt branded into my skin.

On Halloween night I helped Gabrielle get ready for her party. Her costume was a tight gown of black embroidered lace, and a rich red velvet cloak.

"I'm Little Red Riding Hood!" she said, and twirled around her bedroom.

I laughed at her enthusiasm. "And who is your wolf?"

"That remains to be seen. I'm sure someone will rise to the challenge."

The mood in the household was giddy that night, and I resented that I was to spend it reading. I stayed in my room for a few hours and listened to the sound of a storm gathering outside. The drumbeat of raindrops against the windows added to my agitation, and at the first crack of thunder I realized that I couldn't stand the sight of my bedroom walls any longer. I decided to go down to the kitchen and seek out a sweet.

As I descended the back stairs, I heard a peal of laughter from somewhere within the house. There was a level in the stairwell where one could veer off into the main quarter of the building, or continue down to the kitchen. Normally, I stayed on course to the kitchen, but that night the sound of the party was just too alluring.

I crept silently on tiptoe along the hallway and listened to locate the direction the voices were coming from. Directly in front of me was the top landing of the grand staircase. I peered down towards the entrance: no one was there. Without the bustle of daily activity, the marble-lined foyer reminded me of a tomb.

I lifted my skirts, cursing their rustling sound, and scurried over the landing to the safety of the hallway on the other side. The voices were louder there, and the faint scent of pipe tobacco wafted towards me. I knew at the end of the hallway

I would find a spiral staircase that led down to the private suite of themed rooms. I had made it this far; the task at hand would be to get down the staircase unseen.

Once more I lifted my skirts and began to quietly make my way just as Rebecca's fair head appeared. She emerged from the stairs wearing a pastel, ruffled confection meant to look like a milkmaid, or Little Bo Peep. Her hair was fashioned into a cascade of golden curls with eyelet bows. The look was juvenile, if not altogether unbecoming. I spun around to find a doorway I might duck into, but there were none. I pressed my back against the wall and prepared for the inevitable.

Rebecca approached, her usually pretty face contorted with rage. "You! What are you doing here? You know you are not allowed in this part of the house."

Her lips were rouged, but the scarlet stain was smudged past the side of her mouth towards her jaw. The mother-of-pearl buttons that made up the front of her costume had been fastened in haste, causing her neckline to gape, and exposing a portion of her right shoulder.

"Well," she said, and crossed her arms over her chest when she realized I was staring. "Answer me. Why are you here?"

I smoothed my hands down my skirts, and sought the first lie I could muster. "I am looking for the library. I thought it was in this part of the house."

"You're looking for the library?"

"Yes. Gabrielle recommended a novel called *Jane Eyre* she thought I would enjoy," I said. "I thought I could just slip into the library and fetch her copy without disturbing anyone."

Rebecca smirked. "*Jane Eyre*, you say?"

I broadened my smile. "Have you read it? It sounds intriguing."

"I don't believe your story for a moment. You know you are not supposed to be down here," she said, and was about to say something more when she glanced over my shoulder and stopped. "Good evening, Declan."

I turned around and found him standing behind me at the entrance to the hall. My shoulders dropped. I hadn't seen him since my attempt at kite-flying in the park.

"Good evening, Rebecca. Ava," he said as he strolled towards us. "Has the little lamb lost her way?"

I wasn't sure if this was in reference to Rebecca's costume, or if he had overheard my lie, but Rebecca responded with a cackle.

"Oh, you," she said, and swatted his arm. "Are you coming to the party?"

"In a moment," he said. "I need to speak with Ava. You go ahead."

She hesitated and then turned to me. "Now I don't remember why I came up here in the first place," she hissed. "Just go back to your room." She spun on her heel and returned down the spiral stairs.

I waited until she was out of earshot. "Good evening, Declan. I didn't know you were here tonight."

"I wouldn't miss Gabrielle's annual Halloween party. Why aren't you there?"

"Gabrielle won't yet allow me to attend any of her parties."

"I see."

"Yes," I said. There wasn't anything else to add and an uncomfortable silence took over.

"What do you think of my costume?" Declan asked, in a poorly disguised effort to change the subject.

Declan was dressed formally in a black, cutaway jacket. As I searched his person, the only difference I could detect from his normal appearance was that his hair seemed more neatly arranged, and smoother. He watched my confusion with growing amusement.

"I'm a respectable gentleman!" he said at last and laughed.

It was such a bad joke that I laughed, too, despite my better judgement.

"In all seriousness," he said. "If memory serves me correctly, the first time I met you was in a remarkably similar situation."

He was standing close enough that I could smell the faint scent of his cologne; it was reminiscent of the forest and something slightly sweet and smoky. I found it hard to look him in the eye when he was this near.

I brushed imaginary lint from my skirt. "Yes, that night I had sneaked into the library to gather more novels to read."

"And tonight?"

I was not about to admit I was trying to sneak into Gabrielle's private wing. "I am in need of another novel," I said.

"Yes, I heard. *Jane Eyre*."

I nodded.

"Well then, we can't have the lady wandering all alone in search of Gothic literature," he said, and held out his arm.

I studied his face. He was amused at my predicament, but not unkind. The faintest set of lines had begun to form in the corners of his eyes, which only added to the warmth of his gaze.

He interpreted my pause as confusion, and leaned towards me in a conspiratorial manner. "I'm going to escort you to the library," he said slowly, as if I did not understand his words.

I lifted my hand and rested it in the crook of his offered arm, as lightly as possible. He immediately pulled his arm in, wedging my hand between his biceps and chest. I fought to keep a smile from spreading across my lips.

"Let us be off," he said.

We walked back towards the landing and turned right, down the grand staircase to the first floor. As we made our descent, the arched window over the front door illuminated with lightning, and a clap of thunder soon followed.

"You have chosen a perfect night for *Jane Eyre*, I see," he said.

"I have?"

"Yes. An unexpected storm, the whistling wind, things that go bump in the night: the hallmarks of Gothic literature. All we need now is a strange apparition haunting the halls."

I giggled. "That might be Rebecca."

Declan threw back his head and laughed, squeezing my hand even tighter. "I think you're right."

We entered the library, and Declan released my hand to pour himself a snifter of brandy from the crystal decanter Gabrielle kept by the fireplace.

I began searching for the book amongst Gabrielle's massive collection that stretched floor to ceiling along three walls of the room. The books were arranged alphabetically by author, and I realized quickly that in the fabrication of my lie, I had forgotten who wrote *Jane Eyre*. I didn't want to ask Declan, as I suspected he already questioned the veracity of my story.

Declan settled in one of the leather wingback chairs and sipped his drink. I was acutely aware that his eyes watched my every gesture.

"Why was Rebecca angry with you?" he asked, and swirled the liquid in the glass.

I looked over my shoulder at him and shrugged. "I have offended her in some way. She doesn't like me."

"No. She is threatened by you, as you are far prettier than she'll ever be."

I tried to keep my focus on the book titles as I ran my

index finger along their spines, but a frisson of excitement passed through me.

"I think Rebecca is very attractive," I said. "When her face isn't twisted up in anger."

Declan let out a muffled laugh while he sipped his drink. "Oh, she's very attractive naturally, and possesses many abilities that make her even more so, but she doesn't have the raw material that you do."

My cheeks grew warm. "Thank you, Declan," I said, without turning to look at him.

"It's not necessarily a compliment," he said. "It's what you do with those materials that matters."

All at once my feelings of affection changed to embarrassment. I turned away from him and walked towards the farthest bookcase.

Silence passed for a few minutes. I heard his footsteps and glanced over my shoulder to see him coming towards me.

"Are you having trouble finding it?" he said.

I ignored his question and continued to search. Out of the corner of my eye I saw him place his glass on a small table to my left.

"Here, allow me," he said. I felt him press against my back, as his right arm reached around my shoulders to the bookshelf. His muscular hand closed around a blue-spined book directly in front of me, embossed with the words "*Jane Eyre* by Charlotte Bronte" in gilt script.

I stood still, and for the briefest moment, felt the warmth of his breath against the back of my neck, and the late-night stubble of his jawline as it grazed my cheek. My fingers dug into the bookshelf as I became aware of the sound of my own heartbeat. I was certain he buried his face in my hair, just for a second, and inhaled, and then the moment passed.

I felt him step away, giving me just enough room to turn around. As I faced him, he did not smile at me in the playful way I had expected, but stared with a meaning I didn't totally comprehend.

"Your book," he said, and held it up.

I took it from his hand. "Thank you."

We were standing so close as to almost be touching. He didn't make a move to step away from me, but leaned to the side to collect his drink.

He lifted the glass towards my lips. "Would you like a taste?"

The intensity of his gaze was too much, and I looked down towards the floor. "No, thank you."

"Pity," he said, and drained the contents of the glass as he walked away. He moved towards the entrance to the room and deposited the snifter on a tray as he passed. "Let us get you back to your side of the house, and I will return to the party."

I realized I was standing with my back against the bookcase, holding the copy of *Jane Eyre* pressed to my breasts.

"Shall we?" he said from the doorway, and held out his arm.

"Yes, of course," I said, and hurried to join him.

We made our way back up the grand stairs, and he escorted me as far as the servants' stairwell.

"Now, I assume you know how to get back to your room from here?" he said, flashing the same broad smile as he had initially.

I still felt flustered. "Yes, thank you, Declan."

He bent over and kissed my hand, lingering for a moment longer than necessary. "Then I shall bid you good evening," he said, and bowed.

He turned and walked across the landing, down the hallway to the spiral staircase. I watched until he disappeared from view, and then raced back to my room.

CHAPTER 4

The following weekend, Gabrielle was to spend Saturday night at the home of one of her benefactors, a widower renowned for his wealth, as well as his eccentricities. Every November he threw a lavish party with Gabrielle as his hostess. She and Rebecca would set out for his home on Saturday morning, and then return the following day. The prospect of this delighted me: it was the first time since my arrival that I would have a day all to myself.

"I do hope you will use today productively," Gabrielle said, as she put the finishing touches on her traveling ensemble. "Practice your French, perhaps? Aurelie, who assists Mrs. Kreisler in the kitchen, is fluent. I'm sure she would be all too happy to converse with you."

"Yes, I have spoken with Aurelie before," I said, and tried to keep resentment out of my tone.

"Good, then that's settled." Gabrielle picked up her hat, a velvet toque of pale, cerulean blue, and placed it on her head. "Will you help me, darling? Rebecca is already downstairs."

She handed me a long gold hatpin. Its end was carved with a gryphon clutching an amethyst orb in its beak.

"Where would you like it placed?" I asked, and stood behind her as we both faced the full-length mirror.

She pointed to a spot above her right ear, and I went to work, attempting to slide the pin in between her hair and the velvet without stabbing her scalp in the process. "There," I said, proud of my handiwork. I stepped back and looked at Gabrielle's reflection in the mirror, but she didn't look at herself; she was staring at me.

"How beautiful you are, Ava," she said, as though viewing me for the first time. She turned to face me and placed a hand on either side of my neck. "You have always been pretty, but you have truly bloomed in the months since you've been here." Her right hand slid up and caressed the side of my cheek, sending shivers down the backs of my arms. "The fineness of your skin, your rosy mouth. You are like a porcelain doll. The man you end up choosing will be very lucky indeed."

I blushed, and tried to look away, but she held my chin with her thumb and forefinger. "You need to be more confident in your beauty." She stepped to my side so that we both faced the mirror at the foot of her bed as she wrapped her arm around my waist. "Look at yourself."

My mother had raised me to be clean and neatly presented on all occasions, no matter what I wore. She told me, "Kind thoughts and good deeds are the true beauty secret." And that my inner light would shine out to all who met me, *etc., etc., etc.*

But in Gabrielle's house of opulence I couldn't turn a corner without being met with another towering edifice of mirrors. Some might have viewed it as a sign of Gabrielle's vanity, but I saw it as an occupational hazard. Part of her job requirement was to be comely, and one day it would be mine.

Every time I passed my reflection it seemed to either confirm my assets or highlight the lack thereof. Never in my life had I spent so much time dwelling on my looks as I had in the past six months.

I stared at the young woman facing me: she had dark chestnut hair, pinned up loosely, framing a heart-shaped face with large, golden brown eyes. Gabrielle was right; something about my appearance had changed. My face had become fuller, leaving behind the wan quality I always seemed to possess, and my cheeks, once sallow, were pink with health. My body was fuller, too, with more significant curves than I'd noticed before. I looked at my reflection as if seeing myself for the first time. I was surprised by what I saw: I was beautiful. It was like discovering a marvelous secret, and a ripple of pleasure radiated through me.

I glanced away from my reflection to Gabrielle's, and the spell was quickly broken. She was who I wanted to be, and it didn't matter if I was now beautiful, as she would always be more so.

Unaware that my mood had shifted, Gabrielle pulled her arm tighter around my waist.

"Look at us, the fairest lilies in the field," she said, beaming. She rested her head on top of mine and sighed with pleasure.

I bristled.

At last she broke away. "All right, enough of my procrastination. I must go."

I accompanied her down to the front door where the carriage was waiting out front, along with Forrest.

"I'll see you tomorrow," she said, and hugged me goodbye. "If you must leave the house to get some air, please ask Janie to accompany you." This command, disguised as a request, was tossed over her shoulder as she walked out the door.

"Of course, Gabrielle," I said, forcing a smile. I waved as they pulled away.

Janie appeared and asked if I'd like an early lunch. I thanked her, but declined, and returned to my room.

A range of emotions roiled inside of me. I loved Gabrielle and was grateful to her. She had taken me in, fed me, given me clothes, and opened up a whole new world to me. A whole new life. But in my desire to live a life of freedom, I had unwittingly entered one of even more restrictions. Usually, Gabrielle treated me as her equal; but there were times, as of late, when I felt as though she was my governess, and I her willful charge.

Then there were my feelings for Declan. I did not want to fall in love with anyone; if I was to be a courtesan, I needed to engage with more than one man. But since our exchange in the library Halloween night, I could not imagine anyone other than him. All others paled in comparison.

I paced the room, looking out my window into the walled back garden. I didn't even have a view of the street, or city beyond: just more of Gabrielle's controlled world. A wave of bitterness swept over me, and the air felt stifling. Quickly, before I could reason myself out of it, I put on my coat and affixed my hat and raced down the stairs. I decided to use the front door. With their mistress gone for the day, I suspected most of her staff would congregate in their quarters near the kitchen.

"Are you going out, miss?" a voice sounded behind me.

I turned to see kind Mrs. Kreisler, the cook, standing in the foyer and smiling.

"Yes," I said.

Mrs. Kreisler stepped towards me, wiping her hands on her white apron.

"Does Miss Lyons know you're going out alone?"

I looked into her pale eyes, so honest and good, and the elaborate lie I had planned soon vanished.

"No, she doesn't," I said.

Mrs. Kreisler tilted her head with concern. "I don't know that she'd want you to, would she?"

"Please, Mrs. Kreisler," I said, "I haven't done anything on my own in months. If I don't go out for a little while today, I might go mad. Please don't tell Gabrielle."

Mrs. Kreisler chuckled. "I understand. We'll make a deal: promise me that you'll be back before dusk, four o'clock, let's say, and I'll pretend that you've spent the day upstairs, studying."

"Thank you, Mrs. Kreisler. I will be back by four, I promise."

She nodded and saw me out, closing the door behind me.

Outside on Seventy-Sixth Street, I turned right, towards Fifth Avenue, and decided to walk downtown. I had no idea of what I would do, or where I was headed, I just liked the idea of this temporary freedom. The autumn air was brisk, and the sunlight filtered through the trees, creating dappled patterns on the sidewalk.

I crossed over to the Central Park side of Fifth Avenue and continued walking, lost in my own thoughts. I had walked just over ten blocks when a regal, black brougham pulled up alongside the sidewalk and stopped. The door opened and out stepped Declan, wearing an elegant navy suit and overcoat with a trilby hat.

"Good morning, Ava," he called out. "Are you off to fly kites?"

His sudden appearance startled me. I was both elated to see him and annoyed by his greeting. As I drew closer, I saw that his lips were curled into a mischievous grin.

"Good morning, Declan," I said, "I have today off from my studies, and I am taking a walk."

His expression changed to one of concern. "Unaccompa-nied? Or is Janie hiding in a bush nearby?"

"Not that it is any of your concern, but Gabrielle is gone for the day and I'm taking a walk by myself."

Declan studied me for a moment. "Would you like to accompany me on an errand?"

"What kind of errand?"

"There is an artist whose studio I need to visit. After-wards I'll take you to lunch. How does that sound?"

I was so thrilled, I could have cried. "That sounds perfect."

"Excellent," he said, then paused. "There is the issue of a chaperone. It won't do for you to be seen around town unac-companied with a bachelor. I suppose we could stop by Gabrielle's and see if anyone is available to join us."

That was the last thing I wanted to do. "Declan, do you have plans to lead me down the path of moral turpitude this morning?"

His eyes crinkled with amusement. "My schedule is already quite full—I haven't left time for debasement today. Perhaps tomorrow."

We stood facing one another, trying not to laugh.

"Fine," he said at last. "Get in the carriage. We won't bother with a chaperone. Somewhere my grandmother is spinning in her grave."

Declan motioned to his driver and helped me into the vehicle.

As I took my seat, I admired the beauty of the interior. It was outfitted in gleaming mahogany and burgundy velvet cushions embroidered with the Aldridge family crest in gold thread. This was the first time I'd seen Declan since Halloween night and I felt both excited and shy to be sitting with him in such a confined space.

"Providence has smiled upon me that our paths would cross this morning," he said, as the carriage began moving.

I smiled at his compliment. "Where is this studio?" I asked.

"Tenth Street between Fifth and Sixth Avenues."

"Tenth Street?" I said. "I've never been that far downtown before."

"Really?" he said.

I nodded.

"Gabrielle has kept you rather cloistered, hasn't she?"

"I hadn't thought of it in quite those terms, but yes."

"Has she told you why? She undoubtedly has a reason," he said.

"Yes," I said. "She told me that if I wish to follow in her footsteps then I must keep myself 'scarce' and appear 'rare'."

"Ah. She knows whereof she speaks, but that must be frustrating."

"Yes," I agreed. "Especially in a city like this, when there is so much going on right outside the door."

"But I've been on outings with the two of you: to the Metropolitan Museum, and the Natural History Museum."

I nodded. "Oh, yes. I've had vast exposure to the museums, and Central Park, and her dressmaker, and hairstylist, and many restaurants, but I don't get to go out after dark, and I've yet to attend one of her parties. My most exciting outings thus far have been our lunches at Delmonico's."

"Lunches at Delmonico's are exciting to everyone," he said with a chuckle. "As for her parties, they are entertaining, I won't lie. I'm sure you'll be invited in time."

"She says I will be. It's almost painful to hear all the festivities at night when I'm not included."

"I take it, then, that Gabrielle does not know you've gone out by yourself today," he observed.

"Mrs. Kreisler knows. I promised her I'd be home by four o'clock."

"I see."

We both remained silent. I stared out the window and watched the buildings pass to my left. Declan gazed out his own window, as Central Park passed by in a riot of autumn color. The carriage swerved, causing him to slide into me until our sides were pressed against one another. Neither one of us moved away.

I looked down to my hands and smiled, trying to think of something else to say.

"I won't tell Gabrielle of our outing today, and I'll ask you to keep a secret for me, too," he said.

"Of course," I said. "Anything."

"I'm taking you to meet my friend, George Montgomery Tilton. He's the artist who painted the portrait of Gabrielle that hangs above the fireplace in the drawing room."

I knew the painting immediately: it portrayed her wearing a Japanese kimono and golden silk slippers with pointed toes. She reclined on an emerald green, velvet settee; her red hair cascaded over her shoulders, and a pile of lilies lay on the ground at her feet.

"Gabrielle has shown me that painting," I said. "It's beautiful and a true likeness of her. She said that it caused the artist who painted it a great scandal."

"Yes, it certainly did," he said with a grin. "Up until that point, George painted portraits of society women. His work was always very good, but quite formal. Then he painted Gabrielle in a much more expressive manner. His critics were in shock to see this change in style, but also of subject matter —that he painted a courtesan."

The carriage hit a bump in the road, and we both jolted upwards. Declan's arm shot out reflexively across my body and his hand rested on my thigh.

"Are you all right?" he said, as he retracted his hand.

"Yes," I said, feeling flustered. I couldn't turn my head to look him in the eye.

"Be careful, Edwards!" he called out as he rapped on the window in front of us. The faint voice of his driver called back an apology.

Declan continued with his story. "But that scandal was a boon for George; suddenly everyone wanted him to paint their portrait. With that one painting, he had tapped into his clients' most secret desires: to be seen as sirens or goddesses to be worshipped. Or, in the case of the men, as brave adventurers."

"And is he painting your portrait?" I asked with a sly smile. "Is that why you're visiting him today?"

Declan laughed. "No. I've had more than my fair share of adventures in this life—I don't need George to create that image for me," he said, and lightly touched my hand with his fingertips. "This is where I need you to keep my secret: I have commissioned George to paint a portrait of my uncle Albert for Gabrielle."

"What an extraordinary gift!" I said.

"George was the artist who brought Gabrielle and Albert together years ago in Paris. And my uncle commissioned him to paint many portraits of Gabrielle, but never one of himself, much to her disappointment."

A leaf fluttered in through the window, landing in Declan's lap. He reached down and held it up for me to see. "A maple leaf," he said, and brought it closer towards him to study. "Its color reminds me of your eyes."

The leaf was a golden brown and did remind me of amber. He tucked the leaf into his breast pocket, behind the square of russet-colored silk that resided there. We held each other's gaze for a few moments, but I was the first to look away and resume watching the passing cityscape.

At last the carriage stopped at a busy intersection. Declan helped me down and rested his hand on the small of my back. He instructed Edwards to return home as we would flag down a hansom for our return trip.

"Come, let's go meet George, and I will introduce you to the bohemian heart of New York," he said.

Between the reassuring pressure of his hand at my waist, and the warm timbre of his voice, I felt a buzzing sensation ricochet through all the veins in my body, making me ebullient and light. His hand remained on my back as he guided me towards an unassuming red brick building on the north side of Tenth Street. Declan rang the bronze door bell, and an elderly manservant ushered us into a vast studio, the likes of which I had never seen before.

The walls ran two-stories high with a mosaic of skylights in the ceiling above, bathing the space in ethereal, late morning light. Structurally, the walls echoed the red brick of the outside façade, but throughout the room, portions were draped in luxurious, jewel-toned fabrics in a multitude of prints, or affixed with wide swathes of elegant wallpaper, also in varying patterns. The furniture was a happy jumble of intricately carved armoires, tables and assorted chairs. I recognized the green velvet settee from Gabrielle's portrait off to my right, with a stuffed ostrich standing guard to its left. Surfaces overflowed with metal urns and bowls, exotic instruments, and bejeweled artifacts that I couldn't identify. It looked as though giant hands had taken sections of the Natural History and Metropolitan museums and shaken out the contents at random.

"The prodigal son has returned at last!" called out a loud voice.

I turned to see a tall, imposing man emerge from behind one of the tapestried drapes. He wore a long gray smock over dark trousers; the hems of both were edged with what looked to be small splatters of dried paint.

He let out a booming laugh and outstretched his arms as he walked towards Declan. They embraced, and he slapped Declan multiple times on the back. "I feared we'd lost you to the wilds of Zanzibar ... or the arms of a pretty little bonbon in Montmartre."

I clapped my hand over my mouth to keep from laughing; Declan's friend George clearly had not seen me.

Declan cleared his throat and gestured towards me with his eyes. "Ava, allow me to introduce you to my friend, and avowed lech, George Montgomery Tilton."

George turned around, and showed visible shock to find me standing there. "Please forgive me, miss. Whatever lechery resides within me is greatly exaggerated by Mr. Aldridge."

The great artist walked towards me and clasped my hand between his giant paws. He was an attractive man of about forty, with close-cropped dark hair peppered with silver, and a neatly trimmed beard and mustache to match. His eyes were a warm brown against a bronze complexion, and his overall presence seemed joyful, and extremely gregarious.

"Ava, what a pleasure it is to meet you," he said, and did not let go of my hand.

Declan joined us. "Ava is Gabrielle's cousin."

"No," George said, and looked from Declan back to me. "Dear God, the Lyons must be the most gorgeous family in the world."

I couldn't contain myself any longer, and burst out laughing. "It's lovely to meet you. I so admire your portrait of Gabrielle on the green settee."

George appeared to not hear me, and studied my face with great concentration. "Come here into the light, let me see you better," he said, and began to pull me towards a brighter spot a foot away.

"George," Declan said in mock anger, "Ava is not your subject. I must return her to Gabrielle unmolested."

George waved his words away. "You have kept this glorious creature hidden from me—I will have my time."

In the light, he studied me at various angles. From anyone else this behavior would have been horrifyingly rude, but George seemed kind, and so genuinely excited about the mere existence of my face that I was flattered.

Declan wasn't nearly as pleased. "Do you want to paint her as an *odalisque*, George?" he said, and crossed his arms over his chest in irritation. He obviously had witnessed this act before.

"No," George replied, not taking his eyes from me. "Gabrielle is the odalisque. Ava, I would paint as the fairy queen, bewitching all who cross her path."

"As a child, Gabrielle always said I reminded her of a fairy," I offered.

George nodded thoughtfully, with downcast eyes. "She would. She is the wisest of us all." At last he let go of my hand, and turned away from me, towards Declan. "And why have you not drawn, Ava, sir? What is your excuse?"

"You're an artist?" I asked. I realized I did not know Declan well, but this seemed a completely unforeseen facet of his personality.

Declan let out a surprised laugh. "No, George is the artist. I used to scribble."

"Do not listen to him, he is being modest. Years ago, Declan made elegant, lyrical portraits in pen and ink. They were truly very good," George said, and walked over to his friend. "Not as good as mine, of course, but then, whose are?"

Declan clapped George on the back. "If you weren't so talented, you would be completely insufferable."

"I see you've spoken to my wife recently," George responded.

"Where is Charlotte?" Declan asked. "Is she here?"

"No, she and the children are visiting her mother in Connecticut. I know she will be sorry to have missed you."

"Will she be back in time for Gabrielle's party on Thursday?"

"No, unfortunately not," George said.

"Gabrielle is hosting a party for George this coming Thursday," Declan said to me. "She knows he'll be unveiling a new piece, but she doesn't know that the piece is for her."

"She will be so moved," I said, and already felt depressed that I wouldn't be there to witness the unveiling.

"Ah, that reminds me," Declan said. "George, when you meet Ava at the party, you must pretend it is the first time. Gabrielle doesn't know that I brought her here today, and I want to keep it that way."

George mimed a locking motion over his lips. "I won't say a word."

"The party?" I asked, but Declan knew what I was really trying to communicate: that I wouldn't be invited.

"You will be there," he said, and rested his hand on my upper arm.

"Of course you will be there!" George added. "Now we should attend to your reason for coming all the way down here. Declan, I'll take you in the back to see the piece. Ava, you must forgive my superstitions: I don't allow anyone who hasn't been involved with a painting from the beginning to view it until I feel it is finished."

"I understand."

"But I don't want you to be bored, so come over here with me," he said, and led me towards a large, throne-like chair carved with gargoyle's faces, and with a tufted, blue velvet cushion. "Have a seat here …" His voice trailed off as he rummaged in one of the armoires.

I sat down on the chair and rested my arms on its elaborate armrests. The seat was so high that my feet dangled off the ground like a child's.

"Ha! Here it is!" George said with triumph, and handed me a thick leather album. "I thought you might enjoy seeing photographs from my time in Paris. You will definitely recognize some of the faces."

"Is there anything in there that I will regret her seeing?" Declan asked.

"Of course! What fun would it be for her if there wasn't?" George said.

Declan shook his head, and leaned over me. "This won't take long."

I smiled up to him. "Take all the time you need—I suspect this will be very entertaining," I said, and tapped the album with my index finger.

"That's what I'm afraid of." He touched my arm, and then they both disappeared behind one of the fabric panels.

The cover of the album was chocolate brown leather, embossed with swirls of gold paint and the word *Souvenirs*. I turned the deckled pages and saw pretty photographs of city blocks and flowers. And then a group of young men congregated around a table, laughing. The ceiling above them slanted in such a way that it looked to be a garret apartment.

The pages went on like this: scenes of attractive people I didn't know and places I'd never been, until at last I recognized a young man's face—Declan. It looked to be in the same garret space as the previous pictures, but he was photographed alone, seated on an upholstered chair with one leg resting on the other. He wore a button-down shirt, the sleeves rolled up to his elbows. On his leg balanced a pad of paper, and in his right hand he held a pen. At the angle in which the photograph was taken, I could see there was a drawing of some sort on the pad. His head tilted down as he focused on the image before him, his expression one of complete concentration. I stared at this photo longer than the others and traced my fingertip over the muscles in his forearms.

I turned the page, and the album became more intriguing. The first photograph was of Declan again, but this time seated on a wooden chair in an entirely different room. A fleshy young woman sat on his lap, wearing what looked to be a performer's costume. It was sparkling and ruffled, and her skirt was short, showing her stockinged legs, from her knees down to her laced boots. She had fair, curly hair and a mischievous grin for the camera. Her arms were thrown around Declan's neck, and his arms clasped about her waist. He studied the camera with a mysterious expression: neither happy, nor unhappy. His lips curved slightly as though he were about to ask a question. It was then that I noticed: he did not have a scar on his face.

Seeing him in the arms of this woman gave me such a strange mixture of emotion; a funny sense of possessiveness, but also curiosity. I wondered who she was.

The pictures that followed were of other women, all dressed like the blonde on Declan's lap, laughing, drinking, and then finally, performing a dance. And then a picture of the most curious building I had ever seen. It was an entrance that appeared to be a mouth: fanged teeth framed a wooden doorway, above which was carved a stone nose, and glaring eyes. The whole front of the building was sculpted in such a way as to appear as though it was melting, or dripping, like wax from a candle. I leaned over and made out the words hung above the entrance: *L'Enfer.* "Hell", if my newly acquired French was accurate.

The next photos appeared to be taken inside this place

called Hell, as the walls had the same dripping quality, and were decorated with stone demons, or gargoyles. I realized it was a café, with patrons seated at square tables beneath the sneering creatures. The largest photo on the page focused on a man and woman seated in front of the photographer. The man was Declan, and he leaned forward over the table, caught in mid-laugh with his eyes closed, the image slightly blurred from his movement, but I could see the angry scar now marked his face. To his right was Gabrielle. She was elegantly dressed in a dark, fitted jacket and feathered hat. Her hands were raised in a defensive gesture and her face contorted in mock terror as if the stone gargoyle above her was about to attack. I laughed at their antics; even in these black and white images from years ago, Declan and Gabrielle seemed filled with color and larger than life.

"Any discoveries you'd like to share?"

I nearly jumped. I had become so engrossed in the picture album that I didn't hear anyone re-enter the room. I looked up to find Declan staring down at me.

"No," I said. "But I do have a question."

"Even better!" George bellowed as he entered the room, drawing the curtain behind him.

"What is this 'Hell Café' you all went to?"

Declan laughed. "*Le Cabaret de L'Enfer*, I presume?"

I nodded.

"Actually, I think I prefer the name 'Hell Café', Ava," George said, as he collected the album from my outstretched hands. "You might be on to something there."

He crossed back to the armoire and opened one of the drawers, placing the album within. "It was a fun, and somewhat naughty café in Montmartre we would visit from time to time. So many of the cafés and cabarets were named after occult conventions, it got to the point that if you weren't going to a place where you could have a drink and theoretically conjure a demon, was it even worth going?"

We all laughed.

"We should leave you and let you get back to your work," Declan said, and helped me from the chair.

George approached and I held out my hand. "It was lovely to meet you, George. Thank you for sharing your photographs."

He looked down at my outstretched hand and laughed. "Nonsense, Ava! You are family now," he said, and kissed me gently on either side of my face. "I look forward to seeing you again on Thursday."

"That's right," Declan said. "But remember: you have never met Ava before. Your introduction at the party will be the first time you have ever laid eyes on her."

"Ava? Who is this Ava you speak of?" George said, and hugged Declan goodbye.

Back out on Tenth Street, we turned left and began walking east.

"You certainly made an impression," Declan said.

"He's delightful," I said with a chuckle.

"Yes, he is. For all his bluster, he's one of the most genuine people I know. He has painted everyone from kings to dock workers, and he treats everyone the same."

"Are you pleased with the portrait?"

"It's magnificent. George poured himself into this piece; it's more than I could have hoped for."

"I look forward to seeing it," I said.

"You need only wait until Thursday," Declan said. "You will be at the unveiling."

I sighed. "I hope so, but Gabrielle might not allow me."

Declan stopped in the middle of the sidewalk and held my elbow. "You will be at the party—I will ensure that you are. Do not give it a second thought."

His eyes bored into mine with such intensity that I knew better than to argue. His gaze swept down to my mouth and I smiled. I felt mischievous, too, and I tilted my head closer to his as though I wanted to whisper something in his ear. He leaned down.

"Where are we having lunch?" I asked.

Declan's eyebrows raised in surprise. "I see that you have your priorities in order."

"I take lunch seriously."

"As well you should," he said, and took my hand and placed it in the crook of his arm as we began walking again. "I am taking you to a little Viennese café about a block from here."

We walked along Tenth Street until we reached Broadway, and Declan began to steer me left. Just as we were about to turn, I spotted one of the loveliest buildings I'd ever seen.

"Oh, Declan! What is that church?" I asked, as I stared rapt at the towering marble spires.

"That is Grace Church, where yours truly was christened thirty years ago," he said.

"It's beautiful. It reminds me of a castle out of a fairy tale."

Declan cocked his head and looked with intent. "It's so familiar to me that I forget the beauty of its structure."

I glanced back up at him. Declan was undeniably handsome in a classical way, but between his wavy brown hair rustled by the wind and the scar running the length of his cheek, something about him seemed almost feral. Despite his hat, a lock of hair had come loose on his forehead; I fought an urge to reach up and touch it.

"You know, I somehow can't envision you in a church," I said.

"Ah, then my history precedes me. Do you think the

marble would crumble if I set foot inside? That the altar would erupt in flames?"

"No, nothing like that. I guess that when I think of you, it's somewhere more exotic or bohemian, like George's studio. Not anywhere as mundane as a church."

"And how often do you think of me, Ava?"

My blushing alone told him all he needed to know. He didn't wait for me to answer.

"Come then, the café is right here," he said.

As we approached the entrance, a middle-aged woman with jet black hair emerged, followed by three younger women who looked like copies of her. They all wore large, elaborate hats, overflowing with flowers and feathers; they reminded me of full-blown peonies struggling to remain upright under the weight of their blossoms.

"Why, Mr. Aldridge! What a surprise!" the older woman said and outstretched her hand.

Declan took it and nodded his head. "Mrs. Dalton. It's lovely to see you and your daughters."

"We stopped to have Mrs. Baeder's torte before we returned home."

"It is my favorite!" said the tallest of her daughters.

"You have excellent taste, Miss Dalton," Declan said. "It is the finest in the city."

The young woman blushed a deep scarlet at his words and became glassy eyed. Clearly Declan had an admirer. I had let go of Declan's arm as soon as they approached, but Mrs. Dalton's eyes darted back and forth between us as he spoke.

"Miss Ava, allow me to introduce you to Mrs. Dalton, and her daughters Miss Dalton, Miss Beatrice and Miss Penelope."

"How do you do," I said, and nodded my head.

"It's lovely to meet you, dear. My hearing must be lapsing as I didn't catch your surname."

I noticed that Declan had not given my full name; he didn't know my true surname, only Gabrielle's ruse of introducing me as her cousin. I suspected his omission was intentional.

"My last name is Lyons," I said.

Mrs. Dalton had smiled at me beatifically, but upon hearing the name 'Lyons' I noticed a small shift in her expression: the smile remained, but it had left her eyes, and her face reminded me of a mask.

"*Lyons?*" she said, studying me. "You aren't related to Gabrielle Lyons, by chance, are you?"

I smiled back. "Yes. Gabrielle is my cousin."

"I see," she said, and maintained the same fake smile. Behind her, her daughters tittered to one another. I turned to them and caught them looking me up and down. It reminded me of the behavior I'd witnessed with Gabrielle, but this time I was the one on the receiving end.

Mrs. Dalton had dismissed me on hearing I was connected to Gabrielle and had begun interrogating Declan.

"You naughty boy, you've missed my last two parties!" she said.

"Yes, I was overseas," he said. I could hear in his tone that he was struggling to remain polite.

"Well, you're back in the city now, and I won't accept your declining the next," she said. "What brings you downtown?"

Declan turned to me and rested his hand on my back. "I am lucky to spend this afternoon with Miss Lyons and when I discovered she had never visited the Baeders' café, I knew that must be remedied."

Mrs. Dalton stared at Declan's arm. "I see. Well, we should be on our way back uptown. Girls, say goodbye to Mr. Aldridge."

The girls giggled and said their goodbyes, walking away in a neat line. We watched their retreat in silence. I glanced over to Declan and could tell from the way his jaw was set that he was angry.

"You didn't need to protect me," I said.

"Yes, I did. She's a small-minded gossip, and we've now given her enough fodder for the remainder of the month. If not the season."

Mrs. Dalton and her daughters had been rude to me, but I was determined not to stoop to their level. "They're all very pretty," I offered.

Declan nodded. "Yes, they are. Unfortunately, that is all they are. The daughters seem to possess one brain that they take turns using."

I laughed before I could stop myself. "That's a mean thing to say."

"Yes, it is. But in my defense, I don't think it is their fault. They have been unlucky enough to have a mother who believes that as long as one is attractive, one needn't bother with cultivating a personality," he said and then dropped his voice to a lower and ominous octave. "The *matchmaking-mama*: one of the many reasons I moved to Paris when I was younger."

"'Matchmaking-mama'? What does that mean?"

"Come, let's go inside. I will enlighten you over lunch," he said, and opened the door to the café.

We entered a small restaurant with fewer than twelve tables. The walls were brick, with a stamped-tin ceiling in an ornate design. Despite its humble size, all the tables had starched white cloths and small crystal bud vases holding clusters of yellow flowers.

A petite older woman approached us. She had snow white hair pulled tight in a bun at the nape of her neck and I imagined she had been striking in her youth. On seeing Declan her face lit up with joy.

"Declan! What a lovely surprise!" she said and reached up to clasp his face between her hands.

He looked equally elated to see her and leaned over to kiss her gently on the cheek as he said his greetings.

"I'd like to introduce you to my friend, Miss Lyons. Mrs. Baeder and her family make the finest food in the city, if not the world."

I nodded hello and smiled.

A light pink flush rose in her cheeks. "It's lovely to meet you, Miss Lyons. Any friend of Mr. Aldridge is always welcome here."

Mrs. Baeder took our coats and Declan's hat and ushered us to a round table set by a bay window that looked out onto Broadway.

Once we were settled she produced two menus, but Declan stopped her. "I hoped you and Mr. Baeder would surprise us. Although, I have promised Miss Lyons your famous torte."

She beamed. "Of course! You honor us. We'll bring you the best of what we have today," she said, and left us to begin preparing the meal.

"Now, I am to tell you about the matchmaking-mama," he said and arched an eyebrow.

I laughed. "Yes, who is she?"

"Not a 'she', sadly, but a 'they'. They are a special breed of mother who make it their mission to hound the young men they find suitable in a fevered hunt to secure the best marriage for their daughters."

"That doesn't sound too terrible. It's understandable that they'd want their daughters to have a good marriage."

"And there it is: you said 'good' marriage and I said, 'best'. One would assume that in a good marriage, it is a union based on mutual affection and respect. In a best marriage, at least from the matchmaking-mama's perspective, it is a relationship of increased social status or wealth. Ideally both. After a few seasonal rounds of forced interactions and inspections in ballrooms, everyone involved begins to feel like cattle. I am certain it is as miserable for the young women as it is for the young men."

"That sounds awful," I conceded.

"Yes. It is. I lasted one season before I left the city and moved to Paris," he said.

The server appeared at our table with rolls and the first course, which appeared to be a hearty soup. I was hungrier than I'd realized and had to stop myself from gobbling down everything in an unseemly manner.

"Have you ever visited Paris, Ava?"

I shook my head. "No, I've never been anywhere. Coming to the city was the farthest I'd ever traveled."

"Yes, you said you had sought out Gabrielle after something unpleasant occurred. The way you both have described Langley Falls, I imagine Manhattan is a dramatic change."

"It seems almost impossible that two such different places could exist in the same state," I agreed.

"You had never been to the city before, and yet you made your way to Gabrielle. On your own, or did someone help you to get here?"

Under other circumstances I would have found such questions intrusive and impolite, but coming from Declan, I felt elated that he would take such an interest in me. And so, as our second and third courses arrived, I told him the whole tale of my escape—including my brother's betrayal and my near brush with being married to the village cretin.

Declan stared at me incredulously. "You have the heart of an adventurer, Ava. I've witnessed you running off in the park, trying to sneak into the party on Halloween—yes, I knew what you were doing—this morning's walk and now this extraordinary tale."

My cheeks burned. "Declan, you're embarrassing me."

His voice softened. "That is not my intention. You are a kindred spirit."

"I am? How? You now know quite a lot about me, but I know very little about you."

"Ask me anything you wish."

I had so many questions: what happened to him in Paris? Why did he give up drawing? Who was the blonde woman sitting on his lap in the photograph? How did he get the scar? As my mind scrambled to think of what to ask, I searched his face and in doing so, my focus must have rested on his scar momentarily.

"Surely you have noticed the scar on my face," he said, as he held my gaze.

I immediately looked down at the table, feeling my cheeks burn again. "Yes I noticed."

"There is no reason to blush, Ava. You did not comment on my scar—I did. And I made peace with it long ago. Eventually, everyone has scars, and after a certain age you realize that external ones are far preferable to internal ones."

I lifted my chin and looked at him.

"I was just about your age and in Paris. I met a young woman named Mireille. She was a dancer, and artist's model, and I thought I'd found the great love of my life."

"The woman sitting on your lap in the picture album!" I blurted out before I could stop myself. I clapped my hand over my mouth in horror.

Declan's eyes widened and he seemed momentarily stunned. "Yes, I know the photograph you're referring to, and that was Mireille." He turned and glanced out the window. "Why on earth has George saved that picture? Nostalgia will be the death of him."

Looking back to me, he resumed his story. "My father had just died when I moved to Paris. Albert thought it would serve the dual purpose of giving me a fresh start and fulfilling my dream of becoming an artist. I met George my first week there and Mireille soon after. All the pieces of my life seemed to fall neatly into place so quickly. I spent my days drawing or whiling away the hours in cafes with friends—I'd even found a garret apartment to rent. It was the true romantic vision of what an artist's life should be. But I wasn't a real starving artist, of course: this was a minor detail I kept close to my vest. I was wise to the ways of the world, or so I thought, and aware that there were people who would be all too willing to relieve me of my funds."

"I take it Mireille was one of those people?" I asked.

"Yes. As the months passed and our relationship deepened, I confided in her. I wanted to marry her. I knew there would be a scandal if I married a dance hall girl, but I didn't care. Then one night, while I was in a cabaret waiting for Mireille's performance to end, as I had countless nights, a man stormed in and punched me. I had never seen him before: I assumed he was a madman, perhaps out of his mind on too much absinthe. But he wasn't—he was Mireille's husband. I punched him back, but as the situation escalated, he slashed my face with a broken bottle."

I gasped, and instinctively reached across the table and touched his hand.

He caressed the back of my hand. "It was a horrifying time in my life. We all have moments that are defining: befores and afters. When I think back to the man I was then, he was a fool. And now, when I look in the mirror, I have a physical reminder that one can pay dearly for foolishness."

My eyes filled with tears. I retracted my hand. Declan's attack and betrayal may have occurred a decade ago, but I could still hear the pain in his voice, as much as he tried to hide it.

Declan saw me wipe at my eyes and his expression

changed, as if startled from a dream. "That is not a tale I usually tell. You are disarming, Ava."

"I am honored that you would trust me," I said. "Did you return to New York after that?"

Before he could answer, a tall, blonde woman appeared at our table with coffee and a delicious-looking chocolate cake. Declan introduced her as the Baeders' daughter; she exuded the same warmth as her mother.

"I remember you devouring this torte as a child, with chocolate smeared all over your face!" she said to Declan, and then winked at me.

"The enthusiasm remains the same, I assure you, but hopefully I've found greater decorum with age," he replied.

She chuckled and returned to the kitchen.

"Did you parents bring you here as a child?" I asked, confused by the familiarity with which they spoke to one another.

"No, the Baeders worked for my father," he said, and handed me a dessert fork. "Now, enough talking, you must try this."

"Oh, my!" I said, as I took a bite. "I think this is the most delicious thing I've ever tasted." It was a dense, two-layer chocolate cake with a layer of raspberry cream, all encased in a glossy, dark-chocolate shell.

Declan picked up his own fork and joined me in tasting the torte. "Mrs. Baeder would make this every weekend when I was a child."

"The Baeders cooked for your family?"

"Yes, but Mrs. Baeder was also a mother figure to me. After my father's death, he left a nice sum to them in his will and they were finally able to open the restaurant they'd dreamed of having,"

I watched as he lifted the little silver pitcher to pour cream into his coffee, his hands elegant in the gesture. He was such an enigma, in many ways. I'd been told of his reputation as a rake, but to me, he was kind, and thoughtful.

"Do I get to ask you another question?" I said.

"Yes, as long as I get to ask you another question in return."

I nodded. "That seems only fair."

"Then ask away," he said.

"You've mentioned your father, but not your mother. Did you lose her when you were young?"

"Yes, she died giving birth to me."

"Declan, I'm so sorry," I said.

"As am I," he said, "I would have loved to have known her. I am told I have her eyes, and that is what caused my father to interact with me as little as possible when I was a boy."

"Because of your eyes?" I asked with confusion. Sitting across the table from him, I did admire the intensity of his gaze. I knew the color of his eyes to be dark gray, but in the diffused lighting of the café, they appeared almost black.

"My father never truly recovered after my mother's death, and my appearance was a cruel reminder of all that he had lost. He put his focus on work and sent me off to boarding school as soon as he was able. It was Albert who stepped in as my father figure, and when my own father died when I was eighteen, I can't say that a great deal of my life changed." He searched my face for a moment. "It is a far different tale than that of your parents, if I remember correctly."

"Yes," I said. "It is different, but both relationships share a common thread of lives being destroyed by love."

Declan tilted his head to the side and his lips curved into a wry smile. "That is a fascinating observation, Ava. And one I would not have made. Have you ever been in love?"

I laughed softly, surprised both by the directness of his question, and the realization that I was oddly at ease in having so intimate a conversation with a man I barely knew.

"I don't know," I said, and paused. "Although I guess if I don't know, that means I haven't."

Declan nodded. "That's very astute. But it does surprise me. You must have had admirers back in your village."

"I did, but I can't say that I was in love with any of them. Or at least, what I felt doesn't seem to match my understanding of what it means to be in love."

"What does being in love mean to you?"

I tried to articulate my thoughts and looked down and traced my finger along the lace edge of the doily that lay at my place setting. "When I think of the phrase 'in love' I think of my parents. My mother gave up everything to be with my father: her home, her family, all that she'd grown up with and had ever known. My father didn't seem to pay as heavy a price as she did, but I know he carried with him the guilt of all she'd surrendered."

"Your understanding of being in love is not a particularly happy one," he observed.

"Their devotion to one another, and their respect, were deeply moving."

"I sense a 'but' in that sentence."

"*But*," I said, "I don't know that I would have made her choice. I have never had feelings for another that were so all-encompassing that I was willing to sacrifice everything for them. My mother paid a big price for her love."

"And this is why you are considering becoming a courtesan?" he said.

I hesitated at his question and looked around the café to make sure none of the other diners could hear our conversation. "I hadn't thought of it that way, but perhaps that's one of the reasons."

Declan saw my unease and leaned forward. "I would never have such a personal conversation with you if I knew others could hear it. I value privacy, too."

I smiled at his reassurance and took a sip of coffee. "Was that the question you wanted to ask me? My views on love?"

"No, that was me being greedy. My question is about your mother's family: did you ever meet them?"

"Only once, when I was a small child. They had a very grand house, but I don't remember any specific details."

"What was their last name?" he asked.

"Vannoy."

"Vannoy? That's a very old New York family," he said. "They used to have an estate along the Hudson. Perhaps that was the house you visited."

I shrugged. "Maybe. I don't remember anything beyond the house being very large and having a gravel driveway."

"There was a member of that family named Oliver Vannoy whom I met years ago. He was a renowned bon vivant; if he's still alive, he'd have to be in his eighties. I wonder if you're related."

"I truly know nothing beyond what I've told you."

"And what is your last name?"

"Richards. Say, why are you asking about all this?"

He leaned forward suddenly. "Because you fascinate me."

All the blood in my body rushed to my face. "Me?"

"Yes, I have a sense about you that I can't put into words."

"What do you mean?" I asked, flustered.

"Given what you've told me, I understand why you'd be tempted to follow in Gabrielle's footsteps, but I don't think it's the path destined for you."

"What does that mean?" I felt almost offended and I didn't even know why.

"Ava, I'm not insulting you when I say that. I think you have far more options than you are aware of. And you saw how Mrs. Dalton behaved towards you when she heard you were connected to Gabrielle. That is but a taste of what you will have to endure should you continue on this particular path."

"Declan," I said, keeping my voice even. "I've had a lovely day with you, but I am not enjoying the direction this conversation is taking."

"I meant no offense, Ava. Take this as an observation from one who has come to care about you," he said.

The tone of his voice was warm and as much as I didn't want it to, it affected me. I nodded and smiled. It had been a wonderful day and I didn't want it to end badly.

"Come," he said. "There is one bite of the torte left. You must have it."

⚜

The sky was just starting to darken; night came so early in November. With luck, I would be back at Gabrielle's house at the stroke of four.

We were silent in the cab ride uptown. Between the exceptional food and the swaying motion of the carriage, I fought to stay awake. I glanced over at Declan; he, too, seemed lost in his own thoughts.

When we reached Seventy-Sixth Street, Declan paid the driver and helped me down to the street. "I feel like a cad not walking you to the door, but if we wish to keep our outing a secret from Gabrielle then it won't do for her staff to see us together."

"You're right," I said. "Thank you, Declan. This was such a lovely day."

"The pleasure was all mine," he said.

Just then a great gust of wind came from the direction of the park, bringing with it a scattering of leaves and small branches. I felt something snap against the side of my neck and I turned quickly in surprise. I laughed as I brushed myself off and looked up to see if Declan was doing the same.

He wasn't. He leaned over and gently pulled a twig from my hair, loosening a few strands. He brushed his fingers along my temple, tucking the hair back behind my ear. I could feel my heart hammering in my chest—other than that moment in the library Halloween night, I had never been this near to his face. I felt the warmth of his hand against my skin and for a moment I thought he would graze his lips against mine. Time seemed to elongate and stand still, and all my awareness distilled down to the sound of my own heartbeat and the rhythm of his breathing. And then he turned his head and pressed his lips against my cheek.

I had been kissed on my cheek by countless others in the course of my twenty years: parents, relatives, friends and sweethearts. It was not until that moment that I learned something so seemingly chaste could feel so very different when delivered by the right person. It felt as though a line of fire burned from my face down to my thighs. *God help me if he'd kissed me on the lips*, I thought.

Declan pulled away at last. "I'm going to wait here to ensure you get in safely."

"Thank you," I near whispered and began to walk towards the front door on wobbly legs.

"I'll see you this Thursday at the party," he called to my back.

I stopped and turned towards him. "I hope so, but that will depend on Gabrielle."

"You *will* be there. You have my word," he said. "Now get inside before this wind blows both of us away."

I ran up the stairs and was soon ushered inside by a relieved Mrs. Kreisler.

CHAPTER 5

G abrielle returned the next day as planned, and Sunday afternoon, she and I sat in the solarium having tea and reading newspapers. A discreet radiator had been included in the design of the room, and it seemed a great indulgence to be able to sit and enjoy the garden's atmosphere on a cold autumn day, protected behind our walls of glass.

Janie entered and handed an envelope to Gabrielle. "A letter just arrived for you, Miss Lyons."

"Thank you, Janie," she said, and opened the letter. It was two pages long and as she read, a smile spread across her lips until at last she let out a very guttural, and unladylike, "Ha!"

"You have a champion, my love," she said, and waved the letter in my direction.

"I do?"

"Yes. I am hosting a party for an artist friend this Thursday night, and Declan has insisted that you be in attendance."

A warmth spread throughout my chest: he had been true to his word.

Gabrielle laughed once again. "Here, let me read you some of this. He begins by chastising me for not utilizing my telephone, making this letter necessary in the first place."

"Do you even own a telephone?" I interrupted. I didn't think I had ever seen one in all my explorations around the house.

"I do. In my private quarters upstairs, but I despise it. That awful ring, so indiscreet," she said with a shudder. "Now, back to Declan's letter. He says, 'It has come to my attention that a dictator's heart beats within your glittering, and ample, chest.' And then, 'Would Albert approve of you keeping Ava chained to her desk on the third floor? Like some beast of burden, or real-life Bertha Mason from *Jane Eyre*? *For shame, Gabrielle.*'"

At the reference to the mad woman in the attic from *Jane Eyre*, I realized that Declan had included that detail for my benefit; he had known Gabrielle would read his letter aloud.

Gabrielle finished the last sentence and began laughing so hard that she had to put the letter down and wipe her eyes. I had never seen her like this, and more than Declan's words, it was Gabrielle's reaction to them that caused me to laugh in return.

"Oh, that man!" she said at last. "No one else would dare speak to me in this fashion, but Declan knows that he can get away with it."

She took a sip of tea and shook her head. "And it would appear that among his other talents, he possesses the gift of prophecy, for I had planned on having you attend this party."

I almost dropped my tea cup. "I'm allowed to attend the party?"

"Yes, darling," Gabrielle replied. "The time has come for you to make your 'debut' of sorts."

"Gabrielle, thank you!"

"This is a special occasion. The artist I am hosting is

73

George Montgomery Tilton. You have seen his work: he painted my portrait that hangs above the fireplace in the drawing room."

I nodded, feigning ignorance.

"George is the friend who introduced Albert to me, and I know he will adore you. In fact, I suspect he'll want to paint you, as well."

I smiled, thinking about the way George had studied the contours of my face the day before. "I look forward to meeting him," I said, and prayed I wouldn't slip up Thursday night.

"Are you finished with your tea?" Gabrielle asked. "We need to plan your dress for the party."

I indicated that I was. "Do I have anything that will be suitable?"

"No, but I do. We have an appointment with Monsieur Marcel tomorrow morning and he said he could take in one of my dresses for you in time. Let's go upstairs, I have a few ideas I want to show you."

Gabrielle's wardrobe was the stuff of dreams: an endless rainbow of lace, beading, feathers, embroidery and silks by the finest makers. That she would have one of her dresses altered for me was an extraordinary gift. My mind reeled at the possibilities of what I might get to wear. I sat on the edge of her bed while she and Janie rummaged inside the cavernous dressing room that lay beyond one of the gilded doors. I had feared Rebecca might be part of this project, but luckily, she'd had "quite a night" according to Gabrielle and was lying down in her own bedroom.

Janie emerged first with a fluttering, pale mauve gown that, to my eye, looked drab. Gabrielle followed with something lacy and pink that reminded me of Rebecca's milkmaid costume from Halloween. After two more trips, six dresses lay on the bed and I had moved from my perch in order to stand and gain a better vantage point. None of the choices appealed to me.

Gabrielle stood at the foot of her bed, hands on her hips as she appraised the selection. "Which do you like the most?"

"They're all very lovely ... it's difficult to choose," I said.

She erupted with laughter. "Ava, you do not lie well! What about them don't you like?"

"They're all very beautiful!" I said quickly; the last thing I wanted was for Gabrielle to think me ungrateful. "I guess I had hoped to wear something a bit more vibrant. With more color."

"I understand that, but I have chosen pale colors for a reason: I want you to appear every inch the ingénue," she said and walked over to where I stood, placing her hands on my shoulders. "There will be important men at the party and I want them to look upon you and dream of their own youth, and feel revitalized. Imagine yourself as the human incarnation of early spring, and all that she promises. What colors would she wear?"

I understood her idea, but I was still disappointed. And presenting oneself as "the human incarnation of early spring" felt like a tall order for one very mortal young woman.

"Wait," she said," I just remembered something."

She strode back into her closet and I heard the sound of drawers opening and closing.

Janie followed. "Do you need help, Miss Lyons?"

"I found it!" Gabrielle said. She appeared in the doorway wrestling a gigantic lavender box. "Here, Janie, help me get this to the bed."

They cleared a space for the box, and then Janie gingerly removed the top. Gabrielle reached inside and pulled out an ivory gown made of the most beautiful lace I'd ever seen. She carried it over to me and held it up to my shoulders.

"This is the first dress I bought for myself when I had

money," she said, and turned me around to face the mirror behind us. "But I think with a few changes around the hips and sleeves, Monsieur Marcel will be able to make it look very current."

I watched my reflection while Gabrielle hovered behind me, holding the dress in place. It was magnificent: the lace work was of so fine a netting that it looked to be spun by a spider. There were details of seed pearls and minute crystals that glimmered in the light and reminded me of early morning dew. The perfect dress for a fairy queen.

"I can see from your smile that you like this one," Gabrielle cooed.

"It's breathtaking," I said.

"Yes, it is. And it should be: it was my very first order from Charles Worth."

I gasped. I knew the name Charles Worth: he was the famous British designer who had founded the House of Worth in Paris, and made gowns for nobility and the extremely wealthy. After Gabrielle had left Langley Falls she would send boxes to my mother and me at Christmas, filled with books and fashion periodicals where Worth designs were often featured. I remembered fantasizing about the kind of women who wore his dresses, and now I would be one.

"Gabrielle, I can't accept this! You can't alter a Worth dress just for me, it's too much."

"I won't ever wear this again, and I want you to have it. This dress brought me luck years ago and I know it will do the same for you, too." She squeezed my shoulders and then called out to Janie, who was standing by the bed. "Janie? What do you think of this dress for Ava?"

Janie smiled and stepped towards us. "It's perfect, Miss Lyons."

"See?" Gabrielle said, "Janie has spoken: it's perfect."

The next day we took the dress to Monsieur Marcel. He'd had a rivalry with Charles Worth years ago, and was elated at the prospect of altering a Worth design (or "correcting it" as he put it). He immediately went to work sketching his planned changes and said the dress would be delivered to me by Thursday morning.

As the day drew closer, Gabrielle explained the plan of the party. It would begin at nine o'clock, but I would not enter until closer to ten.

"You will arrive when the height of the party is just beginning, and stay no more than an hour and a half. Ideally no more than an hour," she said.

"Why, Gabrielle?" I said. I wasn't sure which was worse: listening to a party I wasn't allowed to attend, or being forced to leave a party early when I was having fun.

"These men will be meeting you for the first time. I want everyone present and settled when you arrive, and more importantly, you will only be present for the height of the party. Therefore, you will be associated with the best part, when everyone is enjoying themselves the most."

Thursday evening arrived. Janie helped me dress and style my hair, and then ushered me into Gabrielle's room for her final approval.

Gabrielle had her back to us as she inspected two trays of jewelry that lay open on her dressing table. She wore a daring gown of pale, peach-colored silk in the Aesthetic style, its unstructured silhouette held close to her body. Over top of that floated a sheer mantle decorated with delicate gold beads in an intricate spiraling design. Even though the dress covered her, at a distance she appeared nude.

She looked up when we entered. Her hair was piled in a

pleasing disarray upon her head and she wore long, elaborate earrings of finely wrought gold and multi-colored stones.

"Ava!" she exclaimed. "You are magnificent!" She kissed me on the cheek and then we both instinctively turned towards the mirror.

As I took in my appearance, I felt as though I was looking at another woman. One who led a far more glamorous life than my own. The dress fit me perfectly, and gave me more of an hourglass shape than I actually possessed. Monsieur Marcel had cut away the sleeves and replaced them with two small swags of green silk ivy leaves that arced around each shoulder. Gabrielle was thrilled with this addition as she felt it only enhanced her concept of me as early spring in human form. My hair was swept up loosely, and I wore no jewelry.

"Now remember, when you walk into the room tonight, think of yourself as the peacock, displaying her glorious plumage for all to see!" Gabrielle said, and stretched out her arms to mimic the arc of a peacock's tail.

I laughed at her theatrical gesture. "With all due respect, Gabrielle, isn't it the male peacock who has the beautiful feathers?"

"Ah, yes. You are correct ... then think of yourself as the peacock's daughter!" she said and took my hand, leading me over to her dressing table. "The only thing you need now is a piece of jewelry."

The two trays displayed before me were only a small portion of Gabrielle's collection, all housed in a safe in her dressing room. Watching her select her jewels for the night and talk about the history of each piece was often my favorite part of my evenings with her before she went out.

Gabrielle eyed my appearance once again and then bent down and began examining her options. One tray held blue stones and the other green. She selected a wide bracelet made of many small diamonds accented with emeralds and clasped it around my left wrist. "It's perfect," she said. "That bracelet was given to me by Albert early in our relationship. It, too, will bring you luck tonight."

Gabrielle left to greet her guests, and I sat in my room. I attempted to read, but failing that, I pulled back the heavy drapes and stared out my window into the pitch black. I had not heard from Declan since we'd said good bye to one another on Saturday, but our conversations and images of him replayed constantly in my head. Since that kiss, it felt as though a fire had been ignited within and I found myself entertaining thoughts I'd never quite considered before. I laughed at the realization that his kiss on my cheek had stirred more in me than my dalliance with Lincoln Hanley behind the woodshed.

At nine fifty-five on the dot, Janie appeared at my door. "It's time, miss. I'll escort you down to the party."

I followed Janie down the grand staircase. The party was held in the drawing room, but some of the guests milled outside the entrance near the foyer. The smoke from their pipes, cigars and cigarettes was already heavy and the volume of smoke added a dreamlike quality to the proceedings. The men all stared and nodded as I passed them by. At the entrance to the drawing room, I realized my eyes were beginning to tear from the smoke, and I had to stifle a cough.

Gabrielle appeared at my side, and wrapped her fingers around my elbow. "Oh dear, this won't do," she said when she saw my watering eyes and heard my sputtering.

She left me to cross the room towards a cluster of men sitting by the window. The primary offender, a heavyset man with thick black hair sat in the center, smoking a cigar. Gabrielle leaned over him and said something that caused the group to laugh. She teased the cigar from his fingers and he reached for her other hand, pressing it to his lips. She said something more, and I watched entranced as she bobbed her eyebrows up and down for effect. This brought another round of laughter and then she walked back towards me, waving the cigar.

"Janie, will you please dispose of this?" she said, and handed the cigar away. "Now, let's make your introductions."

She pulled me into the room and introduced me to the first man we encountered. His name was Alexander, and he was very tall, with a powerful build. His hair was the color of straw and everything about him seemed to gleam. He was what I imagined the god Apollo would look like.

"Ava, what a delight it is to meet you. Gabrielle has spoken of you often, and you are even more charming than she described," he said.

Gabrielle told me earlier that only first names were ever used at her parties. This helped to protect the identities of her famous guests and lent a more intimate atmosphere. For all I knew, Alexander might have been one of the most powerful men in New York.

"It's lovely to meet you," I said.

We made polite small talk, and he asked me how I was enjoying New York, and what exhibits Gabrielle had taken me to see.

More men joined us, and Gabrielle introduced me to at least ten gentlemen. I struggled to remember everyone's names. As they circled around me, I realized I'd never received this much attention from so many people at once.

I made sure to make eye contact with all of them, and kept my focus on each man as he spoke, but out of the corner of my eye I searched the room for Declan. At last, a man named Harry stepped away and left an open space through which I could see to the far side of the room. A flash of red caught my eye and I realized it was the lithe form of Rebecca. She wore a crimson-colored gown that glimmered in the low lighting and had a near-scandalous neckline. Her head was thrown back, laughing, and her hands rested on the broad chest of the man she spoke to. As my gaze moved upwards, I realized the man was Declan.

My stomach clenched. Declan's face was in profile, and as I studied the scene I realized nothing about his body language suggested engaging with her. Though she ran her fingers over his lapels, his arms remained at his sides. Nevertheless, a sense of unease flooded through me.

At that moment, Declan turned his head and looked directly at me. Our eyes locked, just as they had the first time we met, and a slow smile began to spread across his face. Without saying a word to Rebecca, he turned and walked towards me, blocking my view of her with his torso.

"Ava," he said, and leaned over to kiss my hand. "How stunning you are tonight."

We continued to study one another, and my surroundings seemed to fade away. I wished everyone else in the room would disappear, or that Declan and I could slip out alone unnoticed. The way he looked at me, I wondered if he wished the same.

"I say, Declan," said a man to my left. "I suspect Ava is always stunning."

It was a kind compliment, but it quickly startled me out of the trance I'd slipped into.

Declan nodded. "It's true. She is."

"You all have consummate taste," Gabrielle said. "If I were a man, Ava would be my ideal."

Everyone surrounding us laughed. "You as a man! I can't even imagine it," said a stocky gentleman with slicked back red hair.

"One day Cornelius, I shall surprise you by showing up in a top hat and cutaway coat," she said, and twirled an imaginary moustache with her fingers.

The men roared and I marveled at Gabrielle's skills in

action: she gave every man present equal attention, and affection, but made them all feel as though they were her favorite.

"Gabrielle, my dear, forgive my interrupting you, but I think we should begin."

I looked up to the tall man who had spoken and saw he was wearing a red fez and an elaborate embroidered robe: it was George. He recognized me at the same moment and a great smile spread across his face.

"Yes, of course, George. But first I want to introduce you to someone very dear to me," Gabrielle said, and wrapped her arm around my back. "This beautiful creature is my cousin Ava. I've so wanted you two to meet."

George leaned down and clasped my hand in his giant fists. "Ava, how wonderful to see you again!"

"Again?" Gabrielle responded immediately.

Out of the corner of my eye, I could see Declan smirk at George's blunder. I feared I might laugh.

George's eyes widened. "You seem so familiar. Didn't we meet in Paris?"

I played along with his ruse. "I've never been to Paris, but you seem familiar to me, too."

"My mistake. Perhaps I am remembering another incarnation," he said, and bent down to kiss my hand.

"Past lives notwithstanding, what's important is that you've now met one another in *this* life," Gabrielle said as she studied us both. "George, I think Ava would be a wonderful subject for you."

"I agree. You remind me of a fairy queen, Ava."

"That's what I've always said!" Gabrielle exclaimed and playfully swatted him on the arm.

George winked at me before she could see and I struggled to maintain my composure. I looked up to Declan and saw that he was enjoying this performance as much as I was.

"Let me go and begin the introductions," Gabrielle said, and made her way through the crowd of men to the fireplace

Declan stepped between George and me. "Good job," he said and slapped George on the back.

George started to open his mouth in response and then dropped his head forward. "Thank heavens I don't make my living by keeping secrets."

As Gabrielle took her place, everyone around us began shifting. "Come, let's get closer so that you can see," Declan said. He placed his hand on the small of my back and guided me through the crowd.

Gabrielle stood in front of the fireplace, next to an easel holding a large rectangle draped with red velvet cloth.

"Thank you all for joining me here tonight to celebrate the work of our beloved George," she said. "This is a very special night because the unveiling of a new painting is much like a birth. I know of no other artist who puts such passion and devotion into his work, and so it is he who should introduce us to this new creation. George?"

He walked to the fireplace to join her, kissing her hands as she stepped to the side. He drew himself up to his full height, and with the added inches of the fez he wore, George made an extraordinary and imposing sight. I wondered if he'd ever painted a self-portrait, as he seemed an exceptional subject.

"Thank you for joining me tonight gentlemen. And ladies," he said, and bowed towards Gabrielle. "It is a very special night, but for reasons other than what you think. Gabrielle, I am going to invite Declan to explain."

Declan had kept his hand on my back and when he shifted a finger or moved ever so slightly, I felt a shiver pass over my skin and through me. As he removed his hand to step away, I felt a void.

"Thank you, George, and thank you, Gabrielle. I'm sure you are confused," Declan said.

Gabrielle did look bewildered.

"We will remedy that in a moment," Declan said to her, and then turned to address the crowd. "I think everyone here remembers my Uncle Albert with great fondness." A wave of nodding heads passed through the room. "He was an exceptional man, and none of us would be here tonight were it not for him. He loved good friends, and good wine, but most of all he loved Gabrielle."

With his back to the firelight, Declan's hair appeared haloed in gold. Combined with the intensity of his gaze as he spoke, he reminded me of an avenging angel. I couldn't imagine ever growing tired of looking at him.

"Albert was taken from us too soon," Declan said. "I can't bring him back, but there are great artists, like George, who are able to tap into something eternal and capture a man's essence to keep with us always."

At Declan's cue, George removed the red cloth and revealed the painting. It was a life-size portrait of Albert from the waist up. He wore an elegant jacket and waistcoat in brown tones and had a small tiger lily in his buttonhole. George's abilities were indeed breathtaking: Albert appeared to be almost alive and watching all of us with amusement.

Gabrielle staggered in front of the painting, but with her back to me, I couldn't see her reaction. She hugged Declan and then George, whispering something to each of them. At last she turned around and tears streamed down her face. Five men came forward at once and presented her with their handkerchiefs.

"I could make a quilt!" Gabrielle exclaimed, and accepted a blue silk cloth from Alexander. "To say I am surprised is an understatement," she said and dabbed at her eyes. "Declan is correct: none of us would be here tonight were it not for Albert. This house was one of his greatest visions, and now it will have a portrait that truly honors him."

Members of Gabrielle's staff moved silently throughout the room, dressed in white and carrying glasses of champagne on silver trays. A dashing man with a neatly trimmed Van Dyke beard appeared at my right. He took two glasses from an approaching server and handed one to me.

"It's a striking portrait, don't you think?" he said.

"Yes. He looks almost alive."

"He does," the man agreed. "And so apropos for Albert; I've never met anyone as vital."

I nodded and smiled.

"I arrived late and didn't have the pleasure of being introduced to you. I am Jonathan," he said, and leaned towards me so that I could hear him over the din that was slowly building.

"It's lovely to meet you," I said. "I am Ava."

"Yes, I know. You're Gabrielle's cousin. You've caused quite a stir here this evening," he said, and looked at me with a seductive glint in his eye.

"I have?" I felt like I hadn't been at the party long enough to cause a stir.

Before Jonathan could answer, Declan raised his glass at the front of the room. "To Albert!"

"To Albert!" we repeated and sipped from our glasses. I hadn't tasted champagne until I came to live with Gabrielle, and its tart fizziness never ceased to thrill me.

Declan raised his glass again. "And to George: the finest artist I know, and an even finer friend."

"To George!" we said.

And then Declan lifted his glass again.

"Again, Declan?" a loud voice cried out from the back of the room. Everyone laughed.

Declan laughed too, his glass still lifted. "Yes, Archibald. If I can sit through another damned version of your 'triumph in Greenwich,' you can endure another toast."

I had no idea what he was referring to, but everyone else

clearly did, and bellowing laughter soon surrounded me. I'd noticed that everyone was becoming louder with the addition of champagne.

"As I was saying," Declan continued. "To Gabrielle: her radiance blesses us all."

"To Gabrielle!"

I looked back to her and saw that her tears had dried. She caught my eye and came towards me.

"What a night this is!" she said, and kissed me on the cheek.

Jonathan still stood next to me, and Gabrielle reached over and caressed his face. "I feared you wouldn't make it tonight."

"I would never miss this."

"Have you met my cousin, Ava?" she said.

"Yes, she is a delight," he said as his gaze lingered on me.

"She is indeed. Now if you'll forgive me, I'm going to steal her from you."

Jonathan nodded. Gabrielle guided me towards the painting and Declan, who had watched this whole exchange.

"You must see the portrait, darling. I know you never met Albert, but George has captured him perfectly," she said.

It was painted in warm, autumnal tones punctuated by the icy gray of Albert's hair and the vermillion orange of the tiger lily on his lapel.

"The tiger lily looks real enough to pick!" I said. "Was it his favorite flower?"

"In a manner. It was a private joke between us, a play on my last name of Lyons. Albert called me a lioness, and loved to wear little symbols just for me. But he couldn't think of a flower that symbolized a lion."

"Perhaps a sunflower?" Declan offered. "Although that might be unbecoming on one's lapel."

Gabrielle glared at Declan in a teasing manner. "Albert

decided on the tiger lily, joking that it was the closest thing he could find to a lion. And his term of endearment for me became 'Tiger Lily'."

"It's stunning, Gabrielle. I'm sad that I never met Albert. I can tell I would have liked him."

"He would have adored you," she replied, and Declan nodded in agreement.

George appeared, his cheeks rosy and eyes sparkling from the champagne. "Has Gabrielle shown you the secret in the portrait?"

I shook my head and he positioned me at a slight angle to the painting. "Lean in and look into his eyes."

I leaned forward until my face was a few inches away from the canvas's surface. Albert's eyes were painted in smoky shades and as I tried to make sense of the shapes in front of me, a form began to emerge: with just a few smudges of pearl gray and black, George had painted Gabrielle's face reflected in Albert's pupils. It was not something I would have noticed on my own, but once pointed out it was uncanny.

"That is amazing!" I exclaimed. "How did you do that?"

"George is a magician," Declan said and winked.

"I believe every piece has its own desires and my job is to listen," George responded mysteriously.

We stepped to the side to allow others to view the painting.

"Gabrielle, where are you going to display the portrait?" Jonathan said, as he joined us.

Declan removed the almost-empty champagne glass from my hand and replaced it with a fresh one. He rested his other hand on the small of my back, moving his thumb up and down slowly along my spine. It was difficult to concentrate on the conversation.

"I'm going to place it in the foyer," she said.

"Really?" George said, "I had assumed you would have it in your private chambers."

"As did I," Declan added.

"No. It would be too tempting to sit and stare at it all day," she said, and reached up to touch George's arm. "It is magnificent. You have captured him perfectly—I feel as though he's about to speak."

The din in the room was becoming louder, and some of the men had lit cigars. Through the increasing fog I spied Rebecca in a far corner, leaning over Gabrielle's newly acquired gramophone as a jaunty little tune began to play. A few men sang along and raucous laughter followed.

"Follow me into the foyer," Gabrielle said.

We followed her out of the room into the marble- and mahogany-lined entranceway. She gestured with a champagne glass towards the wood panel to the left of the front door.

"I want the painting right there. Albert's portrait will be the first thing visitors see."

As we exited the drawing room others followed, and soon the party seemed to split into two. Screaming laughter and loud singing echoed out from behind the wall. Just then, as if by some unspoken cue, members of Gabrielle's staff appeared carrying the coats and hats of many of the men present. They all said their goodbyes and began the process of leaving.

"What will happen now?" I asked Declan. My time at the party had gone by quickly and I sensed I would soon be escorted back to my room. I felt like Cinderella waiting for her coach to turn into a pumpkin.

"Most of the men will head downtown to the club. Those who are in Gabrielle's inner circle will move on to a private party in the other wing," he said.

"Oh," I said, and could feel my cheeks burn at the mention of the private rooms I had yet to see. "I guess I will need to go back upstairs then."

"Not necessarily," Declan said. "Why don't we have a nightcap in the library before you retire. I'll introduce you to another novel you might enjoy," he said, and slid his hand down my arm until he clasped my hand.

"All right," I said. "But should I say goodbye? I don't want to be rude."

"The way the champagne has been flowing tonight, I doubt anyone will notice our absence," he said and led me through the crowd.

In the library, a fire burned in the fireplace, and all the electric lights had been turned off, leaving everything aglow by candlelight. I sat down on the leather chesterfield while Declan poured a finger of whisky into a glass.

"Will you join me this time?" he said, holding it out to me.

"Yes." I returned his gaze and held out my hand.

I took a sip and the liquid felt like fire racing down my throat. At first, I thought I might cough, but then the sensation changed and became an embracing warmth.

Declan poured himself a glass and joined me on the sofa. "How did you enjoy your first party at Gabrielle's?" he said. "Did it live up to expectation?"

"It was fun ... though not as lively as I'd expected."

He nodded. "It was more subdued this evening. Most everyone is still hungover from the election Tuesday night."

I chuckled. "Gabrielle was adamant that no politics be discussed this evening. She said if she heard the names 'Cleveland' or 'Harrison', the guest would be asked to leave."

"Gabrielle is wise," Declan laughed in return. "And the party was also more subdued because it involved art and had a purpose. Most of the men here tonight don't care a whit about culture, but they have enough awareness to feign interest."

"They were all lovely to me."

"I don't know that I would refer to any of them as 'lovely'," Declan said with a snort. "Now that you've seen who Gabrielle's benefactors are, do you still want to be a courtesan?"

I opened my mouth to answer but I didn't begin to know what to say.

Declan leaned towards me. "You don't have to answer that. But I do have one question: has Gabrielle yet shown you the private wing, or shared with you any of the more mundane aspects of how she runs her life?"

"No," I said. "I have a general idea, but not the specifics."

He downed the rest of the brandy and set his glass aside. "I don't understand why she is coddling you so. If this is truly a path you wish to pursue, then she should give you all the information you need to make an informed decision."

I groaned and tilted my head back to rest against the tufted leather. "Declan, are you truly bringing this up *again*?" When he had suggested we retire to the library for a nightcap, I had not envisioned that it would be to interrogate me about my life's choices.

He thought for a moment and nodded. "Yes. I am bringing this topic up again. Ava, for the life of me, I don't understand why you would ever consider becoming a courtesan."

"Why wouldn't I? It's been a good choice for Gabrielle."

"You are not Gabrielle. You are different," he said.

"And what does that mean?" I said, and crossed my arms over my chest. Suddenly, I really did feel like Cinderella having stayed too long at the ball.

"From what I gather, Gabrielle has provided you with a solid education these last few months. Surely, there must be something that you've learned that piques your interest."

I stared at him. "What are you talking about?"

He shifted closer to me. He'd removed his jacket and loosened his tie, and from the emphatic way he was speaking I could tell the alcohol was affecting him.

"I mean, through no fault of your own, you didn't have access to a formal education growing up. You do now, and you are a natural student: you've picked up French easily, you're a voracious reader, and you have an adventurous and inquisitive spirit—"

"But not desirable enough to be a courtesan," I said, cutting off his words. "Verging on a bluestocking, is that it?" Fury raged through me. In one humiliating instant, I decided that what I had interpreted as attraction was in reality Declan's desire to turn me into some kind of Pygmalion-inspired project.

Declan looked shocked, and his voice lowered. "That's not at all what I'm saying. The courtesan's life is very specific, and in most instances, very short-lived. Gabrielle is not the norm."

I'd turned my face away from him to stare at the fire.

He grabbed my forearm; I looked down to see his strong, elegant fingers encircling me. "I want more for you," he said, and focused on me with an intensity that seemed almost angry.

"Why?" It was an honest question. I was a young woman with no money, from an obscure little town, who, to an outside observer, had nothing in common with the man seated beside me.

He studied his hand clutching my arm. "I told you: you are a kindred spirit."

"And what about Rebecca?" I said.

"What about Rebecca?" he repeated.

"Is a courtesan's life good enough for her?"

"Rebecca's choices don't concern me," he said.

"It didn't look that way when I arrived at the party."

Declan stared at me as if I were insane. "What on earth are you talking about?"

"At the party, her gestures suggested there was something between you two."

"You mean because she rested her hands on me while we spoke?"

I nodded.

"Where were my hands during the conversation? Was I touching her?" he said.

"No," I said

Declan reached up and ran a finger along one of the ivy leaves that arched over my shoulder. "And where is my hand now?"

As his hand brushed against the bare skin of my shoulder, I froze. A cascade of goosebumps spread down my arm and, even in the low lighting, I knew he saw. He hesitated and then slowly began to move his fingertips along my collarbone, causing a trail of fine hairs to stand on end wherever he grazed my skin.

"I wonder how far their path travels ... to places I cannot see." He shifted his position on the sofa until he faced me and ran his fingers up to caress my neck. "I can feel your pulse racing. Have I scared you?"

"No. I'm not scared of you," I said in a near whisper.

He moved closer, never moving his hand from my neck. With his other hand, he reached out and ran his thumb down my cheek. "Look at me."

He leaned in and I closed my eyes.

"Oh!" blurted a high-pitched voice from behind me. Startled, I opened my eyes and turned to see Janie looking embarrassed. She stepped backwards into the doorway. "Forgive me, Mr. Aldridge, Miss Ava. Miss Lyons is looking for you, miss."

The spell was broken. Declan let out an exasperated

groan, and leaned away from me. "Thank you, Janie. Tell Miss Lyons that we'll join her in the foyer in a moment."

Janie nodded and left the room.

"The search party has been sent for you," he said as he stood up. He held out his hand and helped me to my feet.

What had just happened? For one moment I had thought this evening was going to end in a kiss—not in my being shuffled upstairs so soon. I didn't want my time with him to end. "You were going to recommend another novel for me to read," I said, weakly.

"Ah, yes, that's right," he said, and seemed agitated. "Must it be a novel?"

"No," I said.

Leaving my side for a moment he dashed over to the bookshelf. Watching his broad shoulders and long form as he reached up to select a book, I remembered how he pressed against my back on Halloween night. I blushed at the memory and felt such disappointment that Janie had interrupted us.

Striding towards me with a big grin, he presented me with a small, red-bound book.

"*A Thousand Miles Up the Nile*," I read aloud. "What is this?"

"It is the travelogue of an explorer named Amelia Edwards. I suspect it will appeal to you for many reasons, and we can discuss it when I return next month."

"When you return? Where are you going?"

"I need to check on an investment and then I'll spend Thanksgiving with the Bryn Mawr branch of my father's family."

Declan saw my disappointment and lifted my chin. "I'm not going to Timbuktu, just Philadelphia."

"Oh," I said. At that moment Philadelphia sounded as far away as Timbuktu. And as much as I didn't want to have feelings for this man, I was alarmed at how crestfallen I felt at the thought of not seeing him. Maybe it would be for the best. Maybe his absence would help to purge my feelings for him.

"In the meantime, I'll look forward to our discussion when I return," he said and held out his arm.

Taking his arm, I followed him out of the library to the foyer where Gabrielle waited.

CHAPTER 6

"**D**arling, are you listening?" Gabrielle said.

We were in Gabrielle's carriage, on our way back to her house after having visited her favorite milliner and her best glovemaker. Pale blue hatboxes lay stacked on the seat next to me, and as I startled from my daydream I realized I was hugging one of them.

"I'm sorry. I really was listening. You were talking about the beading on the velvet cape Monsieur Marcel is making you."

Gabrielle laughed. "You were daydreaming far longer than I realized! I was speaking of our Thanksgiving plans."

I blushed. "Forgive me, Gabrielle. I'm a little tired today."

"Yes, I can tell. You don't usually have dark circles under your eyes. Are you feeling well? I hope you're not coming down with something."

"I drank more champagne last night than I'm used to."

"That will do it." Gabrielle nodded.

In reality, I hadn't been able to sleep the night before. I lay awake picking apart my feelings for Declan: alternating between relief and despair that I wouldn't see him in the coming weeks.

We arrived at Gabrielle's and found Janie waiting for us in the foyer, alongside a pretty young maid named Cordelia. Cordelia was Janie's cousin, and the newest addition to the household staff.

"All the flowers and gifts are displayed in the drawing room, Miss Lyons," Janie said with a bright smile.

"There are some for you too, Miss Ava!" Cordelia interjected.

"For me?" I said, with surprise.

Deliveries of flowers and gifts were a daily occurrence for Gabrielle, particularly so after she hosted a party. She kept an account with her favorite florist on Twenty-Eighth Street, but she rarely used it as her benefactors were so liberal with their floral displays of affection.

"I told you, you made a marvelous impression last night," Gabrielle said. "Let's go take a peek."

The drawing room was one of the most beautiful rooms in the house, all its details lost in the smoky haze and low lighting of last night's party. Its wallpaper gleamed with images of ornate flowers and birds plucking strawberries. The walnut shelving between the fireplace and the bow window displayed Gabrielle's collection of blue and white porcelain, their glazes seemed to glow in the late autumn sunlight. As I surveyed the room, I saw that the long sideboard to the left of the window overflowed with roses and small, wrapped packages.

"Miss Lyons, I organized all of your gifts to the left and all of Miss Ava's to the right," Janie said, following behind us into the room.

"That's perfect, Janie. Thank you," Gabrielle said.

Excitedly, I rushed to my collection: five flower arrangements and three rectangular boxes, all wrapped in the same peach-colored paper and stamped with the name "Maillard's". I gathered the notes attached to them, my hands shaking slightly. All were from men I couldn't quite recall.

Gabrielle appeared at my side. "Who sent them?" I handed her the notes and she read through, nodding her head with each one. "Who I expected. They're testing the waters," she said.

"What do you mean?" I said, as I lifted one of the peach boxes, curious as to its contents.

"None of them are part of my inner circle, but they attend my parties and are friends of my benefactors. I have not said that you are a courtesan, but they want to position themselves first in line, should you be."

Declan's words from the night before came back to me. I knew so very little about how Gabrielle actually constructed her livelihood. "I thought all the men at the party were your benefactors, except for George and Declan, of course."

Gabrielle let out a sharp breath. "Dear lord, no! I would be too exhausted to get out of bed in the morning."

"I am confused, then. How many benefactors do you have? And who were all the men here last night?"

"All the men at the party last night were benefactors to a degree, but my true devotions are for six men, four of whom were not able to attend the party."

I stared at Gabrielle agog.

"Six men are responsible for keeping me in the life to which I am accustomed. The others are friends, or colleagues of that core of six. They attend my parties, I may dine with them occasionally, but I am never intimate with them. Some want to become more to me, but it is my policy to never have relationships with more than six men at a time."

"Why?"

"One for each night of the week, keeping one night for myself. It's a matter of sheer practicality."

I was shocked by Gabrielle's candidness, and looked back to see if Janie was still present. She had moved to the doorway, and stood as a silent sentinel, her eyes on the floor ahead of her.

"Janie knows all of this," Gabrielle said when she noticed my glance towards the doorway. "I don't know what I would do without her."

I sensed an opportunity to ask Gabrielle all the questions I had been unable to ask before. But I still felt strange doing so with another person present, even one as trusted as Janie.

"Janie, would you please bring us some tea? We'll have it in here. The light is so exquisite today," Gabrielle said, as if hearing my thoughts.

Janie nodded and left the room.

"Have a seat. I can tell you have questions."

I sat down on the blue settee, taking the gift with me.

"Let's have chocolate with our tea," Gabrielle said, and lifted the box from my lap.

"Oh! Are they chocolates?" I said, an octave higher than usual in my excitement.

"Yes, and very good chocolate, but so very common of them to send it to you," she said, removing the outer wrapping and lifting the top off the box.

"What do you mean?" I asked, selecting a piece.

"You are a young woman, and they assume all young women like candy. I would be far more impressed if they had bothered to learn something about you—your favorite flower, your interests—and send a gift unique to *you*. But no, they sent chocolate," she said, and waved her hand dismissively.

I had just bitten into a caramel, and suddenly felt guilty for enjoying it. "But I do like chocolate," I said, trying not to speak with my mouth full.

"So, do I," she said, and selected a square from the box. "But my point is, if they want to impress you and set themselves apart from other men, they should put greater creativity and insight into what types of gifts they send you."

I understood her point, but I felt protective of the gifts that were sent to me. They were nice gestures, even if the men who sent them hadn't inspired any interest in me. I didn't want to admit to myself how much I'd hoped there might be something from Declan in that pile, and how disappointed I was when there hadn't been. I wondered what type of gift he would have sent, if he had. Gabrielle was right: it would have been something more interesting than a box of chocolates.

Gabrielle reached over and squeezed my hand. "Do not let a man's gifts sway you if you are not interested in him. The relationship between courtesan and benefactor is a delicate one, but at its very core there must be mutual attraction of some kind."

I cleared my throat. I wanted a cup of tea, but hoped Janie would not enter until I said what I needed to. "Declan expressed concern that you haven't shared the more day-to-day aspects of what it means to be a courtesan."

"Did he," she said.

I didn't look up to meet her eyes, but I felt her gaze. "Yes. He said I needed more information if I were to make an informed decision."

"And did Declan elaborate on what exactly that information should be?"

I glanced up, expecting to see anger in Gabrielle's expression, but found amusement instead. "Well, for example, I've never seen the wing of private rooms. I have an idea of what goes on there, of course, but certainly not specifics."

"You're right." Gabrielle sighed. "Declan's right. I don't have time today, but on Monday, Rebecca and I will give you a tour of the wing and discuss more details."

Her words shocked me. I hadn't expected she would

relent so easily. I didn't relish the idea of spending time with Rebecca, but I was excited to finally see what lay beyond that door.

Gabrielle walked over to the sideboard. She ran her hands over her assortment of gifts and then selected one, opening it to reveal a necklace displayed on navy-colored velvet.

I gasped. From my distance on the sofa I couldn't see the necklace's specifics except that it was elaborate and sparkled. I jumped up to join her.

She lifted the necklace from the box and held it up for me to see. It was a garland of diamond flowers with enameled bees perched on three blossoms. "It's a masterpiece!" I said.

"Yes, it is."

"Who is it from? You haven't opened the card." I handed her the small square of cream-colored linen.

"I don't need to see the card to know who it's from," she said, and I noticed a trace of sadness in her voice. "It's from Alexander."

"Apollo!"

"Excuse me?" Gabrielle said, looking confused.

"Last night when you introduced me to Alexander, he was what I imagined the god Apollo would look like: tall and broad and golden."

She smiled. "I'm going to tell him you said that. He'll love it."

Gabrielle opened the card and read its contents. "This is one of the unfortunate aspects of being a courtesan."

"What's wrong?" I asked.

"Alexander wants me to marry him."

"Oh!" I exclaimed and clasped my hands together. "That's wonderful!"

"No, darling, it isn't."

"Why not? You don't want to marry him?"

She shook her head. "No. He means more to me than any

of the others, to be very honest, and we have great fun together, but I can't say that what I truly feel for him is love. And more importantly, what he truly feels for me isn't love."

"What do you mean?"

"We have a wonderful time with one another, but ultimately, I know that he desires me because he wants to conquer me as he has so many businesses in this city. No," she said and shook her head once again. "I have been down this road before—men like Alexander will eventually move on. They can't tolerate the competition any longer and they won't accept my unwillingness to give up this life. "

She rested her hand on my arm. "This is what I meant when I told you to guard your heart; it is the difference between being sad when Alexander leaves rather than devastated."

Gabrielle had been ebullient all day and now in the late afternoon light, she was the one to look tired.

"Are you all right?" I asked.

She turned back to me with a smile that seemed forced. "Yes, of course. Look, here's Janie. Let's have our tea and speak of happier subjects."

The moment passed and we had tea. As we parted, Gabrielle said she'd have all my gifts sent up to my room. I looked forward to a night curled up in bed reading the Egyptian travelogue and eating chocolate. And trying not to think about Declan.

❧

At one p.m. on Monday afternoon I sat on Gabrielle's bed, waiting as she put the finishing touches on her hair. Rebecca sauntered in a few minutes later. She wore a dress of forest green, embellished with orange ribbons that reminded me of carrots. She caught me staring at the strange ribbons and glared. I quickly averted my eyes and tried not to giggle. I had been living in Gabrielle's household for more than six months now, and Rebecca had only two expressions for me: glaring or smirking. If the day came that she actually smiled, I feared I wouldn't know how to respond.

"There you are!" Gabrielle said to the reflection of Rebecca in her mirror. "Let's get this tour underway."

We followed Gabrielle through the small gilded door at the far end of her bedroom. On the other side lay a dark narrow hallway that led to a spiral staircase like the one I had tried to reach on Halloween night. We descended and entered another doorway at the base of the stairs.

I followed Gabrielle through, with Rebecca behind me, closing the door. As I tried to get my bearings, I realized the room we were standing in was identical to Gabrielle's bedroom we had just left.

"Are we somehow back in your room?" I asked, more than a little confused.

Gabrielle laughed. "No, not quite. To my gentlemen, this is my private bedroom. They don't know that my real chambers are upstairs. The two rooms are identical, with the exception of this mirror," she said, gesturing towards a large mirror mounted on the wall that faced her bed. It was an ornate affair with a frame of rococo roses cast in bronze, whereas the mirror upstairs had a frame of mythological figures carved in wood.

"And this chest of drawers," she said, gesturing towards the piece. "You will notice it has six drawers: each man has his own drawer."

We left her bedroom through a gilt door identical to the one upstairs, and she ushered me into the most beautiful hallway I had ever seen. A line of doors stretched out before me on either side, each one painted in a different color or carved in a unique style. The ceiling was vaulted and the wood floor had an intricate woven pattern inlaid with golden stars.

"The Scheherazade room," Gabrielle said, as I followed her through the first doorway.

The bed was massive and low, draped with paisley textiles in jewel-like tones. On the walls hung large oil paintings of voluptuous women in varying degrees of undress. Minaret-shaped hanging lanterns of brightly colored glass and metal were scattered about the room, casting dappled, rainbow patterns across all the surfaces.

Gabrielle wrapped her arm around my shoulders. "Look up into the face of the woman holding the basket of persimmons," she said.

I searched the walls until I found the painting. It depicted a woman wearing a gauzy gown tied at her shoulders. She held a basket of fruit in her arms and looked out at the viewer with a coy half-smile.

"There are holes cut out in the eyes," Gabrielle said. "On the other side of the painting is a small room where a person may sit and look through into this room."

I started to ask why, and then quickly realized the answer. "Do many of your benefactors like to be watched when they are in here?" I asked, and then added, "Or watch others ... I guess?"

"Some. Right now, I have one gentleman who enjoys being watched when he is intimate with me. Do you know the tale of Scheherazade, Ava? She told a tale every night for a thousand and one nights to save her life. In honor of her ingenuity, this room also serves as a security measure: if you are unsure about someone, this is where you bring them for the first time."

"And who watches you?" I asked, but as soon as the words were out of my mouth I knew that answer, too. "Oh."

Rebecca smirked at me from the corner. "Have you ever

watched another, Ava? Perhaps when you were down on the farm?" she said.

"No."

"Too bad," she said.

"Rebecca, get the door. Let's move on," Gabrielle said.

The next room had a pastoral theme. All the walls were painted with a fine mural mimicking grass, trees and sky. There was a small, freestanding structure of whitewashed wood that reminded me of the house I'd grown up in, in Langley Falls. If I squinted my eyes, I could have been standing in the fields in back of my childhood home.

"As you can imagine, this is not my favorite room," Gabrielle said. "But it's remarkable how many industrialists have fantasies of a 'simple life'."

I wondered how far the fantasy went. Did Gabrielle have to bring in cows for milking? Did she set up a butter churn in the corner? I smiled to myself at the absurdity of it all.

We toured the next few rooms, and all were beautiful and luxurious, but not nearly as scandalous as what I'd imagined. There was a grand, walnut-paneled dining room lined with paintings of satyrs chasing nymphs, a billiard room, three other bedrooms, and a "spiritualist" room that housed a crystal ball the size of my torso. The private wing of the house had been a tremendous source of fascination for me over the last six months, and it appeared my imagination was greater than the reality.

Then we came to a dark door carved with dragons, and I followed Gabrielle down into a room unlike anything I'd ever seen. The lighting was low and the walls were lined in red velvet. There were ebony and glass cases containing leather whips and metal devices whose purpose I could not fathom, and an ornate cage that looked large enough to house a person.

"What is this place?" I said. "It looks like an elegant torture chamber."

"Some people find great pleasure in pain, or enjoy the sensation of being bound, or want to explore the nature of control. Rebecca is an expert in all these arts. This is her domain."

While Gabrielle spoke, Rebecca strode over to one of the cabinets. She opened the glass door and brought out a kind of whip; it had dozens of short, leather strips attached to a black lacquer handle. She began slowly pacing the room and slapping the leather against her palm.

I watched her for a moment and then returned my attention to Gabrielle. "Do many people enjoy being whipped?"

Before she could answer, there was a knock. Slowly, the door opened and Janie stood silhouetted against its frame. "Excuse me, Miss Lyons. There is a messenger from Mr. Bainbridge's office. He requires your signature."

I noticed that Janie did not step down into the room but moved backwards into the hallway once she'd delivered her message.

"Thank you, Janie," Gabrielle called out, and then to me, "I'll be back in a moment."

I wanted to chase after her. Rebecca stood in the corner studying me and slapping the whip against her palm in rhythm. I was certain this was an attempt at intimidation, so I began to explore the room in as nonchalant a manner as I could muster.

Moving around the perimeter, I noticed objects whose purpose intrigued me, but I kept my questions to myself so as to avoid engaging with Rebecca. There was a table of sorts, round and covered in black velvet. I leaned over to examine its surface and discovered it had a series of leather straps affixed to it. The leather was tooled in a scrolled design and quite beautiful. I reached down and ran my fingers over its intricate surface: like kid gloves. I had not expected such softness.

"Ever seen one of these before?"

I gasped and stood up quickly, nearly whacking Rebecca in the head as she leaned over me. She stood uncomfortably close, and her perfume enveloped me and felt smothering. It was a scent redolent of vanilla and I wondered why someone who presided over a room filled with tools to inflict pain would choose a fragrance reminiscent of a bakery.

"You startled me," I stammered.

"Yes, I can see that. But you didn't answer me," Rebecca said. "Have you ever seen one of these before?"

I shook my head. "No."

"That's what I thought. Well, there's a first time for everything, let me show you." Rebecca stepped aside and put her whip down. She reached under the table and I heard the sound of scraping metal. Slowly the table began to shift vertically until its surface was perpendicular to the floor: a large circle of over six feet in diameter, with leather straps hanging down.

"Step up and I'll show you how this works" she said, pointing to a small platform at the base of the circle.

"No, thank you."

Rebecca laughed. "Are you scared? I won't hurt you."

"No, I'm not scared."

"Come now, I thought this little tour was to expose you to all the secrets of our world. Don't you want to learn what happens in this room?"

I paused as Declan's words came back to me. I did want to have a better understanding of all that Gabrielle did, and for that matter, all that Rebecca did.

Rebecca saw my hesitation and moved closer. "Don't you trust me?"

"No. Not at all," I said, before I could edit myself.

She laughed again. "I appreciate your honesty. But you needn't fear me: I won't hurt you. Even if I wanted to, Gabrielle will be back at any moment."

She had a point there. What could she do to me in the next few minutes?

"When I was learning these particular skills, my mistress insisted that I experience all that my clients would. I could never do to another what I hadn't experienced myself."

"You had a teacher?" I asked, shocked.

"Yes, of course," Rebecca said. "She was a vicious thing, and extremely old by the time I was her pupil, but men traveled from all over the country, if not the world, to experience her talents."

Suddenly Rebecca became infinitely more interesting. I realized this was the most we had spoken to one another in six months. I let her lead me over to the big velvet circle.

"Good girl," she said as she helped me step up onto the platform. "Put your back against there and I'll strap you in."

"I don't need to be strapped in," I said. "I can get a sense of this just by standing up here."

Rebecca pursed her lips and reached up to caress my cheek. It was jarring to be touched by her and I had to keep myself from flinching. It was what I imagined it was like to be caressed by a wolf.

"You're a very pretty girl, and that may be enough at first, but in the long run, you will need other abilities," she said. "Gabrielle has told me something of your story: you ran away from home and came all the way to New York to become a courtesan. But at this point, it's just play acting, isn't it? Dressing up in lovely dresses, and having lunch at Delmonico's, all by the grace of Gabrielle. What is your actual contribution?"

Rebecca retracted her hand, but fixed her gaze on me like a predator stalking her prey. "Are you strong enough to endure this kind of life?" She shook her head before I could answer. "I doubt it. I'll believe it when I see it."

I was furious. Why did everyone question me? "Strap me in," I said, pressing my back against the velvet surface. I knew Rebecca was manipulating me into doing what she wanted, but I didn't care. I needed to prove myself.

She started by buckling the largest leather strap around my waist. It was uncomfortably tight, and I told her so.

"It needs to be tight so that you don't fall out."

"Fall out? What do you mean?" I said, trying to keep rising concern out of my voice.

"You'll see. The key is to remain relaxed. Stretch out your arms, I need to buckle your wrists."

I was on this contraption to prove a point, but I didn't want to be maimed in the process. "You're not going to throw knives at me, are you?"

Rebecca arched her brow. "Would you like me to?" she cackled. "No, I'm not going to throw knives at you."

She bound my wrists to the board above my head, along with the belt around my waist and another wrapped around both of my calves. This alone was far more stressful than I'd expected: I was completely at Rebecca's mercy.

"Now relax. Just enjoy the sensation of being held by the straps," she said.

"But I don't enjoy this sensation."

"Oh, shush. Men pay hundreds of dollars to have this experience with me and I'm giving it to you for free. You should be thanking me." She picked up the little whip again and raised it towards my face.

I flinched and tried to struggle against the straps.

"Ava, stop it. I said I wasn't going to hurt you and I meant it. Now close your eyes." Her voice had taken on a new commanding tone.

I closed my eyes and tried to calm my racing pulse.

"That's it. Good," she said. "Now unclench your left hand and open your palm to me."

I did as I was told and soon felt something soft being traced in figure eights over my skin. It felt like hair, but coarser. I realized it was the end of the whip. Rebecca continued moving the leather strands gently over my hands and spoke in a soothing manner. "Close your eyes. Feel the belt around your waist, supporting you. Allow yourself to relax, Ava."

Rebecca's voice was deeper than Gabrielle's and had an endearing, crackling-rasp that I'd never noticed before. I listened to the sonorous rhythm of her voice and slowed my breathing. Focusing on the sensation of the soft leather as she stroked the whip over my hand, I tried to forget that I was strapped to a board in a room that appeared to be a dungeon.

"Open your eyes. There now, that wasn't so bad, was it?"

I shook my head.

"Now open your palm again and I'll show you more of what I'm known for."

She held my hand open and in a lightning-fast move slapped the fleshiest part of my palm with the end of her whip. She moved so quickly, and with such precision, that it was over before I realized what she'd done. I didn't feel pain so much as tingling. She walked over to my other hand and did the same. The skin on the palms of my hands had a new vitality.

"That's just a taste. Imagine that sensation on other body parts," she said.

"Thank you, Rebecca, this was far more enlightening than I'd expected," I said, and meant it. "If you'll please help me down now. The wrist straps are starting to hurt."

"Nonsense, they aren't any tighter than a corset, and you wear a corset daily."

"Yes, but I don't wear a corset on my wrists."

"You're a sharp thing, I'll give you that," she said, and then stepped behind the board. I heard a series of switches being flipped and Rebecca reappeared. "Gabrielle isn't back yet, so now I'll show you what this really can do." She reached up higher on the board and pulled it down. To my horror, I realized the wheel was being turned, taking me with it.

"No, Rebecca! Stop, I don't like this," I called out.

"Don't be a ninny, Ava. I'm moving slowly. Don't you want to be versed in all these arts?" she said. The kind tone she'd adopted with me had been replaced with a more hostile one. "What will you do if Declan wants to strap you to the wheel? Will you whine and complain then?"

"I doubt very strongly that Declan would want to strap me to this thing," I snapped.

She snickered. "Don't be so sure about that. Declan has always been a man of sophisticated tastes."

She continued turning me as she spoke until I was almost upside down. My protests fell on deaf ears and my writhing against the straps was ignored. I heard a faint ping as one of my hair pins dropped to the ground. Between Rebecca's too-sweet perfume and being painfully strapped to the board with my head in the wrong direction, I was nauseous.

"Rebecca, stop this!" I pleaded.

She leaned over until her face was an inch from my own and I felt her breath on my cheek. "I want you to remember everything you're experiencing right now when you think you're cut out to work alongside the likes of Gabrielle," she sneered. "Or me, for that matter. You are nothing but a little girl playing dress-up and a total waste of our time."

"Enough!" roared a loud voice.

Neither of us had noticed Gabrielle's return. She stormed over to me as Rebecca stepped out of her way.

"Go back to your rooms, Rebecca. You are dismissed for the rest of the afternoon. I will speak with you privately tonight," Gabrielle said. She turned the wheel until I was right-side up again and locked it into position.

While Gabrielle unbuckled the straps on my wrists, Rebecca slowly returned her whip to its cabinet and then walked out of the room without saying a word.

Once I was free, Gabrielle helped me down off the platform and immediately wrapped her arms around me. "Are you all right? Would you like some ginger tea? Or, no, perhaps lemonade? I always find lemonade calming."

I assured her that I was fine, but massaged my sore wrists. Gabrielle led me out of the red room, back into the hallway where Cordelia waited.

"Miss Ava! You look to have seen a ghost!" she exclaimed.

I saw Gabrielle stiffen at this familiarity and Cordelia did, too.

"Forgive me, Miss Lyons," she said, and quickly crossed her hands in front of her apron and looked down at the floor.

"It's all right, Cordelia. Just refrain from outbursts like that when I'm entertaining."

"Oh, no Miss Lyons, I'd never! My granny taught me long ago that—"

Gabrielle raised her fingers to cut off her story. "Cordelia, please let Janie know that I'd like lemonade and cookies to be brought to my office."

"Yes, Miss Lyons," she said and left to find Janie.

"We'll go collect ourselves before we complete your tour. I want to hear exactly what that was that I just walked in on."

I followed her back through her false bedroom until we reached the narrow hallway that led to her real bedroom. She approached a non-descript wooden door I hadn't noticed earlier and pulled out a set of keys.

"You are one of the few people I've ever allowed into my office," she said.

"I had no idea you even had an office," I said, as I watched her work a series of locks.

Gabrielle opened the door and paused in the doorway. "Of course I have an office. I run a business."

Her office was housed inside the tower that looked out over Fifth Avenue. The room itself was relatively small, but it had a soaring, domed ceiling decorated with the constellations in gold leaf against a dark blue background. There was an ornate, oversized desk with carved lions standing guard at each corner. The walls were lined with bookshelves and there was a brown leather chesterfield sofa. It reminded me of a miniature version of the library downstairs.

Gabrielle took a seat on the sofa and gestured for me to do the same. "Now tell me what happened. How did you end up strapped to the Catherine wheel?"

I described all that had occurred and, more importantly, all that Rebecca had said. My wrists smarted, but it was her cruel words that bothered me more than anything.

Gabrielle listened, betraying no emotion, and then pinched the bridge of her nose, squeezing her eyes shut. I reached forward to touch her arm, alarmed by this gesture.

She opened her eyes. "I'm fine," she said and stood up to pace the room. "I can't account for Rebecca's behavior. This is unlike her. What she did was inappropriate in so very many ways."

Gabrielle leaned down and grasped my hands. "And what she said to you was uncalled for and untrue. You are not a waste of my time. I would not have you in my home if you were."

"How old is Rebecca?" I asked. "I've always thought she was my age, but the way she spoke to me today, I sensed she might be older."

"I don't know her exact age. I would estimate her to be between thirty-five and forty."

"No!" I exclaimed. "She looks no more than twenty!"

The side of Gabrielle's mouth curled up in a grin. "I agree. I've often wondered what deal she made with the devil to remain so well preserved."

There was a knock at the door. "Your lemonade, Miss Lyons," called out a soft voice from the other side.

Gabrielle opened the door and gestured for Janie to set the tray on the table in front of me.

Janie put the tray down and quickly glanced at me with concern. I could only imagine what Cordelia had reported back to her.

"Thank you, Janie," Gabrielle said as she saw her out. "After we're finished, I'll place the tray outside the door to be collected."

Gabrielle sat down again and we spent the next few minutes drinking and eating. The lemonade did help with the lingering nausea and I felt better than I'd expected.

"Your color has returned to normal, but you still look tired," Gabrielle said, studying me. "Given what you've just experienced, would you like to complete your tour, or should we reconvene another day?"

"I want to finish the tour," I said. I feared if I didn't, Gabrielle might change her mind and I'd never have this opportunity again.

"There are many logistical issues to show you, then." She crossed over to her desk where she pulled out a thick, leather-bound portfolio. "What I am about to show you has never been seen by anyone other than Albert. Declan knows of its existence, but he has never seen it. If this book were to ever fall into the wrong hands it could destroy the lives of many. You are never to repeat to anyone the contents of this book. Do you understand?"

"Yes, Gabrielle." My pulse had begun racing at the prospect of what the book contained.

Gesturing me over to her desk, Gabrielle opened it to a chart spread over two pages. "At the top, you'll see the man's name, his address and references, and any physical characteristics or personal traits I need to remember. Next to that is a list of his preferences, and then over in this column is every service or experience I have shared with him and on what date. To the far right of that is what I received in return: P stands for property, J for jewelry, S is for stock and dollar signs are self-evident."

I didn't know where to look first. I recognized quite a few of the names listed, and agreed with Gabrielle's assessment of the scandal that would ensue were this book ever to fall into the wrong hands. The amount of money she received was far more than I'd ever imagined—I suspected Gabrielle made more in three months than my father had in ten years. Then I read down the list of Services Shared. They ran the gamut from "quiet evening reading poetry" to "the regular French routine" to "frolic with 5 others from Kate Woods' House."

My cheeks burned, but I wasn't even sure what many of the entries meant. "What does that mean, Gabrielle?" I asked, pointing to the last that mentioned Kate Woods.

She peered over my shoulder at the specific entry. "Sometimes a gentleman will want to be intimate with a group of women, all at once. When that is required, I seek girls from a high-end establishment whose Madam I have an arrangement with."

"'Intimate with a group'—do you mean an orgy?" I asked.

Gabrielle laughed. "I had no idea that you knew that word! But yes, that particular evening could be defined as an orgy."

My mind was spinning. I'd heard of such things, largely from sneaking looks at the books my brother Rees had kept stashed under his bed that he didn't think anyone knew about. "And, you are all nude together?"

Gabrielle caressed my cheek. "Of course, darling."

I felt like my face was on fire.

Gabrielle's hand remained on my cheek, but her manner softened. "I have shocked you, I can tell. Please know, Ava, this is not the only way to be a courtesan. I'm sure there are some out there who don't participate in group experiences. You will need to decide what you are comfortable with and what your personal boundaries are."

I felt foolish for being so shocked. What did I think was going on in this wing of the house? Tea parties? Quilting bees? No, I was pathetically naive.

Then an awful thought struck me: did Declan participate in the orgies? Rebecca said he was a 'man of sophisticated tastes'—whatever that might mean. My nausea returned. Frantically, I started to search down the list of names, fearing what I might find, but I stopped myself. I was being absurd. What Declan did or didn't do wasn't my concern. Or shouldn't be.

Gabrielle closed the book and locked it in a drawer. "Tomorrow night I will be seeing the gentleman with the voyeur fantasy. Normally, Rebecca sits in the little room and watches us, but I think you should have that job this time. What do you think?"

"I ... I don't know," I said. I knew I was being tested, but between what had happened with Rebecca and what I'd just read in the book, I couldn't think straight.

Gabrielle nodded. "We're finished in the office. Let me show you the final two rooms, and you can decide."

I helped her carry the tray with our empty lemonade glasses into the hallway and watched as she locked the multiple locks that studded the door to her office.

"Our next room is right here," she said, pointing to a wooden door directly in front of us. She unlocked two locks and pushed in the door to a small room no larger than a closet.

In the dim light I made out an unfurnished space, save for an ornate floor lamp and one spindle-legged chair. The chair was positioned facing a pair of burgundy brocade drapes that stretched up to the ceiling. Gabrielle threw open the drapes with a flourish, to reveal a plain white wall that had a small, rectangular niche cut out in the center.

"Come sit down and look through the eye holes," she said, beckoning me.

I positioned my face at the holes, and peered through. Sure enough, they looked down upon the large, purple bed in the Scheherazade room. "What would you like me to do exactly?" I asked.

Gabrielle rested her hand on my back. "I want you to watch. Only for a few minutes, no more than ten. There is a small button inside the niche, probably near your right ear. Reach in and find it."

I withdrew my face and felt around until I found the small metal knob.

"Excellent," she said. "As soon as you are seated and ready, you'll press the button. That will sound a small chime in the room below that lets me know you're there."

"And all I have to do is sit and watch?" I asked.

"Yes. Although technically, you don't even need to watch. Once you've sounded the chime you can close your eyes. I will ask you not to leave immediately, however. There is a chance we might be able to hear your movements. But you'll know exactly when it's time to go."

It sounded like the simplest job in the world. And if I was honest with myself, I was curious to see firsthand what went on in that room.

"I'll do it," I said.

Gabrielle clapped her hands. "Wonderful! I'll give you all the specifics tomorrow evening."

She helped me up from the chair and then closed the drapes and ushered me out the door.

"This will be left unlocked for you tomorrow," she said as she busied herself with the keys. "Now. I have saved the best room for last. Come."

I followed her back down the spiral staircase, through her fake-bedroom and out into the beautiful hallway once again. We walked to the far end, to an alcove on the left. Inside the alcove was a door decorated with a swirling whiplash design that reminded me of the ocean.

"The Aphrodite room," Gabrielle said, and led me inside.

There was an oversized bed carved with mermaids and studded with gemstones, and a white marble fountain in the corner adorned with more oceanic motifs. But all of this paled in comparison to the focal point of the room: a breath-taking, twelve-foot-high, stained glass window depicting Aphrodite rising from the sea. It looked down upon the bed and bathed the whole room in its otherworldly colors.

"Albert had this commissioned for me from Tiffany Studios when we first returned to New York. This room was built to house the window."

I watched her looking up at the window, her profile awash in blues and greens from sunlight streaming through the glass. "It's you!" I exclaimed. "You were the model for Aphrodite."

"Of course. This is my home. If anyone is going to be portrayed as the Goddess of Love, it will be me!" she said with a wink.

We left the bedroom and I followed Gabrielle through yet another door that led out into the main section of the house, just by the grand staircase. As we came to the foyer, we discovered Janie and Cordelia waiting.

"Miss Lyons," Janie said, "A package just arrived for Miss Ava."

"For me?" I asked.

"Yes, miss," she said, and held out a small, square box wrapped in brown paper and twine.

"It's from Philadelphia!" Cordelia blurted out as I took the package.

"Philadelphia?" Gabrielle said, smiling at her outburst. "Open it right now. I don't think I can stand the suspense." She led me over to the large marble table that sat in the foyer.

I looked at the return address, but it was simply a street address with no name. I slipped off the paper and twine and found a deep blue box and cream-colored card within. With shaking hands, I opened the card.

Dearest Ava,

A small token to guide you on your path—think about what I said.

Yours,

D.

Feverishly, I tore open the box and found a necklace within. It was an oval-shaped pendant made of gold, adorned with a diamond-covered star with elongated rays, all suspended from a delicate gold chain.

Gabrielle leaned over my shoulder. "How lovely! A compass rose in diamonds," she said.

"A compass rose?" I asked, "I thought it was a star."

"It is. It's a directional guide and represents the four winds. Put it on, I know we're all anxious to see it on you."

I lifted the necklace out of the box and Janie rushed to help fasten the clasp behind my neck.

The three women sighed as I turned to face them.

"It's perfect," Gabrielle said, and came over to study it more closely. "Eighteen-karat gold and, oh, look at this."

She'd turned the pendant over to reveal a compass set into the other side. "How marvelously clever."

I held the compass side up in my hand and the four of us moved as a group in a circle, watching the changing direction of the arrow and giggling at what appeared to be our impromptu dance.

"I assume I know who this is from, but are you going to enlighten me?" Gabrielle asked when we came to a stop.

I handed her the card and watched as she read.

Gabrielle looked up and waved the paper in my direction. "See?" she said, with a triumphant grin. "Not chocolate!"

CHAPTER 7

Gabrielle held very few, if any, modesties concerning her body—I learned that soon after my arrival in the spring. This fact was confirmed as I sat in her chamber the next evening while she readied herself for the night ahead. She wore a dressing gown of tawny silk chiffon bordered at the hem by exotic ivory birds with flame-orange beaks. The fabric gathered at her waist with a column of three tiny buttons and was almost entirely see-through. She wore nothing underneath.

From my seat on her bed, I watched as she selected a crystal flacon from her dressing table and dabbed the perfume at the nape of her neck and between her breasts. These intimate gestures fascinated me. Growing up, I'd never seen my mother in anything less than her corset and chemise, and perfume was strictly for special occasions. I was not used to seeing another person so comfortable in their own body, and watching Gabrielle, I felt flushed and didn't know where to look. I wondered if any of this would ever feel normal to me.

"Where did you go, Ava?" Gabrielle said. "I was speaking

to you, but you clearly didn't hear me." She stood in front of me and caressed my face with her hand. The touch of her skin sent a shiver across my shoulder blades.

"I'm sorry. I was lost in thought."

"It happens to the best of us," she said, and sat down next to me, resting her hand on my knee. "As I was saying, Rebecca is going to stay with her family in Brooklyn for the rest of the month. Her parents are going through a difficult time, and she is distracted and not herself. It will be good for all of them to be together. In the meantime, Janie will take over some of her responsibilities."

I'd wondered what happened when Gabrielle spoke to Rebecca the night before, but felt it was wise not to ask. "Surely, Janie's new responsibilities will not extend to the Dragon Room downstairs," I said.

"No, not those responsibilities," Gabrielle said and squeezed my knee. "As Janie will be aiding me more, I want Cordelia to take over as your lady's maid. I suspect you both will enjoy that arrangement."

"Oh, yes! I like her tremendously." I always looked forward to seeing Cordelia, and knowing I wouldn't see Rebecca for the rest of the month added to my happiness.

"Excellent. Then that's settled," she said, and stood up. "I'm going to finish getting ready, but I want you to be in the viewing room at eleven p.m. sharp."

"I will be there," I said, rising at my cue to leave.

Gabrielle searched my face. "You know you don't have to do this tonight if you don't want to. If seeing me in such a ... private way is going to make you too uncomfortable—"

"It won't," I said, interrupting her before she could finish her sentence. I was tired of being coddled, and if I wanted Gabrielle to treat me as her equal, she needed to see me as such.

"All right then," she said, and stroked her fingertips over

Declan's necklace. "It looks like it was made for you. Declan has exceptional taste."

I flushed and looked away. It had not left my neck since I'd put it on the day before. "It's the most beautiful thing I've ever owned. I don't know how to thank him."

"You don't need to worry about that. Seeing you wearing it when he returns next month will be all the thanks he needs."

"I won't let you down tonight," I said, before I slipped out of the room.

"I know you won't."

⚜

The following hours were spent in my room, where I alternated between staring at the wall, worrying my thumb over Declan's necklace, and attempting to read *A Thousand Miles Up the Nile*. Back in Langley Falls I had so many chores to do that when I had a moment to myself it felt like a wondrous treat. At Gabrielle's, I had no chores and as my classes were becoming less frequent, I had too much time to think. I was in a strange in-between place: anxious for my *real* life to begin, but not knowing what that meant anymore.

Cordelia stopped by to see if I needed anything before she retired; her happy chatter was a welcome break from my ruminations. I didn't know if I should remain in my day dress while I was in the viewing room, but in the end, I decided to change into my nightgown as no one was going to see me anyway. I accepted Cordelia's help in undressing and then sent her on her way for the night.

At eleven p.m. I was seated in the chair in the closet-like room, leaning forward and looking through the eye holes. All I saw was darkness, but then I remembered I needed to press the little button. At that, dark lenses retracted and I could see down into the suite below me.

Gabrielle was already positioned on the bed, reclined against a shimmering pile of pillows. Her hair was loose and fanned out over her shoulders in a cascade of copper waves. She was nude, save for what looked to be a rope of diamonds fastened around her waist. In the dim lighting it was difficult to see details, but she looked the part of an odalisque from a painting come to life.

I held my breath, and my heart pounded in my ears in anticipation of what was about to happen. I was more nervous about watching than I'd expected.

A man entered the room from an arched doorway to my right. He was nude as well and appeared quite a bit older than she due to his silver hair, but he had a strong barrel chest and muscular legs. He didn't look like any of the men I'd met at last week's party, but admittedly, they'd all been wearing clothes and I was viewing him overhead and from behind. Gabrielle said something and held out her arms. The man crawled onto the bed and pulled her to him in a passionate embrace. They kissed, and his mouth traveled down her neck until he reached her breasts.

I watched transfixed as they kissed and snaked around one another, casting the pillows to the four corners of the bed. This went on for quite a while until he pushed her onto her back, spreading her thighs as he positioned his head between her legs. I mashed my face into the viewing holes, trying to get a better look. At the angle I was watching, I couldn't see all that he did, but I saw her evident pleasure. My pulse raced, and to my shock, I felt my own sensations creeping up from between my thighs.

And then without warning, the black lenses covered over the eye holes again and I saw only darkness. I slumped back in the chair, unsure what to do next. Watching Gabrielle and her partner was not nearly as strange as I'd expected, and my reaction had caught me off guard.

I'm a pervert now, I thought and tried not to giggle. My part had ended, so I pulled the curtains shut and left the little room, quietly closing the door behind me.

To get back to my bedroom I would pass through Gabrielle's. I knew I should go to bed, but I was restless and the chance to look around her chamber without anyone else present was too much of a temptation. I crept over to her dressing table and examined the assorted bottles scattered across; their cut-glass and metal toppers sparkled in the soft lighting. I selected the flacon that held her perfume, and rubbed a drop onto my wrist, inhaling deeply. She always smelled of night-blooming jasmine, and orange blossoms, with something spicy woven throughout. This scent was so much a part of her that it felt as though her ghost was present. I paused and looked around me, but I was alone. Next, I picked up her brush, it was square shaped with a sterling handle of ornately detailed nude women. Running my palm over the rough bristles, I looked up and saw my reflection in her mirror.

Could I envision myself in this life? The longer I lived here, the harder it was for me to tell anymore. Would I ever feel comfortable being watched when I was intimate with another? I pivoted my face from side to side, examining from which angle I appeared prettier. As I turned my head to the left, I spied Gabrielle's dressing gown lying on her bed. She hadn't worn it downstairs.

I walked over to the gown, leaving the vanity behind. Caressing the fine fabric between my fingers, I held it up to the light to admire its translucency. Suddenly I had an idea: I shed my own nightgown and robe and pulled on hers.

Gabrielle's full-length mirror hung on the wall opposite her bed. It was carved with the goat god Pan chasing maidens along the bottom and winged cherubs scattering roses at the top. It was both beautiful and bizarre: Gabrielle called it "the intersection of the sacred and profane." I approached the mirror to see how I looked in her robe. Gabrielle was a few inches taller, so the fabric puddled at the hem, but overall, it suited me. Walking a step closer, I opened the robe and looked at my body. Pan seemed to leer at me with approval, but the angels appeared disappointed. I tried to imagine how a man would see me. How Declan would see me. Did I possess any of the seductive powers Gabrielle held? Watching her with that man, so lost in her abandon, had stirred me, and I still felt the ache between my legs.

All this unfulfilled desire—I was tired of carrying its weight. Yearning for Declan. Longing for my "real" life to begin. And wishing I was more like Gabrielle. All these desires were making me agitated. Making me brazen.

In a fit of inspiration, I dragged the chair from Gabrielle's dressing table over to the mirror, and sat down. Opening the robe, I examined my body from different angles; the elongated s-shape of my calf through thigh, the shallow swell of my abdomen. Then I pulled my legs up and rested them on the arms, opening myself to my own image. I slid my hand down and began stroking the cleft between my legs as I watched the woman in the reflection do the same. I saw a deep flush rising across the curve of her throat and I closed my eyes for a moment, focusing on the sensation building beneath my fingertips, when I heard a gasp.

My eyes shot open and I looked up to find Gabrielle standing behind me. She was nude, save for the diamonds still affixed around her waist. I was mortified, and about to jump up from the chair.

"Stay there," she said, flapping her hand towards me. "Wait one moment." She disappeared into her closet and remerged wearing an indigo kimono and carrying a shawl.

"Come, sit with me over here," she said, and led me to the divan by the fireplace.

My whole face burned with embarrassment and I didn't know how I'd ever look her in the eyes again. I sat down next to her and accepted the shawl she handed me, swaddling it around myself.

"The shawl is not for my sensitivities, darling. You can be stark naked in front of me and I won't care, but I sense you would be more comfortable."

I was humiliated, and I thought I might cry. "Gabrielle, I am so sorry, and so embarrassed—"

"Stop right there. You have nothing to apologize for and nothing to be embarrassed about. One of my rules is that shame does not exist in my house. It has a way of collecting in the walls like a poison and I won't have it," she said. "Besides, considering what you just watched and what I just walked in on, I think we're even."

I looked up into her face and saw the amusement in her eyes and felt instantly relieved.

"Normally, this is when I'd ring Janie for tea, but given the circumstances and how we are currently attired, I don't think that's the best choice. Dear Janie can only take so much!" she said and let out a big laugh.

I joined her laughing. Suddenly this whole situation was the funniest thing I could possibly imagine, and I collapsed forward, laughing so hard that hot tears streamed down my face and my shoulders shook. And then, in one instant, the laughter changed to sobs.

"No, no, no," Gabrielle said, and slid towards me, smoothing her hand over my back. "Oh, Ava, you're quite overwrought. Look at me, please."

I let out a shuddering cry and lifted my eyes to meet hers.

"What has brought this on?"

"I ... I don't really know. This has taken me by surprise," I said, as I attempted to wipe the tears away with the heel of my hand.

Gabrielle leaped up and went to her dressing table, reaching into one of its drawers to pull out a silver flask.

"Here, take a sip," she said, handing me the flask as she rejoined me.

"What is it?" I asked.

"Whisky. My grandfather swore it could cure all ails."

I nodded and took a sip, the now-familiar fire filling my throat.

"Of course, my grandfather was also an alcoholic," she continued.

I nearly spat out the whisky as I fought to contain my laugh.

She grinned, taking the flask from my hand. "There. I made you laugh. It can't be all bad."

I wiped the remaining tears from my face. "I don't know where that came from."

She reached over and clasped my fingers. "You have been through a tremendous ordeal in a very short span of time. The death of your father. Your brother's betrayal. Coming to stay with me ... Maybe I have been too hard on you."

"No, Gabrielle," I said. "I am so grateful to you. I don't want to think what my life would be if I hadn't come to you."

"I know that," she said, and absentmindedly ran her fingers along the sleeve of her robe that I was wearing. "This looks better on you. I want you to keep it." She stood up again and put the whiskey back in its drawer. "I have put off introducing the sexual elements to you, hoping you would change your mind from pursuing this path. I admit, my intention tonight was for you to be unnerved by what you saw in the viewing room. But that did not occur, and I see now this is a war I am not winning."

"Why don't you want me to follow in your path? You have

created all this," I said, gesturing to our luxurious surroundings.

Gabrielle sat down again. "Because I want more for you."

"You sound just like Declan."

"I do?"

"Yes, he said the same thing to me," I said.

"Did he really? You've made quite the impression on him."

"He told me that he and I are kindred spirits."

Gabrielle cocked her head to the side. "I have watched him become involved with a seemingly endless stream of women over the past nine years, but always extricating himself before it turned serious. I have never known him to give anyone a piece of jewelry—certainly not anything like the necklace he sent you."

"Do you think Declan is interested in being my benefactor?" I said. "I know that's why the other men sent gifts."

"No, absolutely not. He gave you a very meaningful gift. He wouldn't be interested in sharing you with another man."

"But if I am to be a courtesan," I said, struggling to find the right words, "I don't know then how I should handle Declan."

Gabrielle looked surprised. "Is there anything for you to handle? Darling, you're overthinking this. Enjoy whatever time you spend with Declan and don't worry beyond that."

I nodded at her sage words, but knew I wouldn't be able to implement them.

"I've entered the slow time of the year. I'm sure you've noticed that I'm not as busy as I was over the summer," she said.

It was true. Throughout the spring and summer, Gabrielle's life seemed to be one big champagne-soaked whirl, but in the last week, she'd only gone out three times.

"You have fewer classes now, and I sense that has been a disservice to you; it's giving you more time left alone with your own thoughts. But I have more free time now, and we can figure out some novel activities to remedy that," she said. "My schedule moves opposite to the New York social calendar. During the summer, when most of the wives and children have been ensconced in their country homes, the men run wild. When the holiday season begins on November first, my schedule becomes slower."

"Because most of the men need to be involved with their families?" I offered.

"Exactly. Or work obligations."

"Is that ever difficult for you?"

"No. I know what to expect. Besides, Thanksgiving is my favorite holiday and the one I celebrate with *my* chosen family," she said, and squeezed my arm. "I'm not willing to give that up for anyone."

The sip of whisky had seemed to help. I felt calmer and my thoughts were clearer. "I'll finally get to meet your friends from Paris. They're all coming for Thanksgiving, aren't they?"

"Yes. When we met years ago, we were all so far from home, and so poor at the time, but our first Thanksgiving together turned out to be one of the loveliest holidays of my life. The wine was flowing heavily that night, and by the end George had drafted a proclamation stating that we were to gather every year on Thanksgiving for the rest of our lives. And most years, that has come to pass. This year is particularly special because our dear friend Marguerite is in town to perform at Madison Square Garden. She isn't always able to join us because of her touring schedule."

"I'm looking forward to meeting her," I said.

"Yes, I am anxious for you to meet. You're both so dear to me. Now, do you feel better?" she said and waited for my response. "Good. Then you should go to bed, and I need to get back downstairs to Reginald."

"Your gentleman is still down there?" I asked, shocked.

"Yes. He's asleep," she said, and leaned over to look at the little gold clock that sat on her dressing table. "I have at least another fifteen minutes until he wakes up." She stood up and helped me to my feet.

"But Gabrielle," I said. "What is the plan for me at this point? Will I attend another party?"

"I will throw my annual gala for my benefactors in December. It is the most significant party of my year. I explained to you about some occasions involving multiple people ..." she said as her voice trailed off.

I noticed she was choosing her words very carefully.

"Good heavens—look at what you've seen tonight! I needn't be so precious with you anymore. My annual gala is an orgy, Ava," she said bluntly.

"I see."

"You are welcome to attend of course, but I understand if it is not something you wish to participate in. You'll have a few weeks to think about it and decide."

I nodded. I had no idea what to say.

"But in the meantime, you and I will plan Thanksgiving!" she said. "It will be potluck and, as you know, I do not cook."

I laughed, remembering Gabrielle's inabilities in the kitchen from my childhood. "But I do!"

"I know you do. I was hoping you would make your mother's magnificent apple cider pie, or give Mrs. Kreisler the recipe."

"I'd love to make it," I said.

"Wonderful!" she said and leaned over to kiss me goodnight. "Now get to bed."

As I made my way back to my room, I realized that Gabrielle and I had just had a conversation that spanned the topics from family recipes to orgies, all while half-dressed. My life had already become something I couldn't have fathomed back in Langley Falls.

My nightclothes were still in Gabrielle's room, so I selected a new nightgown and climbed into bed. As I lay in the dark, I felt the reassuring weight of Declan's compass pressed against my chest. I prayed it would point me in the right direction.

CHAPTER 8

The bustle of activity leading up to Thanksgiving did a world of good for my overall disposition. Selecting flowers for the house, discussing recipes with Mrs. Kreisler, and making my mother's apple cider pie: these small acts made me feel as though I was contributing *something*. While Gabrielle insisted the meal was potluck, that was a largely ceremonial concept. All of her guests would bring a dish, but the majority of the dinner would be provided by Mrs. Kreisler and the kitchen staff. Thanksgiving was also a more casual affair than any other party Gabrielle hosted throughout the year. She gave her staff the day off, with a skeleton crew returning for a few hours to help with our seven p.m. dinner.

I spent the final moments before the guests arrived fussing over the flowers in the entryway.

"Ava, everything is glorious! Relax and enjoy yourself," Gabrielle said when she caught me fiddling with a chrysanthemum.

I couldn't help it. I wanted everything to be perfect.

George and his wife Charlotte were the first to arrive; his

booming laugh preceded them into the foyer. They appeared in elegant evening attire and carried wicker food hampers. Charlotte was not at all what I'd expected: small and pale, with light blue eyes, she stood barely over five feet. She wore a subdued gown of dove gray silk decorated with a delicate navy trellis motif, whereas George was his peacock-self in a dinner jacket of royal blue sateen embroidered with green ferns. Charlotte was the minimalist to her husband's excess.

"My sweet friend!" Gabrielle exclaimed as she embraced the petite woman. "How long has it been?"

George kissed my hand, and everyone said their greetings.

"Ava, it's a delight to finally meet you," Charlotte said. "I have heard nothing but the loveliest things about you from George."

Gabrielle looked the couple over and then peered past them. "Are the children accompanying us tonight? I didn't know if you would bring them or not."

"No, they are at home with my parents and my sister's family. We had our first meal with them earlier today. George and I decided we would be selfish and have the kind of holiday we used to have, before we became responsible adults. I can drink as much champagne as I wish tonight!" Charlotte said.

"As you should!" Gabrielle exclaimed. "Cordelia, please bring in a bottle of the Piper; we'll start with that. Oh, and your hampers! Janie, please take them into the dining room."

Janie gathered the baskets, while Cordelia went in search of the bottle of champagne to open for Charlotte.

Gabrielle was just about to usher all of us into the drawing room when the doorbell rang again. Forrest escorted in two men: Jack Laird, a musician, and Leopold Blackburn, a jeweler. They too appeared as opposites of one another. Jack was tall and rangy, with dark olive coloring and unruly coppery brown hair. Under his outercoat, he wore only a white button-down shirt and black pants. His clothes were of fine material, that was clear, but everything about him seemed rumpled; as though dressing had been an afterthought.

The second man, Leopold, was immaculate. He was shorter, with skin the color of rice paper, dark hair beginning to silver at the temples, and a well-groomed salt and pepper beard. He wore a pinstripe suit with an unusual dragonfly brooch on his lapel. Both men carried boxes that were soon whisked away by Janie.

"The only person left is Marguerite, and she's sometimes late," Gabrielle said, after introductions were made.

"Sometimes late? We'll be lucky if dinner starts by midnight, knowing Marguerite," Jack said.

Gabrielle stroked his cheek. "Don't start. I want you to be on your best behavior with one another."

"Aren't I always?" he said, flirtatiously.

"No. I remember that dinner in Venice when you and Marguerite all but tried to stab one another with your forks during the dessert course. We will have no repeats of that tonight. Do you understand?"

"Yes, ma'am," he said. "I cannot speak for Marguerite, but I promise to take the higher ground."

"Excellent. That is all I ask for," Gabrielle said, and kissed him on the tip of his nose "Let's retire to the drawing room. There are hors d'oeuvres awaiting us there."

As soon as the words were out of her mouth, the doorbell rang once more. Janie opened it and one of the most elegant women I had ever seen stepped into the foyer. She was tall and statuesque, like Gabrielle, her raven-black hair arranged with a constellation of small diamond stars. Janie took her cloak, revealing a gown of claret velvet, accented with Venetian lace that seemed to glow against her dark skin. She wore a stack of diamond bracelets up her right arm and a large ruby ring on each hand. This was Marguerite Walling-ford Légère, better known as "Madame Légère, The Nightin-gale," to those who followed popular music. She was strikingly beautiful and utterly intimidating.

I smiled at her and fought the urge to drop into a deep curtsy. She glanced at me sharply before allowing George to kiss her hello. Following behind Marguerite were three men wearing Fifth Avenue Hotel uniforms and carrying silver-domed platters.

"No one makes a better entrance than you," Gabrielle said, as she rushed to embrace her friend. The two women held each other for a moment and then Gabrielle broke away, remembering the men holding the platters. "Janie, please show them into the dining room. And will you check on Cordelia? She seems to have disappeared."

"I see you've spent hours in the kitchen," Gabrielle said, as the men walked past her.

"Hours upon hours," Marguerite agreed with a laugh. "One of the great joys of staying in a fine hotel is that one's manager may arrange to have meals provided from their fine kitchen."

"You needn't have gone to such extravagance for *us*," Gabrielle said. "You didn't need to bring anything: Mrs. Kreisler has created an exceptional menu."

"I have no doubt, *chérie*. If I could convince Mrs. Kreisler to come back with me to Paris, I would steal her from you in a heartbeat. But as I haven't succeeded yet, the culinary delights of Chef Sebastian will have to suffice."

In all the commotion, the men from the hotel reappeared in the foyer. "Madame Légère, when shall the carriage return for you?"

"You don't need to have the hotel's coach return for you," Gabrielle said. "You can use mine."

"Or we will take you to the hotel on our way home," Charlotte offered.

"It seems I won't be needing a return coach. Thank you, gentlemen," Marguerite said.

The men nodded, and Forrest saw them out.

Janie appeared in the foyer. "The dining room is set, Miss Lyons."

"Enough of this jibber-jabber!" Jack cried out. "Some of us are ravenous!"

"We don't have to begin in the drawing room with drinks," Gabrielle said to the group. "If everyone would prefer, we can proceed to the dining room."

"It feels very uncouth to forgo hors d'oeuvres, but the smells wafting from the dining room are just too tempting," Charlotte said.

George agreed. "This year let us break with convention and go right to the meal."

"To the dining room!" Jack called, and raised his fist in the air as though he was leading a charge to battle.

This brought another round of laughter and I knew at that moment it was going to be a fun night.

Cordelia finally appeared carrying a tray of champagne glasses and led everyone away. I began to follow, but felt Gabrielle's fingertips brush my arm.

"Wait, Ava," she said. "Marguerite, I would like you to meet my cousin Ava."

Marguerite's eyes widened. "Your cousin? I thought this was the Rebecca I've heard so much about."

"No, no," Gabrielle chuckled. "You won't be meeting Rebecca on this visit."

Marguerite's whole countenance changed when she realized I wasn't Rebecca. "Ava, how delightful to see you," she said and stretched out her bejeweled hand.

"The delight is all mine," I said as I clasped her fingers.

Marguerite held on to my hand but turned to her friend, "Ava is your cousin? Why have I never heard of her until this moment?"

"Surely I've mentioned her to you before."

"No. You haven't."

"Yes, I have!" Gabrielle admonished. "I told you about the little girl who lived next door, who I loved like a sister."

"Yes, of course I remember *that* Ava, but you never said you were cousins."

"How unusual," Gabrielle said, with an airy laugh.

Marguerite studied her. "Yes. How unusual, indeed."

I had no idea why Gabrielle continued to introduce me as her cousin, especially to this group of friends. But as always, she had her reasons. Declan felt the ruse was a way to protect me. Sometimes I wondered if she just liked the fantasy of having a blood relation she was actually close to. That fantasy appealed to me as well.

"Well, Ava," Marguerite said in her mellifluous voice, "then you shall sit by me at dinner." She slipped her hand into my elbow and I escorted her into the dining room.

The table was a masterpiece of silver urns overflowing with flowers and a jewel-studded cornucopia centerpiece spilling forth with sugared fruits and nuts. Against the golden damask of the dining room walls, everything seemed to shimmer and glow.

Janie and Cordelia had set all the dishes on the sideboard. It was an astonishing display of roasted turkey with both chestnut and oyster stuffings, *haricots verts amandine*, fish *au beurre blanc*, and an assortment of Mrs. Kreisler's extraordinary breads. Under the silver-domed platters, Marguerite had brought a potato galette, asparagus *aux hollandaise* and Maryland-style crab cakes, in honor of her birthplace. This sentimental touch made me like her even more. Charlotte and George brought a beautiful, ruby-red cranberry dish decorated with candied oranges, and a cheese-cake decorated with more candied fruits, almost too pretty to eat. Jack brought a selection of cheeses and Leopold a dazzling chocolate cake that, upon closer inspection, I realized was undoubtedly made by Mrs. Baeder. My contribution was a pumpkin pie and my mother's apple cider pie.

"Janie, Cordelia, everything is perfect! We'll be fine on our own for the rest of the night," Gabrielle said.

Janie nodded. "As you wish, Miss Lyons. Please ring for us should you need anything else this evening."

We wished them a happy Thanksgiving as they took their leave. Everyone swarmed the table, finding our name cards. For, as casual as this dinner was supposed to be, Gabrielle still insisted on seating everyone specifically.

"I'm at the head of the table?" Leopold asked

"Yes, of course," Gabrielle replied. "You always set the elegant tone to which we aspire."

I found my seat across from Marguerite at the other end of the table, with Jack to my left and Gabrielle at the head to my right.

"On second thought, I want to change seats with Ava. Here switch places with me," she said. As we moved to take each other's seats she whispered in my ear, "I want to put myself between Jack and Marguerite."

Once we were all finally seated with a plate of food in front of us and a glass of wine in our hands, Gabrielle raised her glass, "I give thanks for all my loved ones tonight; blessings abound! Let us rejoice!" she said before taking a sip, and we all followed suit.

The meal lasted for hours and the food itself was exceptional, but the stories, and the laughter they evoked, were even better.

"Do you remember when I tried to get you that job as a

chorus dancer?" Marguerite said, as she sliced into a spear of asparagus.

Everyone at the table groaned, causing Gabrielle to giggle.

"What happened?" I asked. The wine had made me feel more comfortable participating in their conversations.

"I was performing in a small cabaret," Marguerite said. "The finale was a number called '*Le Beau Rêve*' that involved my singing while a chorus of ten girls danced around me and sort of swished their skirts about and kicked. Gabrielle had no background in performance, but she was beautiful and charming, so I suggested her to the director because it was such a simple dance to learn." She leaned towards me. "What happened was truly awful."

"It was worse than awful," Gabrielle agreed. "I'm so very nearsighted, and I couldn't gauge the distance to the edge of the stage. I became too enthusiastic in my kicking and kicked out a footlight, thus setting fire to the table of a gentleman sitting right in front."

"No!" I gasped.

"No one was hurt," Marguerite quickly added.

"Thankfully!" Gabrielle said. "But that drew to a close my short, but illustrious, career as a dance hall girl."

"It's all right," Marguerite said with affection. "You have many other talents."

"I didn't realize you were so nearsighted," I said. "I've never seen you wearing spectacles."

"And you never shall," Gabrielle said and squeezed my arm.

"Vain," Marguerite teased.

"Said she who is wearing a king's ransom in diamonds," Gabrielle retorted and gestured to her friend's sparkling display.

"*Touché*," Marguerite said, and raised her champagne glass

to Gabrielle. "You and I always were cut from the same cloth. And it's a queen's ransom, *chérie*."

Gabrielle reached across the table to touch Marguerite's hand. "How I've missed you! We can't ever go this long again without seeing each other."

"I agree," Marguerite said, and stroked her hand.

"I was so hoping Gérôme would join you this trip. I haven't seen him in ages, either," Gabrielle said.

"He was supposed to, but his mother became ill right before I left. If she continues doing as well as she has been, he'll join me in Maryland for Christmas."

"I hope she gets well quickly," Gabrielle said, and then turned to me. "Marguerite is married to one of the most dashing men on Earth."

Marguerite smiled and looked down at her plate. "He is. We are very blessed to have found one another."

Jack had been watching this exchange with interest. "You didn't invite me to your wedding, Marguerite," he said. "So much for remaining 'friends'."

Marguerite tilted her face to the side. "And would you have attended if I had?"

They both held each other's gaze a moment longer than necessary.

"That's what I thought," she said and resumed eating.

In the uncomfortable moments that followed, we all focused on our own plates until Leopold stood up and walked over to the sideboard.

"Who would like more champagne?" he said and brought two bottles back to the table.

Everyone asked for a glass.

"When is your performance?" George asked Marguerite.

"Next Saturday, at the theatre in Madison Square Garden."

"I cannot wait to hear you sing again," he said and raised

his glass to her.

"Madison Square Garden?" Jack said as he cut into his turkey breast. "I'm surprised you're not performing at the Metropolitan Opera House."

Marguerite had just lifted her glass but stopped. "Is that supposed to be a joke?"

Jack looked confused. "Of course not. Why would it be?"

"Where have you been?" Marguerite's tone had taken on an angry edge.

"I've been touring in Russia for over a year. What are you talking about?"

Gabrielle leaned towards him. "The Metropolitan wouldn't allow Marguerite to sing there."

Recognition crossed his face as something unspoken that I didn't understand passed through everyone present.

"I'm sorry, Marguerite," Jack said. "I didn't know."

"Why wouldn't they allow you to perform?" I asked Marguerite softly.

"Because of the color of my skin," she replied.

I was horrified and said as much.

"Yes," she said, "but it is a moot point now, as the building burned down."

"The opera burned?" I asked. "Oh, yes. I remember reading about that."

"In August," Gabrielle said. "A workman dropped a lit cigarette in the room where all the paint was stored. It was all New York society seemed to be able to talk about for weeks."

"It was God's will!" Charlotte called out from the other end of the table, her cheeks flushed from champagne. "It was a sin that the Opera wouldn't allow Marguerite to sing, and God burned it to the ground!"

There was stunned silence until Leopold spoke. "I admit, I thought the same thing when it happened."

"I did, too," Gabrielle said. "You have performed all across

Europe for more members of royalty than I can count, yet the *Opera* wouldn't allow you? It was a disgrace."

"It wasn't just me, I should point out. The Opera's views have affected many artists. They didn't allow Sissieretta Jones to sing there either, and she went on to sing at Madison Square Garden earlier this year to great acclaim. Did any of you attend that performance? I so wanted to go," Marguerite said.

"I think Declan did," Leopold said.

"Declan!" Marguerite exclaimed. "I thought he would be here tonight. Where is he?"

"With his family, outside of Philadelphia," Gabrielle said.

George said something to Leopold that caused everyone at the other end of the table to laugh and begin a conversation amongst themselves.

Marguerite leaned across the table towards Gabrielle. "Now, tell me the latest gossip about Declan," she said in a near whisper. "Who is he having assignations with this month?"

My stomach clenched at her words.

Gabrielle winked. "I think for the first time since I've known him, I can honestly say there is nothing to tell!"

She did not look my way as she said this, and I wondered if her answer would have been the same if I hadn't been present.

"No! Really?" Marguerite said.

"Yes, really. It seems our Mr. Aldridge is changing his ways," Gabrielle said.

Marguerite sighed. "I have often thanked my lucky stars that I never fell in love with him. What a heartbreaker he is," she said and then turned to me. "Have you met Declan, Ava?"

"Yes, I have," I said, attempting to keep all emotion out of my voice.

"Ava has become a favorite of Declan's," Gabrielle said.

"He gave her the necklace she is wearing."

"Did he?" Marguerite said and glanced at Gabrielle. "I noticed the necklace immediately. It's exquisite. May I?"

I held the pendant out for her inspection.

"Eighteen-karat gold ... excellent quality diamonds. How clever!" she said when she saw the compass. "Declan has beautiful taste. This is quite a gift."

The dessert course came, and my pies were well received.

"Ava, I just met you, but I'd marry you for this," Jack said as he tasted the apple cider version.

"It was my favorite pie as a child," Gabrielle agreed. "What a delight to have it again."

I felt a kind of pride that I hadn't experienced in all the time I'd been in the city.

As we finished, Gabrielle suggested we move into the drawing room for after-dinner drinks. Charlotte and Leopold sat on the settee talking. Gabrielle and George roamed the room discussing the artwork while Jack trailed behind them, smoking a cigarette.

"Bring your champagne and come sit with me, *chérie*," Marguerite said when she spotted me pouring myself another glass. I joined her in the two wingback chairs by the window.

"How long have you been staying with Gabrielle?" she asked.

"Just over six months."

"That long! And how have you been spending your days?"

Marguerite was clearly trying to interrogate me, but her motives did not seem malicious. Just curious.

"Gabrielle arranged for me to take classes in history, French, dance, art."

"Did I hear my name?" Gabrielle appeared and took a seat on the leather ottoman in front of us.

"I was just asking Ava what she's been up to since staying with you," Marguerite said, and then lowered her voice so no one else in the room could hear. "I love you, Gabrielle, but I don't believe this 'cousin' business for a moment. What are you up to?"

"You and your intuition," Gabrielle said. "Ava is not my cousin, though she might as well be. I don't want the others to know this though."

"You needn't worry about that. Most of the time people only see what they want to see, anyway. But why do you need this ruse?" Marguerite said.

"Gabrielle took me in when I escaped a bad situation. I've hoped to follow in her footsteps and become her protégée," I said.

Marguerite exhaled. "Ah, this all makes sense now: the lights I've seen around you. The figures behind you—they are your parents, aren't they?"

I was confused and didn't know what Marguerite was referring to.

Gabrielle squeezed my hand. "Marguerite is a Spiritualist. It is so normal to me that I forget others don't know."

"It isn't something I advertise," Marguerite said. "Not everyone shares our views."

"They should. It is a gift from God, just like your singing."

"I wish you could convey that to some members of my family," Marguerite said and absentmindedly ran her fingers over her diamond bracelets.

During their back-and-forth, my brain was reeling. "Please forgive me, but are you saying that my parents are here? Right now?"

"Yes. You've had a couple with you through much of dinner. Your mother comes through stronger, though."

I turned and looked behind me. "Is she here now?"

Marguerite focused on a point just beyond my chair. She closed her eyes and smiled. I had forgotten to breathe and realized I was clutching Gabrielle's hand in a vise-like grip.

"She is here," Marguerite said as she opened her eyes. "She said that you are at a fork in the road and don't know which path to take. When the time comes to decide, you will choose wisely and should not doubt yourself. She's fading, but she also said that she knows you wonder if she would be proud of you, and she is. Tremendously so."

Tears began rolling down my cheeks. In all the time I'd been at Gabrielle's, I'd wondered what my mother would think of my new circumstances. Would she be horrified, or would she understand my choices? I knew this wasn't the life she had planned for me.

Gabrielle wiped my tears away with her handkerchief. "Marguerite's visions have that effect. Didn't you say you saw lights around Ava? That's always good, isn't it?"

Marguerite nodded. "Yes, you're being guided. There are unseen forces at work who are aiding you. The lights also indicate that a dramatic change is coming. What do you see, Gabrielle? I know you have visions, too."

At that moment a loud clap of thunder sounded and seemed to shake the walls.

"Well, that was foreboding," Gabrielle said and stood up. "Was it supposed to storm tonight?"

"The rain was just starting when we arrived," George said. "Such strange weather we're having for this time of year."

Charlotte squealed. "Oh, a storm!"

"Let's move our party to the spiritualist room," George quickly added. "The sound of the thunder and wind will provide the perfect backdrop."

"Yes! It will be so atmospheric!" Charlotte agreed.

"That's fine with me," Gabrielle said, "Does anyone mind if we move on to the spiritualist room?"

Marguerite gestured her assent. Jack shrugged.

"I would be delighted. I can visit my old friends," Leopold said.

"In more ways than one," Marguerite said dryly, causing Leopold to chuckle.

I didn't understand the joke.

We followed Gabrielle out of the drawing room, through the darkened labyrinth of the private wing, until we reached the correct door and filed inside, all giddy from champagne.

Charlotte beelined to the giant crystal ball that took place of precedence in the center of the room. "This beauty!" she cried and splayed her fingers across its surface.

There were cabinets filled with more rare gemstones and beautiful oddities. A purple velvet chaise longue lay in one corner and an assortment of jewel-toned velvet and brocade chairs were scattered about the perimeter of the room. I selected a scarlet throne with a firebird print and sat down.

"What exactly is the purpose of this place?" Jack said as he studied a dramatic chandelier of smoky quartz and amethyst drops.

"It serves many purposes," Gabrielle said. "First and foremost, it is a sanctuary where one may try to contact the spirits. It is a cabinet of curiosities and a place of contemplation. And for some of my gentlemen, it is the backdrop to their fantasies."

Marguerite ran her hand over the crystal ball and hummed softly. "Do you know many men with fantasies that involve spirits?"

"Not many, but there have been a few, and I like to be prepared," Gabrielle said with a grin.

Marguerite winked at her.

Jack reclined on the chaise with his arms behind his head. "We're all here. Now what?"

Charlotte had begun swaying around the room and came to a stop. "A séance! What do you think, Marguerite?"

"Is there someone in particular you wish to contact?" she said, without looking up from the crystal ball.

"Hmmm. Let me think," Charlotte said and resumed her swaying dance.

Leopold rummaged in a cabinet with his back to all of us. "You and Albert really did amass an extraordinary collection of specimens. I wish you would put this ruby in a safe though. It makes me nervous to think that you have it out like this," he said and held up a red stone the size of my fist. As the light from the chandelier bounced off its surface, I saw a star form.

"Don't worry Leo, this room is always locked," Gabrielle said, "and Albert designed the security himself."

"Albert!" Charlotte called out, mid-pirouette.

"What about him, love?" George said, and pulled her onto his lap to stop her impromptu (and annoying) dance.

"We should contact Albert!" she said.

Marguerite looked up. "I think that should be Gabrielle's decision."

Gabrielle shook her head. "I already know Albert is here. I talk to him all the time. There is no need to contact him."

Marguerite nodded. "All of you have loved ones around you tonight."

Leopold left the cabinet and joined Marguerite. "Do you feel like doing this? Tonight is your holiday, too."

Marguerite touched his arm. "It's my pleasure. Let's just start and we'll see who wants to come through."

Another crack of thunder sounded, and I thought I saw the chandelier sway. Maybe I had drunk more champagne than I realized.

"This is some storm," Jack said as he stood up from the chaise.

Marguerite suggested we form a circle around the crystal ball. We dragged chairs from around the room while Gabrielle dimmed the lights, and then we took our seats, holding each other's hands. I had never been to a séance before; it was something I'd only read about in novels.

"Close your eyes and take a deep breath," Marguerite said. "Our minds affect our surroundings, so make sure your thoughts are pleasant ones. Find a favorite memory: perhaps it was a beautiful day when the sky was blue, and you were surrounded by flowers. Perhaps it is the memory of your baby's head, heavy on your shoulder asleep. Or your beloved's laugh. Choose a happy memory and sit with it."

I held Marguerite's hand on my left and George's on my right. The pressure of her palm was steady and centered. George's hand engulfed mine and at times felt as though an electrical current ran through his palm. The musical lilt to Marguerite's voice lulled me into a relaxed state. In my mind's eye I traveled through a kaleidoscope of images from child-hood: the graceful trees that arced over my family's house, the quilt my mother made tucked around me in bed, its calico soft against my cheek, scented with lavender and the smell of the wind from when she hung it outside to dry. Everything was silent save for the sounds of our breathing. After an inde-terminate amount of time, Marguerite told us to open our eyes.

"We join here tonight, a circle of friends bound together with love and trust. Benevolent spirits who wish to speak are invited to join us."

I felt Marguerite's hand stiffen and I peered out into the dark corners of the room. In the low lighting the shapes of the stones and oddities played tricks on my mind, turning their benign forms into monsters waiting to pounce.

"Speak, gentle spirit. Tell me your name," Marguerite said. She paused, with her head tilted towards her shoulder. "Amberly. That's such a lovely name, and yes, your brother Jack is right here."

From the other side of the crystal ball I heard a sharp

inhale.

"Amberly!" Jack said in a choked voice.

"Sweet girl, what message do you have for your brother?" Marguerite said.

We all sat silently, waiting while she listened to a voice no one else could hear.

"I see," she said at last. "Jack, Amberly says you blame yourself for her death and have suffered needlessly. Nothing you did caused what happened. She says you were a wonderful brother, and she always looked up to you. She wants you to know that she's very happy now. She's with your grandparents and your dog, Clover. You have carried the weight of this guilt for far too long. It's time for you to let all the bad memories go and move on. She isn't suffering, and she doesn't want you to suffer either." Marguerite's voice cracked as she finished the message. "She knows you play her favorite waltz, and she loves to sit beside you at the piano when you do. She loves you so."

Tears were streaming down my face and all around the table I could hear sniffling and throat-clearing. This was far more emotional than what I'd imagined a séance to be.

Marguerite's hand stiffened once again. "Another spirit is present, but I can't make them out as clearly," she said. "Come forward, friend, and show yourself."

At that moment, the loudest clap of thunder sounded, startling everyone and causing the remaining lights to go out. Marguerite appeared to be in an altered state and did not notice. "Yes, that's it, come closer."

As she said this, I could have sworn I heard footsteps. All the fine hairs on my arm stood on end.

"That's it, just a little closer ... let me see your face," Marguerite said.

The footsteps became louder and my heart pounded in my chest. I clutched at George's hand and felt him respond with a reassuring squeeze. Another crack of thunder and the door to the room swung open, revealing the outline of a tall, dark figure. Every childhood nightmare I'd ever had seemed suddenly real.

Someone screamed, and I closed my mouth, relieved to realize that the sound hadn't come from my lips. The figure in the doorway took a step towards us and I was about to jump up from the table and run when the spirit suddenly spoke in a voice we all could hear.

"Making the ladies scream in terror when I enter a room is not the effect I'd hoped for," the voice said, and a disembodied hand held up a lantern to reveal the face of Declan Aldridge.

Back in the drawing room, I sat on the sofa next to Leopold and Gabrielle as we cradled glasses of brandy in our shaking hands.

"I think you've shaved a good decade off of my life expectancy," George said.

Declan handed him a snifter of brandy. "I apologize for terrifying all of you. That certainly wasn't my intention. Janie let me in and told me you were all in the spiritualist room. I convinced her that I could see myself down in the dark."

Marguerite sat on a loveseat by the fireplace with Charlotte, who rested her head on its back, a cold compress covering her face. A muffled sound came from beneath the cloth.

"My love, we can't understand you," George said and leaned over to fold back the compress from her mouth.

"I said, we all thought you were spending Thanksgiving with your family in Philadelphia," Charlotte said.

"Bryn Mawr," Declan answered, and took his seat next to

Leopold.

Charlotte waved her hand meekly in the air. "Close enough."

Declan chuckled. "Thanksgiving with my relatives was the plan, but I soon learned that my great-aunt had many ulterior plans. Namely, introducing me to every Main Line heiress under thirty."

Leopold shook his head. "What is it like to be you?"

"Usually most enjoyable," Declan replied. "But not this week. I reached my yearly allotment of pained small talk last night when a very sweet girl fresh out of finishing school confided in me that her lifelong dream was to sew ball gowns for her cat. Or perhaps it was for all cats—I may have missed some nuance there."

All of us laughed except Charlotte, who peeled back her compress and eyed Declan. "Did you get to see the cat?" she asked.

"No, sadly, I did not," he said.

"That's disappointing," she said. "It might have been a very attractive cat who was quite worthy of a ball gown."

"Yes. This is true," Declan said

"Something to consider," she said somewhat frostily and then covered her eyes once more.

I bit down on my lip and tried to suppress a giggle.

Marguerite leaned over and stroked Charlotte's hand. "That's right, *chérie*. Fight the good fight," she said, bringing another round of laughter from the room.

"And that is why I will always hold you in the highest esteem, Charlotte. No matter what the endeavor, if it is creative in nature, you will be its champion," Declan added. "But as compelling as winsome felines in hoopskirts may be, I couldn't stand another second of my father's family. So, I invented an emergency back in New York, and caught the first train I was able to get a ticket for today."

"This is where you should have been all along," Marguerite said.

"I couldn't agree more," he said.

Gabrielle seemed agitated during their exchange and stood up, searching the room. "Say, does anyone know where Jack is? He was with us when we left the spiritualist room, but I haven't seen him since."

"Oh, dear," Marguerite said, rising, and a brief look passed between them. "I'll help you find him."

Declan started to stand, too, but Leopold stopped him. "Stay here, you've just spent hours traveling. I'll help them."

Charlotte folded back her compress again. "Do you want me to come, too?"

"No, love," George said, and took Marguerite's place next to her on the loveseat. "Just rest."

The room emptied, and I was left with Declan on the settee. He had greeted me, but in all the commotion of his arrival we hadn't had a chance to speak.

I looked over to him and found him staring at me, smiling. "I'm glad to see you are wearing the necklace," he said.

"It's so beautiful," I said, and instinctively reached up to caress its surface between my fingers. "I wanted to send you a note but didn't know where to send it. I don't begin to know how to thank you."

He slid closer towards me on the sofa and rested his arm along its back. "That you are enjoying it is all the thanks I need."

There was so much I wanted to say to him, but I couldn't find the words. Or at least, not with Charlotte and George sitting directly across from us. I looked down at my hands in my lap and smiled.

Just then Jack burst into the room. "There's the ghost!" he said, pointing to Declan with a strange laugh. "That was quite a scare you gave us." His words came out faster than normal and he moved unsteadily.

"Jack, come sit down," Declan said.

"There you are!" Leopold said as he marched back into the room with Gabrielle and Marguerite close on his heels.

"Where am I?" Jack said and threw back his head, laughing.

It was an odd response and Gabrielle walked over and placed her hand on his cheek. "Are you all right?"

"Why wouldn't I be? We're all together and the night is young!" He broke away from her and spun around towards the piano. "All we are lacking is music," he said and marched over and took his place at the keys.

Gabrielle looked over to Marguerite and once again an unspoken message seemed to pass through everyone in the room.

A torrent of sounds exploded from the instrument and then Jack launched into an upbeat tune for dancing.

Gabrielle and Leopold joined us on the sofa, and we all listened while Jack played passionately, both too fast and too loud. I wondered if this was the waltz his sister had loved.

"If I didn't have this wretched headache I'd get up and dance," Charlotte said as she rested her head on George's shoulder.

Marguerite stood in the center of the room and watched Jack pound away at the keys. As he started the piece over again, she walked over to the piano and stood where he could see her.

"You never did like this one, did you Mimi?" Jack said.

"That's not true," she said, softly. "There are other pieces that I like more."

"Then let's find one you love," Jack said. The tempo changed immediately into a beautiful, lilting melody.

Marguerite smiled sadly. "'*Ombra mai fu*.' My favorite."

Jack continued to look at her while he played. "My favorite, too. Will you sing if I start from the beginning?"

Marguerite paused as if to say something and then slowly nodded.

Jack started the melody over again, and Marguerite's posture became even more regal as she prepared to sing. Her voice began softly, almost as though she was singing a lullaby, and I felt every nerve ending in my body ignite on certain notes. She sang in Italian, so I didn't understand the words, but it didn't matter: her voice was haunting. Declan's hand slid down from the back of the sofa and wrapped around my shoulder, sending a cascade of goosebumps over my skin.

Movement fluttered in the corner of my eye, and I turned to see Gabrielle beckoning towards the doorway to the room. At her gesture, Janie, Cordelia and Mrs. Kreisler slipped inside to hear the music better.

Jack came to the end of the piece and started over again, Marguerite seemed to know he would do this and as she started the song over again, she switched to the lyrics in English.

Let Fate smile upon you
May thunder, lightning and storms
Never disturb your dear peace,
Nor may you by blowing winds be profaned.
Never was a shade of any plant
Dearer and more lovely,
Or more sweet.

Jack kept his eyes steady on Marguerite while he played, never once looking at the keys. She, in turn, kept her focus on him: she was singing to Jack. Between the sweetness of the lyrics, and the way they looked at one another, I felt tears welling up. I looked around the room and saw that almost everyone's eyes were glistening. Declan's face was in profile, but he turned towards me at that moment and I could see by the way he held his mouth that he was affected, too. The fire burning behind me reflected on the surface of his eyes and I felt an unbearable yearning for him.

"Brava! Bravo!"

Leopold leaped to his feet cheering, and everyone else followed suit. I was so lost in my own thoughts about Declan that I hadn't realized the performance had come to an end. Declan held out his hand to help me stand and I joined in the applause.

Jack stepped away from the piano and hugged Marguerite. She kissed him on his cheek and whispered something in his ear. When they broke away from one another, both had tears running down their cheeks. She curtsied with the grace of a prima ballerina and he followed with an elegant bow.

The evening had come to an end. Janie and Cordelia helped everyone with their coats and as we walked towards the foyer it was clear Jack was still moving unsteadily.

"But the night is young!" Jack said, as he wobbled, nearly smashing the flower arrangement onto the marble floor.

Declan rushed over and caught him in time. "Go home and get some sleep, Jack."

"Nonsense!' Jack said, attempting to break away from Declan's grip without success. "Say, let's go downtown to the club. It will be like old times."

"All right. We can do that," Declan said in the measured tone one used with a child.

"I'll join you," Leopold said.

"Now that's more like it!" Jack exclaimed.

"Leo, will you help Jack out to the carriage? I'll be out in a moment," Declan said.

"Of course."

Leopold and Jack said their goodbyes and Forrest saw them out.

"Are you out of your mind, Declan?" Marguerite spun

around with outrage as soon as they were out of earshot. "Surely you're not going to take him to the club! Not in that state!"

"Of course not," he replied. "Leo and I will take him back to my house. He'll stay with me tonight."

"He's taken something," Marguerite said softly

Declan took her hand. "I know. Leopold and I have dealt with this before. Many times."

Gabrielle shook her head. "I'm so sorry the night ended this way. Thank you for taking care of him."

"Please don't worry. Jack will be fine. Leo and I will speak with him," Declan said, and turned to me. "But that isn't why I stayed behind. Ava, if you are available this coming Wednesday, I would like to take you out in the afternoon."

It had become a standard reaction to Declan, but I felt my face become enflamed. "Why, yes. That would be lovely."

Declan smiled. "Excellent. Then I shall pick you up at one p.m."

"Are you going to tell me where you are taking Ava?" Gabrielle said. "I am responsible for her welfare, after all."

"No. You'll just have to trust me," Declan said. "It is a surprise."

"But surely, you'll give her some idea of what the afternoon will entail," Marguerite added. "Ava needs to know how to dress, after all."

I glanced over at Gabrielle and Marguerite standing side by side, their arms crossed and brows arched, almost identically.

"You two could wear down an iceberg," Declan said. "Ava should dress as she always does when she dines at Delmonico's."

"Ah, so you're taking her to Delmonico's then?" Gabrielle said.

"No. I am not."

We all stared at him, expecting further information, and soon realized none was forthcoming.

Gabrielle let out an exasperated sigh. "You are maddening!"

"Always," he agreed and then slipped out the door into the night.

Charlotte and George appeared in the foyer, bundled up for their ride home.

"Did we miss saying goodbye to them? Well, we'll see them at the performance next week," Charlotte said, as she kissed Gabrielle goodbye.

"Marguerite dear, may we see you back to your hotel?" George asked.

"Yes, thank you," she replied.

Janie helped Marguerite with her cloak. As we said our goodbyes, she took my hand and flashed a mischievous smile. "I will expect to hear where Declan takes you on this mystery outing."

"I promise: I will tell you," I said.

"Mystery outing?" Charlotte said. "I'll want to hear about this too!"

"And on that note, it's time to leave," George said, with a twinkle in his eye. "Well, Ava, you survived your first Thanksgiving with us. I shall add your name to the proclamation: you'll join us every year for the rest of your life."

"Good heavens, George!" Marguerite said, "I'm surprised you didn't make us take a blood oath."

Charlotte rolled her eyes. "Oh, he would've if he'd thought of it, so don't give him any more ideas!"

We saw them out into the cold night and could still hear their laughter echoing down the empty street when we closed the door.

Gabrielle looped her arm through mine as we started our slow ascent upstairs. "You're one of us now. It's official."

CHAPTER 9

"Where do you think Mr. Aldridge will take you?"

Cordelia asked me this question every morning for the next six days when she helped me dress and arrange my hair. Eventually it evolved into a guessing game of sorts. As the days stretched on, each guess became more outlandish than the next (cliff diving lessons! lion taming!) until we couldn't pass each other in the halls without giggling.

Gabrielle selected my ensemble for the mystery outing: a striking dress in shades of amber, trimmed with russet. "It really highlights your eyes and hair," she said. "We have no idea where you're going, but you'll look exquisite. Like the Queen of Autumn."

"What happened to 'the human incarnation of early spring and all that she promises'?"

Gabrielle narrowed her eyes and pinched my arm playfully. "Seasons change."

Wednesday arrived, and at one p.m. Declan's elegant black brougham pulled up outside.

"How delightful you look, Ava," he said as he helped me into his carriage.

His eyes swept over me with appreciation and, given the way they lingered, I was glad I had listened to Gabrielle's Queen of Autumn idea. I thanked him and arranged myself on the velvet seat beside him. The vehicle rolled down Fifth Avenue, but I still had no clue as to our destination.

"We have beautiful weather today. There's nothing quite like autumn in New York." He continued to make small talk about the weather as well as the new carriage styles that would be popular in the coming year: he was intentionally prolonging the surprise.

When he began pointing out which types of door knobs he found particularly attractive as we rode past, I reached my limit. "For heaven's sake, Declan! Where are we going?"

He grinned and arched his brow. "Can't stand the suspense any longer, I take it?"

"That is something of an understatement." The last six days had seemed impossibly long, but his ruminations on bronze door knobs had felt even longer.

"I won't torture you anymore. This will explain all," he said and handed me a paper portfolio.

With trembling fingers, I took the portfolio from him and unwound the string that held it closed. Carefully I eased out a small stack of paper and began to read the first page. It appeared to be the receipt for a painting. "*Portrait of Guinea Fowl and Tulips*? I don't understand."

Declan grabbed the paper out of my hand and read the contents himself. "Damn it!" he growled and then commanded his driver to turn the carriage around. "Please forgive my outburst, Ava. My valet handed me the wrong portfolio. We're going to stop by my house, so I can retrieve the correct one."

In the all the time I'd spent with Declan, I'd never once

seen where he lived. Inwardly I cheered at the prospect of getting to see his home. I knew he lived near Gabrielle, and moments later we pulled up to a sprawling stone mansion.

As soon as the carriage stopped, Declan turned to me. "It won't do for you to be seen entering a bachelor's residence. I will only be a few minutes."

"Declan, it's cold out here. Surely, there is a member of your staff who can guard my honor for whatever time I am within your home." I gathered myself and made it clear I wasn't waiting for his answer. Choosing not to argue with me, he helped me down and escorted me through the grand front doors.

The first thing I was greeted with as I entered the great hall were the portraits. Seemingly endless sets of eyes stared back at me from every direction: it was a century's worth of Aldridge family members committed to oil paint. They appeared a judgmental lot and seeing them all together when first walking in the door felt like an assault. Suddenly, I appreciated all the lecherous satyr paintings at Gabrielle's in a way I hadn't before.

Staff members tried to help me with my coat, but Declan waved them away. "We aren't staying," he said.

An elegant man in uniform with thick black hair approached. He had a look of grave concern on his face. "Sir, we hadn't expected you home so soon."

"Miss Richards, allow me to introduce you to my right hand and sometimes brain, Alistair," Declan said.

"You honor me, sir," he said

"But not today. You gave me the wrong portfolio, Alistair!"

"Mr. Aldridge, you asked for the portfolio on your desk."

"Then there must've been more than one portfolio, and I didn't realize it. Come, Ava, we'll stop by my study, and then we'll be off."

I took Declan's offered arm as he escorted me down the long hallway towards his study door. Yet more Aldridge eyes followed us.

Once inside I was delighted to find a beautiful space of warm woods and tasteful appointments, with floor-to-ceiling windows that looked out on a walled garden. Everything was orderly, but comfortably so, with the exception of Declan's desk, which had a snowdrift of paperwork.

"Please warm yourself by the fire, Ava. This won't take but a minute," Declan said as he began searching through a pile of paper.

I took my seat, and Alistair appeared in front of me.

"Would you care for tea, Miss Richards?"

"We're not staying long enough for tea!" Declan snapped.

"Sir, there is always time for tea. To think otherwise is uncivilized."

"Fine, fine. Do what you must, Alistair."

"Very good, sir. Miss Richards, may I bring you tea?"

I was afraid to say no. "Yes, Alistair. Thank you."

He nodded and left the room.

As soon as he was out of earshot, Declan chuckled. "I should know better than to argue with him. He's always right."

Declan's movements were becoming increasingly frantic as he searched his desk.

"Would you like some help?" I asked

"Thank you, but no. It's not here. I must have left the folder upstairs. Forgive me, Ava, I'll be back in a moment."

"Take your time. It's lovely by the fire, and it will give me more time to enjoy the tea," I said with a toothy grin.

He laughed and rushed out of the room.

Left to my own devices, I slowly peeled off my leather gloves and lay them in a neat stack on the ormolu table to my side. I shrugged off my coat, too, for Declan's "few minutes" seemed to be stretching out far longer than expected. The urge to roam around his study was strong, but I knew Alistair would return at any moment. He could not, under any circumstances, find me in a situation that could be construed as snooping.

But Declan's study was filled with rare and valuable art pieces — it seemed a crime not to appreciate such fine works on closer inspection. I stood and walked the perimeter of the room, keeping my hands clasped casually behind my back. There was a globe made entirely of gemstones: the earth's oceans in shades of lapis lazuli and the African continent in malachite. And a magical looking wooden mask with a nacreous finish that shimmered like a butterfly's wing.

Then I looked up into the face of a beautiful woman whose eyes I knew all too well. This had to be a portrait of Declan's mother. She had brown hair flowing loosely over her shoulders and wore a white dress with a pink ribbon tied around her wrist. Everything about her spoke of spring and renewal. The artist had portrayed her in an allegorical scene, if I wasn't mistaken. I leaned forward to study the painting closer. The artist's signature read "Bouguereau". I stared rapt at how he had painted her skin: she seemed to pulse and thrum with life. Something about her expression touched me and gave me a sense of who she was as a person. And the heartbreaking scope of all that Declan had lost with her death.

"It's a magnificent portrait, isn't it, Miss Richards?" Alistair said as he entered the room with a sterling silver tea tray.

I nearly jumped at his words— he moved with the quietude of a cat, and I hadn't heard him enter.

"Forgive me for startling you," he said. "It's just so nice to see someone admiring Mrs. Aldridge."

"Did you know Mrs. Aldridge, Alistair?"

"Yes, miss, I did. I've worked for the Aldridge family since

I was practically a boy," he said as he placed the tray on a table and began the tea preparations. "She was an extraordinary woman. High spirited but kind, always kind. Mr. Aldridge inherited more than just his looks from his mother. Did you notice the angel pulling at her sleeve?"

"I beg your pardon?"

"Forgive me. This painting is a personal favorite of mine, and it is so rarely seen by anyone outside the household. Did you notice the angel off to the right, pulling at her sleeve? It's an element that viewers sometimes miss."

I turned my attention back to the painting, and there indeed was a golden haired angel-child. It held a finger to its lips with one hand and pulled at Mrs. Aldridge's sleeve with the other. I started to step back to get a better look at it.

"Yes, Miss Richards, come back towards the desk where you can truly appreciate the full scale of the painting."

"It's just remarkable," I said. "But how on earth did I miss the angel until you pointed it out to me?"

Alistair chuckled. "Most do. I think something about the expression on Mrs. Aldridge's face is so engaging that is all one focuses on."

"I believe you are correct." I shifted my angle to counteract a glare on the painting coming from the window behind Declan's desk, but in doing so my skirts brushed against one of his piles of paper sending them scattering to the ground.

"Oh, no!" I cried, as I spun around. Instinctively, I dropped to the ground and began gathering up the mess.

Alistair was at my side in an instant. "This is all my fault, Miss Richards. I insisted you see the painting from this vantage point. Please rest by the fire and allow me to take care of this."

But I had already begun gathering papers as he spoke, not

looking at their contents just desperate that Declan not walk in on this scene.

"Please," Alistair said again with great kindness, as he noticed the panic in my face.

I nodded and looked down to the stack I was holding to hand to him. Staring back at me were my own eyes. It was a drawing in sepia colored ink of a three-quarter study of my face, my hair was down, as though rustled by the wind and tangled with maple leaves. George was correct: Declan was talented.

My cheeks became enflamed as I looked up into Alistair's eyes. For a moment I thought I saw a look of surprise there, but he was a consummate professional and it quickly passed.

"I'll take that, miss. Here, let me help you up."

He guided me back to my seat by the fire and poured a cup of tea. Once he was certain I was settled, he resumed straightening the papers.

When Declan finally returned, he found me laughing as Alistair recounted the origin story behind the odd painting *Portrait of Guinea Fowl and Tulips*, whose receipt I had mistakenly seen.

"I trust Alistair has taken good care of you," Declan said, as he entered the room.

"He is a true gentleman," I said and smiled to his valet.

Alistair returned my smile and nodded.

"I'm sorry to bring the tea party to an end, but we are on the verge of being late, thanks to my detour," Declan said and helped me up from my chair.

Between this surprise visit to Declan's private world and learning that he'd made a drawing of me, I'd momentarily forgotten that I still didn't know where he was taking me. I thanked Alistair for his kindness and once back in my coat and gloves, Declan escorted me out to the carriage.

Inside, he handed me the correct portfolio. "Now, all will be revealed," he said.

This time I ripped open the binding. It was a letter written to Declan in a shaky hand which I found difficult to decipher. A word that looked to be my name was sprinkled throughout the text. Towards the bottom of the page was a name and address: Oliver Hastings Vannoy, The Dakota, 1 West 72nd Street, New York City.

"Oliver Vannoy?" I said. "When we had lunch together you mentioned meeting this man in Paris, yes?"

"Yes, Ava," Declan said and touched my arm. "He is your great-uncle and is most anxious to see you. We are headed to his apartment now to have tea with him."

"I have a great-uncle?"

He reached over and took the paperwork from my hands. "I know this must be quite a shock, but I trust it is a good one."

"Yes, I think so, but I am confused. How did all of this come about?"

"The story that Gabrielle told of your mother nagged at me. It was her phrase 'the type of environment that should have been your birthright'. I've told you all along I had a sense about you, and when you said your mother's name was Vannoy, I knew I must pursue this hunch. I contacted the detective my family uses, and the rest was surprisingly easy. Your uncle Oliver had been living in Europe for the last few decades but returned to New York just over a year ago."

Declan took my hand, his grip solid and reassuring. "I've already met with him in person. He is a kind gentleman who wept when informed that you are alive."

I inhaled sharply. "He knew about me and thought I was dead?"

"Yes. It seems your brother Rees is quite the storyteller.

But I don't want to get into all that now. I know there is much Mr. Vannoy wishes to say to you himself."

I felt shock and looked to Declan, searching for answers I knew he couldn't give me.

"This will be a good visit, Ava. I promise," he said.

We pulled up to a very grand building that reminded me of a castle, right on Central Park. An elevator took us up to the sixth floor and then at last we stood outside the door waiting to be let in. My heart hammered in my chest and, as if on cue, I felt Declan's hand on my lower back.

"I'm with you. This will be a good visit," he said again, in a low voice.

An older man took our coats and led us into a drawing room that was both elegant and intimate. Brocade paper in shades of blue lined the walls, which were accented with walnut shelving. Tall windows looked out onto the park and let in the golden, late autumn light.

"My child, let me look at you!"

I had been so drawn to the view of the park that I didn't see the small figure who sat bundled in a wingback chair by the fireplace.

"Mr. Vannoy, I'd like you to meet your great-niece, Miss Ava Richards," Declan said.

My great-uncle had a bright cap of white hair and pale blue eyes that appeared far younger than his eighty years. "I'm pleased to meet you, sir." He looked so very frail and I realized he was struggling to try and stand up. "Oh, no! Please don't stand on my account," I said and placed my hand on his as he held onto his cane.

"Thoughtful like your mother," he said, and rested his hand on top of mine. "I want to be able to look into your face, so if I don't stand up, you must come sit in front of me. Geoffrey! Please bring a chair over for my niece."

The man who had escorted us in, placed a chair directly in front of my uncle and another off to my left for Declan.

"There now, that's better. Let me look at you," he said, and pulled a pair of spectacles out of his pocket. "Oh my, you look just like your mother but with my sister's eyes. You have the Vannoy eyes."

"I do?" I said. "Forgive me, sir, but I know so little about my mother's family."

"Please call me Uncle Oliver. And we have done you a grave injustice which I intend to correct as best I can."

"Mr. Vannoy, I told Miss Richards that you and I met beforehand, but she knows nothing of your history," Declan said.

"You're a good lad, Mr. Aldridge. I knew your uncle years ago and liked him tremendously."

Declan laughed. "I don't think anyone has referred to me as a lad in over a decade."

Uncle Oliver chuckled in return. "When you get to be my age, everyone under forty starts to look like a lad."

Geoffrey wheeled in a cart with tea and a selection of delicate-looking pastries. I was still in shock as to where I was and with whom I was sitting. I wasn't sure I'd be able to eat anything.

"Now, then. If you will indulge me, Ava. I will tell you my story."

"Please, Uncle Oliver. I very much want to hear it."

"I moved to Europe when I was in my twenties; other than occasional trips to see my family, I hadn't lived stateside permanently until a year ago."

"What happened a year ago?" I asked as Geoffrey handed me a cup of tea. I cradled its comforting warmth in my hands.

"I found my thoughts turning back to memories from my childhood. It's the strangest thing: I spent decades wanting to get away from this place, and suddenly I yearned to return. To see it all again. So, I did."

The poignancy of his words combined with the slight gravel in his voice moved me. "I'm glad you did."

His eyes crinkled when he smiled. "Seeing you sitting before me, so am I. Spending all those years abroad meant that I missed out on much of what happened within the Vannoy family—which was one of the reasons I moved away in the first place." A sadness came over his expression. "But it also meant that I wasn't involved when I should have been. My sister was a very hard woman; she took after our father. I heard bits and pieces that my niece Clementine had fallen in love with a stable hand and married him. At the time, I just thought it was quite a bit of gossip, but I was always fond of Clementine and admired her courage."

He shook his head and tears filled his eyes. "Then, years later, I heard that she had been completely ostracized from the family. I was appalled and told my sister as much. I intended to seek Clementine out, but months past. Then years. I never did. And now it is too late. It is the single greatest regret of my life. I was so focused on my own life, I didn't stop to help my niece."

His words stunned me, and I didn't know how to respond.

"When I returned to New York last year, I hired a detective to find your family. I knew my niece had passed on, but hoped I could be of help to her children. I communicated with Rees, who told me that there had been a great illness that took your father and you. That he was the sole survivor."

"What?" I nearly spat out my tea.

"Forgive me my dear," my uncle said. "I know this must be most shocking to hear."

"Ava, I explained to Mr. Vannoy some of the circumstances around your coming to the city," Declan said.

"I know you were betrayed, Ava. It seems we both were.

You see, in my effort to improve things for your family and correct my sister's cruelty, I've been sending your brother a monthly stipend."

I felt as if all the blood had left my body. I wanted to believe Rees had become the terrible person he had due to grief, but I had an awful suspicion that wasn't the case.

Declan reached over and touched my arm. "Are you all right? You've grown quite pale."

"Are you warm enough?" Uncle Oliver asked. "Geoffrey, please bring in a blanket for my niece.

Suddenly, I had all three men fussing over me with tea, blankets and concern over my proximity to drafts.

"I'm fine," I said. "This is just a great deal to take in."

Uncle Oliver nodded. "The Vannoys have always been such a strange family. There is a vein running through of innately good people, like my mother and yours. And then there is another vein that is rotten to the core. My father, sister, and your brother all are members."

"My brother wasn't always this way," I said, as my voice cracked. I feared tears would soon follow. "There was an accident when he was younger that forever changed him."

Uncle Oliver reached out and took my hand; his fingers felt papery and cool. "What happened, Ava?"

I looked from his pale blue eyes to Declan's dark gray. Their expressions of concern were identical. "My father was the town farrier and my brother began helping him at a very early age. One day, one of the horses kicked Rees in the head. We feared he would die, but miraculously he didn't. But he was never quite the same. Privately, between ourselves, my mother and I would speak of 'before-the-accident-Rees' and 'after'."

"How did he change?" Declan asked.

"Before the accident, he was lighthearted and great fun to be around. The first thing I noticed was that his laugh disappeared. He became obsessed with money and those who had more than he. The doctor told us he'd suffered a great trauma and to give him time, that it might take years for his old self to return. But it never did. He just got worse. He became meaner."

Uncle Oliver shook his head. "My sweet girl. I can't undo the past, but I will do my best to ensure your future. Mr. Aldridge reaching out to me was such a blessing. I feel I can finally correct a wrong. I have already contacted my lawyer and changed my will. You, Ava, will inherit all I have. And in the meantime, Rees will no longer receive a monthly stipend from me, but you will."

"Me? Uncle Oliver, I don't even know what to say. I just met you and don't wish to think about your passing."

He smiled radiantly at me. "That is why you shall be my heir. All I ask in return is that you come to visit me now and then."

"Of course," I said, and felt the tears I'd been holding at bay fill my eyes. "You are my family."

We spent the next half hour making polite small talk, and I sampled a selection of the pastries.

"Mr. Aldridge has told me that you are staying with Gabrielle Lyons," Uncle Oliver said.

"Yes," I said, surprised that Declan had shared this detail with him. Or that he was even familiar with Gabrielle.

"I met her years ago. A charming woman, and strikingly beautiful, as I recall. I know you have just met me, but please know that I truly care about you. Mr. Aldridge has not told me anything directly, but I have inferred that you are thinking of following in Miss Lyon's footsteps."

His words were shocking, and I immediately turned to glare at Declan who appeared stunned.

"Mr. Vannoy, in all due respect, I told you no such thing," Declan said.

Uncle Oliver made a supplicating motion with his hand. "I know you didn't, but I could read between the lines. Ava, humor an old man and please go look at my art collection on the wall over there."

I motioned to the wall behind me and he nodded. I left my seat and walked over to the collection of five paintings with a growing sense of unease.

"The two I want you to pay attention to are the square painting on the far left and the one above it."

Both paintings depicted women but were painted in dramatically different styles. One was lush and almost ethereal; the other starker and reminiscent of an advertising poster.

"That smaller piece is by a French artist named Toulouse-Lautrec, and the other is by my friend Simeon Solomon, who has fallen on hard times. The women in both paintings were courtesans. I use the past tense because both women met highly unfortunate ends that in all likelihood could have been circumvented had they chosen different livelihoods."

"Mr. Vannoy, this is unnecessary," Declan said, with an edge to his voice.

I felt as though I'd been slapped. Taking a deep breath, I gazed up at the face of the woman in the more ethereal piece. She was beautiful, but appeared sad as she gazed into a candle's flame. I wondered if I would have found her sad or simply contemplative had I not known her story. The woman in the starker piece stared down at me with a lurid green face, and I shuddered to think what had made her complexion that way. I didn't want either Declan or my great-uncle to see my reaction. Keeping my posture erect, I turned slowly and made my way back to my chair. Between his admission of abandoning my mother and this stunt of making me look at his paintings, I wondered for a moment which vein of the family

Uncle Oliver truly belonged to: innately good or rotten to the core.

"Uncle Oliver," I said, as I took my seat. "I suspect your intentions are honorable, but while we are related, we have just met. It would seem you have made assumptions about me which may not be accurate, but are insulting."

The older man blushed. "Forgive me, my dear. You are quite right. I hold no judgement. You wouldn't believe half of the things I have done in this life. My desire to protect you, and make up for lost time, does not give me the right to behave poorly."

I reached out to hold his hand. "I have so enjoyed my visit with you. I don't wish it to end on a sour note."

"I don't want that either," he said with a sad smile. His pale eyes seemed tired and he turned to look out his windows onto Central Park. "As much as I don't want this visit to end, I fear dusk will be here soon and you two should be on your way home."

He struggled to his feet, ignoring my protests, and gave me a gentle kiss on my cheek. We said our goodbyes, and I promised I would visit again soon.

Geoffrey gathered our coats and saw us out. "He has so been looking forward to this visit. Please come back and see him soon. You have given him a new purpose," he said, before closing the door.

✦

On the carriage ride home, I tried to organize my thoughts which seemed to be scattered by a whirlwind.

In one short afternoon, I'd discovered that my brother, whom I'd loved, had betrayed me even more than I could fathom. I had a great-uncle I hadn't known existed, and I was the heiress to a respectable inheritance. And Declan had done all of this without consulting me. I knew I should be thrilled, and I was, but there was a part of me that was unsettled. Yet again, decisions were being made about my life without any input from me.

"As for the stipend, I gave Mr. Vannoy the name of my lawyer and accountant. Gabrielle uses the same firms as well. They'll set up everything for you. The amount is modest, but certainly enough to keep a roof over your head and food on the table for the rest of your life. You'll never need to fear being without, and I can help you invest it," Declan said.

I'd been staring at his face as he spoke, watching his beautiful mouth form shapes of words, but I didn't hear him. I didn't know what to think.

"Of course," he added, "if you'd prefer, I'm certain Gabrielle would be all too happy to give you investment advice. You needn't pursue any other career path." He searched my face and reached out to take my hand. "You now have a source of income you can depend on."

Depend.

Dependence.

Depending upon.

I'd thought I could depend on my father and then my brother to look out for my well-being. And I'd been wrong. I thought I could depend on my mother living long enough to become a grandmother and I'd been wrong. I looked down at Declan's muscular hand holding mine and fought back tears.

"Things can change without warning," I said. "Nothing is permanent."

Declan's brow furrowed. "Ava, what has occurred? You aren't happy."

My heart pounded, and my thoughts were endlessly fleeting images, nothing tangible that I could hold onto for more than a second. Without thinking, I let go of his hand and pulled off my glove. I reached up and touched his cheek, letting my thumb trace a path down his scar. I marveled at how the taut smoothness contrasted against the rough stubble along his jaw; its pale, pearly shade seemed wonderous. I felt tears spilling down my cheeks.

"What is this?" he said, leaning towards me.

Our faces were inches apart, and in the setting sun of late afternoon, Declan's skin appeared to glow. In an instant something shifted in the way he looked at me and slowly he removed his own glove. He mimicked my motion with his thumb and wiped my tears away. We sat studying each other and then Declan slid his hand to my neck and pulled me towards him. He pressed his lips against mine and kissed me with an urgency I hadn't expected but welcomed. His kiss felt like an anchor and my swirling thoughts finally settled. He tasted like bergamot, from the tea we'd drunk, and his familiar smoky forest smell enveloped me. As he moved his lips from my mouth to my neck, I felt every nerve ending in my body awaken.

He pulled away for a moment. "I've wanted to do this since the night you crashed into me with your books," he said.

"Then don't stop now," I said.

We continued our passionate embrace as the carriage rolled on. At another time, I would have worried about Declan's driver seeing us, or random passersby for that matter, but I was beyond that. All I wanted was to taste Declan's lips and touch his hair and inhale his breath until it was my own.

When we were a few blocks from Gabrielle's house, he pulled away again. "We need to stop before I pass the point of no return. It won't do to have you looking like you've been ravaged—we must put you back together before we arrive."

He helped me re-pin my hat and re-button my gloves. I laughed that he, the renowned rake, was yet again far more concerned with preserving my reputation than I was. As we pulled up to the house, he helped me down from the carriage.

"I thought I would come in with you to help explain everything about the inheritance to Gabrielle, but if you'd prefer, I won't."

"I'd like you to come in," I said, and nestled my hand in crook of his arm as he escorted me through the door.

"No. Absolutely not! That is insane!" Gabrielle said, and slammed down the papers she'd been holding.

She, Declan and I sat in the dining room with the file from the detective spread out between us.

"Please, hear me out," I said. "I need to confront my brother. He told Uncle Oliver I'd died. He tried to marry me off—he tried to make me disappear. I need to tell him to his face that he didn't succeed."

The idea of confronting Rees had come to me suddenly as Declan and I told Gabrielle all that had occurred that afternoon. To move forward I needed to resolve my past.

Gabrielle reached across the table and took my hand, sandwiching it between her own. "Rees didn't succeed in making you disappear. Isn't your knowing that enough?"

I knew she meant well, but her small gesture felt smothering. Gently I pulled my hand away. "No. I want to go to Langley Falls tomorrow and confront him."

They both started talking at once, but I cut them off. "I'll leave in the morning and take the train from Grand Central. I'll return late tomorrow night. Please understand: this is something I need to do."

Declan and I locked eyes. I expected an argument from him, too, but he surprised me.

"Then I'm coming with you," he said.

"I'm coming, too," Gabrielle added.

"No!" Declan and I said in unison.

"With all due respect, Gabrielle, I don't think your coming is a good idea," he said.

"I don't either," I agreed. "No one knows where I have been all these months. If you come with us, they will."

"Fine," Gabrielle said, her lips close to a pout. "But Forrest is accompanying you. He was originally hired to be my bodyguard and he has many useful skills."

Declan gave Gabrielle a withering glare. "I can escort Ava to and from Langley Falls without incident. Forrest's presence is unnecessary."

"Now don't be offended, Declan. I know you can hold your own in a fight: I remember all too well your flirtation with pugilism years ago," Gabrielle said and rolled her eyes towards the ceiling. "But I'm familiar with some of the characters you may come in contact with tomorrow and you are not."

"What are you saying, Gabrielle? You're speaking in riddles," he said.

"I'm saying you could have fists of steel and it would be no match for a few drunk villagers toting guns."

I scoffed. "You don't truly believe anyone would shoot at us, do you?"

"Your brother essentially tried to sell you, Ava. To Otis Fleet. Anything is possible. And arrogance combined with stupidity can be a particularly lethal combination. Forrest is going with you."

CHAPTER 10

The Empire State Express left Grand Central the next morning at eight a.m. with Declan, Forrest and me on board.

It took just under two hours and forty-five minutes for us to reach Albany and from there we hired a carriage for the remaining distance to Langley Falls.

When I'd left in the spring everything was green and lush. Returning now, in December, the gray skies and barren landscape reflected the hole I felt in my heart for all that Rees had done. I knew I *could* have made this trip alone, but I was grateful Declan had insisted on joining me, and I prayed whatever special skills Forrest possessed, they wouldn't be needed.

As the carriage rounded the final bend that would lead us to Langley Falls' Main Street, we passed a copse of twisted old trees lovingly referred to by locals as "The Sisters." Today though, they looked less like kindly town protectors and more like evil witches gathered around a cauldron. Their branches curved into accusing fingers and I imagined their ancient, weather-stripped voices hissing, "Leave! Leave this place at once!"

"Ava, are you cold? You just shivered," Declan said.

I smiled across to him. "No. What's that phrase? *A goose walked over my grave*."

Declan took my hand. "You have nothing to fear. You'll speak to your brother and then we are leaving."

I looked down at his hand holding mine. This was the most intimacy we'd shared since yesterday's kiss. The idea of traveling together was a romantic one, even if the destination was not, but any romantic notions I might have held were quickly dashed by Forrest's looming presence.

"Mr. Aldridge is correct, miss," Forrest said, his rough-hewn face breaking into something approximating a smile. "You have nothing to worry about."

It was just past two p.m. when we pulled up to the house that had been my home for twenty years. The house, once the most stately dwelling in Langley Falls, stood at the end of a private road. To its right was my father's workshop and forge. Its shingle flapped in the winter wind: "Richards & Son, Blacksmith and Farrier." I was pleased to see that Rees hadn't changed the sign.

As Declan helped me down from the carriage, Forrest looked to me for instruction. "Where would you like to go, Miss Ava?"

"My brother might be in the house or he could be in the workshop. It's hard to say at this time of day," I said. Or he might have already headed over to the tavern and was onto his third ale, but I kept that thought to myself.

"Forrest, why don't you start in the workshop and I'll escort Ava to the house," Declan said, and took my arm "Is that agreeable?"

I nodded.

Forrest left and made his way towards the shop as we started on the path to the house.

All the buildings had become increasingly derelict over the years, but seeing them with fresh eyes after being away for seven months, it was far worse than I'd remembered. As I searched the front of the house, I couldn't find a spot where the paint was fully intact. The porch was sagging off its foundation and, if I wasn't mistaken, the window that had been mine on the second floor had been smashed in. It seemed as though the walls were held together by hope and prayers, but the supplicants gave up long ago.

Declan helped me up onto the porch and I peered into the parlor windows. It looked as though a cyclone had swept through. What once had been the loveliest room in our home was now awash in trash, debris and broken pieces of furniture.

I gasped. "It was never like this. When my mother was alive, it was even beautiful sometimes."

"We shouldn't have come," Declan said, and wrapped a protective arm around my waist.

I turned to him and placed my hand on his chest. "Please trust me. I *need* to do this."

"All right. Then let's knock on the door and get this over with."

I steadied my pulse as best I could and raised the rusted brass knocker. It landed with a thud. We waited, listening for approaching footsteps. When none came, I tried a second and third time.

"It would appear your brother is elsewhere," Declan said. "Is there anything inside you need to retrieve? You said you left with little but the clothes on your back. I doubt it would be difficult to let ourselves in."

"Judging by the state of the parlor, I imagine Rees has destroyed anything of mine that he couldn't sell."

"I suspect you're right."

He helped me down from the treacherous porch and we made a slow circuit around the rest of the property. There had been snow recently and we stepped cautiously to avoid the melting ice patches and mud.

Declan took in the sweeping vista of skeletal trees above and around us, at last resting his eyes on a mud puddle near his foot. "You remind me of this place."

I glanced down at the puddle. "How far I've come in the world," I said in a flat voice.

He realized his blunder. "Ava, of course you don't remind me of a mud puddle. I meant this landscape—these other-worldly trees. It's winter now, but this is undoubtedly a sight to behold come spring."

"It is beautiful," I agreed. I looked up at the sagging porch and peeling paint. "Or it was."

Declan continued to gaze into the distance beyond the house. "I presume there is a waterfall somewhere around here, given the town's name."

"Yes. Past that field and through the forest beyond. I wish I could take you there, but it would be too dangerous at this time of year."

"I'm sorry to miss it," he said, and held out his hand to help me hop over a particularly large mud puddle. "Did you play there as a child?"

"I did. When Gabrielle lived here and I was very young, we'd play pirates. She was always the pirate queen."

An image of young Gabrielle came to mind, spindly legged with a tattered ribbon tied around her flaming hair, demanding payment from her captives for their freedom.

I had made it over the puddle, but Declan continued to hold my hand. "And what, pray tell, did the role of pirate queen entail?"

"Essentially, she'd take the boys captive and then they'd

have to buy their freedom from her, usually in the form of these pearly, lavender rocks we prized above all others."

"Not so different from today," Declan said with a laugh and pulled me closer to him.

I laughed in return. "I hadn't thought about that, but you're right! It was practice for what was to come."

"What about you? Did you take over the role of pirate queen after she left?"

"I did a few times, but ultimately I found it boring."

Declan brushed away a tendril of hair that had escaped from my hat. Even encased in leather gloves, the feel of his fingers on my cheek gave me goosebumps.

"What did you prefer doing?" he asked, his voice silky.

"I liked climbing down the rocks and searching for the lavender stones, or looking for frogs or fish in the pools below the falls."

His eyes bored into mine. "You were an adventurer even then."

I reached up and caressed his cheek as he leaned down and brushed his lips against mine.

"Miss Ava!" Forrest called out.

"Without fail ..." Declan muttered.

We both turned to see Forrest storming across the yard towards us.

"Your brother isn't here, miss. I spoke to a man named Martin—quite a character that one—he seems to think you have passed on. I assured him you are of the living and he need only look out the window for proof, but that was too much of an effort for him. He said your brother left at noon for the tavern."

"Thank you, Forrest. Then it's back into the carriage. We'll go to the tavern."

I stepped across the threshold into the stone building, blinking as my eyes adjusted to the low lighting.

"Ava, is that really you?" said an excited female voice.

I searched the gloom and found a pretty, ruddy-cheeked blonde staring back at me. Mary Hanley, the tavern owner's daughter-in-law.

"Oh!" she exclaimed. "It is you! This is the most wonderful surprise!"

Before I could respond, she grabbed my hands as a torrent of words tumbled out of her mouth. "We were worried sick when you disappeared—the whole town was so upset! Rees refused to look for you and lashed out at anyone who suggested it—which we all found strange. Some feared he'd killed you, but I said, *not our Rees*! Mrs. Maubry said you were alive and well, but refused to tell anyone where you were. No one knew what to believe!"

Mary took a breath and pulled away to study me. "Look at you!" Her eyes widened as she took in my elegant traveling ensemble of aubergine wool.

I admit, I had dressed for the occasion. When I left Langley Falls in May it was with a rag of a dress on my back. Today I was wearing an original M. Marcel, and a hat with purple-black feathers that arced over my head like a victor's crown.

"You are so pretty, Ava!" Mary gasped. "Where have you been all this time?" At that moment she noticed Declan and Forrest standing behind me and her eyes widened even further.

Fearing she might strain herself, I touched her arm. "Mary, I'd like you to meet my friends, Mr. Aldridge and Mr. Forrest. They have been kind enough to escort me here today to visit my brother. Mrs. Hanley is married to the tavern keeper's son. This tavern has been in the Hanley family for, oh, four generations now, is it?"

Mary beamed. "Yes. And we hope for four generations more," she said and patted her stomach.

"Congratulations!" I said, "Is this number three?"

"Yes, thank you. Lincoln is praying for a boy. He loves his girls, of course, but he so wants a son."

Declan and Forrest gave their well wishes as other patrons pushed past us into the main room.

"Forgive me, I know you must be anxious to see your brother," Mary said. "Come with me. Rees uses our smaller dining room off of the kitchen for appointments on Thursdays. Right this way."

"Appointments?" I said, as we followed her through the maze of Revolutionary War-era rooms. "What kind of appointments?"

Mary giggled. "Heaven knows! You would have to ask Lincoln. But there are piles of papers and all sorts of men who I've never seen around Langley Falls. I can't say it's been bad for business."

Declan and I glanced at each other.

We came to a wooden door, just open enough to make out that a fire burned somewhere within the room.

Mary knocked.

"Not yet, Lincoln. I'll let you know when it's time," a gruff, familiar voice barked out.

Mary stepped inside and we followed. "You have visitors, Rees," she said.

My brother sat at a long oak table, leaning over what appeared to be a ledger, pen in hand. At the sound of Mary's voice, he looked up and we caught each other's eyes. Recent months had not been kind to him, and I searched for the dashing amber-eyed brother I'd so loved in this puffy, blood-shot-eyed stranger. He tried to hide his shock at seeing me standing there, but I saw.

He put down his pen and leaned back in his chair. "Thank you, Mary," he said.

"I'll leave you to your visit," she said and stepped back into the doorway.

I turned to Declan. "Why don't you both go into the main room and have a drink. I'll join you when we're finished."

Declan and I had already discussed that I would speak to Rees alone. While he was not pleased with this plan, he did agree to it.

"We'll wait for you right outside the door," he said.

They followed Mary out and, pointedly, made a show of not shutting the door all the way.

Rees sat studying me, his arms folded over his chest. "Look who has come back from the grave. I thought you'd died."

"No, you didn't," I said. "You know very well that I ran away. And you know why."

"Death, desertion—details," he said with a shrug. "Have a seat."

"No. I won't be staying long enough to sit down."

He heaved himself up from the table and crossed towards me. "Got a train to catch back to the city, do you?"

I narrowed my eyes. "How long have you known that we have a great-uncle?"

Rees let out a bitter laugh. "You never were one to mince words."

He looked me up and down. "Got yourself a fancy man, have you, Ava? Coming here all puffed up like that whore Maggie Lionel."

I bristled. "Her name is Gabrielle now and she is my friend. She was your friend for many years, too. Her mother was like a second mother to you, or have you forgotten?"

Rees appeared not to hear a word I said. His eyes focused on Declan's diamond star around my neck.

"That's quite the necklace," he said, taking a step closer to me. "Must've cost a pretty penny. What if I were to rip it off your throat right now? It would serve you right for all the trouble you've caused me."

"Do it," I said. "It will be the last thing you ever touch."

There was silence as we stood glaring at one another and then Rees threw back his head and guffawed. "Oh, Evie! I've almost missed you. Almost."

He crossed over to the far side of the room and began rummaging in a bag sitting on a chair.

"Your necklace is safe from me. Besides, I suspect you'll need to hock it once your Mr. Aldridge casts you aside for another."

I froze. "What did you say?"

Rees grinned over his shoulder in a menacing way. "Declan Aldridge. That scarred, peacock of a man who escorted you here. I don't know who the ugly old one with him is, though."

My mouth felt dry. "How do you know his name?"

"I know many things. You have always underestimated me. Just like Mother did. While you were being groomed and primped to eventually marry above your station—where was I? Sweating and toiling at Father's forge. You're not the only one who read, though, Ava. You're not the only one."

"What are you saying, Rees? I don't understand."

"I'm saying, you were raised to aspire—I was raised to settle with my lot in life. Not to expect more. To be happy with my miserable little scrap."

"That's not true at all."

"Yes it is. Mother hoped through some miracle, if she could have you just read all the right books, you might catch the eye of a wealthy man passing through Langley Falls and you'd get the family back on track. But me? I was expected to inherit the workshop and stay in Langley Falls. Forever."

"Rees, you're a man: you could do anything you wanted. You could go anywhere you wanted. You still can."

"And you know what I decided I wanted? That if I was going to suffer, you were, too. Before Father died, he made me promise that I'd look out for you and find a *suitable* husband," he said with a chuckle.

My brother was unhinged. I wished we hadn't come. This wasn't going in the manner I had planned. My breath caught in my throat, but I knew I couldn't let Rees see my unease.

There was a sudden movement behind me, and I turned to find Declan standing in the doorway. "It's become unnervingly quiet in here," he said.

"Everything is fine," I said, relieved to see his face. "We'll be finished soon."

As we made eye contact, I could tell Declan didn't believe me for a moment. He paused to study Rees rummaging in the corner and then turned, leaving the door even further ajar.

I stood very still and watched Rees, too, until I couldn't stand it any longer. "What are you doing?"

"All in good time, all in good time. Ah! Here it is," he said. He pulled out a piece of newspaper and nodded. "When I discovered that our great-uncle had changed the inheritance and given it to *you*, I hired a private investigator of my own. I should have done it as soon as you ran off but honestly, I didn't think you were worth the time or effort. Make no mistake: you're still not. But I could've saved myself quite the financial headache."

"Yes, yes: you think I'm worthless. Get on with it, Rees. We do have a train to catch soon."

Rees handed me a scrap of newsprint dated February 2nd of this year from *The Philadelphia Inquirer*. It looked like it had been handled many times.

"What is this?" I asked.

"Read it."

His nearness and the acrid smell of him set my pulse racing.

Trying to keep my hands from shaking, I held the paper up. In the dim light of the tavern the words were not easy to make out.

The Honorable and Mrs. Abernathy J. Cavendish of Gladwyne, Pennsylvania, announce the engagement of their daughter Flora Marjorie to Declan Albert Aldridge of New York City.

I felt as though I'd been punched in the stomach. Could this really be true? Was Declan soon to be married? I tried to think of a barbed comment for Rees but feared my voice would not remain steady.

"Do you know what Mrs. Astor's Four Hundred is, Ava? Theoretically, it's the number of people she can fit in her ballroom, but in reality, it's the list of New York's social elite, and Declan Aldridge is on that list. You will never be part of his world—not really. You may have this little inheritance now and take elocution lessons and have some fancy dresses sewn up, but you'll never be one of the Four Hundred, and eventually he will hate you for it. Just the way Mother secretly resented Father for making her life smaller. You won't notice it at first; it will be a slow erosion. He will become like a stranger to you and you'll just be his embarrassing, provincial wife. Or if he's smart, which I think he is, he'll unload you long before any of this happens. So, cherish that pretty gewgaw around your neck: I suspect it will be your parting gift."

I looked into his eyes but didn't say a word. Despite the cruelty of his delivery, there were some uncomfortable truths about our parents' relationship in his statement and Rees knew he'd affected me.

An evil gleam entered his expression and he dropped his voice. "You should have taken Otis Fleet's offer when you had the chance, a used piece of goods like you. You think I don't know about you and Lincoln Hanley behind the woodshed? Our mother was barely in the grave and you couldn't keep your legs closed. You may have fooled others, but you've never fooled me. I see your true nature. It makes sense that you'd run to Maggie Lionel—you're just like her. A common whore. You bring shame upon this family."

"What family?" I said and turned to walk out the door.

"You don't walk away from me when I'm speaking to you," he snarled and clutched my arm.

I spun around, sending a metal tankard from a nearby shelf clattering to the floor. "Take your hands off of me!" I hissed. "I put up with your torment for the last five years, but no more. You are dead to me, Rees. I don't have a brother."

Declan burst into the room. He grabbed Rees by the shirt and slammed him against the wall.

"Get away from her," he commanded. "If you ever so much as look in her direction ever again, I will hunt you down and make your life a misery. You have my word."

I heard a clicking sound behind me and Rees's eyes widened. Forrest had stepped into the room and held a revolver in one hand, pointed at Rees.

"You should be ashamed of yourself. Miss Ava is a fine lady," Forrest said. "Mr. Aldridge, I will take care of this and join you both at the carriage presently. It looks like Mr. Richards and I need to have a discussion about manners and expectations."

"Ava, is there anything else you need to say?" Declan said as he took my hand.

"No. There is nothing here."

Declan ushered me out of the room through the dark paneled walls of the tavern. We didn't stop until we reached the carriage.

"Look at me," Declan said. "I don't know what was said in there, but you've grown very pale."

After all the horrid things Rees said, the name Flora Cavendish kept waltzing through my brain. I considered asking Declan about her, but I looked into his eyes, so filled with concern, and no sound came out of my mouth.

Declan pulled me into a tight embrace. "There now. It's all over. Whatever he said to you is a lie."

I stiffened and pulled away. "How do you know what he said to me?"

"I don't, but your brother has proven himself to be a liar. You came here today to confront him, and he was cornered. I know his type: he would undoubtedly lash out."

Declan pulled out his handkerchief and handed it to me. "He doesn't matter now. He isn't part of your future or even your present. Keep whatever good memories you have of him and let everything else go. Please. We're very lucky if we happen to like our blood relations—but it can be rare. I haven't been so lucky: my own experience has been largely one of stifling expectations, crippling strictures and very little love as I see it."

"Yet you still spent Thanksgiving with your father's family?"

"Yes. Family is a complicated subject for all of us, I think. I do care for them and feel a strong sense of duty— but I also know when it's time to leave. I discovered years ago that my true family is a chosen one."

I dabbed his cloth at my eyes. "Gabrielle would agree with you."

"There's a reason we've nicknamed her The Oracle over the years. She understands people in a way most of us don't."

"I thought Marguerite was the oracle," I said.

"Her, too. I have to tread carefully with both of them."

I smiled and took a deep breath, but felt a fresh wave of tears building. "I shouldn't have come today. I should have listened to you and Gabrielle."

Declan took my hand. "You were right to come, Ava. Now you *know*. Whatever occurred with your brother was not what you'd hoped for, but now you know who he truly is. And seeing this town in person, and all that you've had to overcome, my esteem for you is even higher than it already was."

The door to the tavern opened and Forrest swept out. He nodded to Declan.

"If we leave now, we'll be able to get on an earlier train," Declan said, and helped me into the carriage.

Once we were all settled inside, the carriage began its retreat from Langley Falls. I watched the passing storefronts through the blur of my tears. As we rounded the bend that took us past The Sisters, silently I said goodbye.

"I trust everything is taken care of," Declan said at last to Forrest.

"Yes, Mr. Aldridge. Mr. Richards will not be bothering Miss Ava again."

I gasped. "You didn't kill him, did you?" Rees was officially dead to me, but I didn't wish him dead to the world.

Forrest shook his head. "No, no. Nothing like that. Just warned him what would become of him if he ever bothered you again."

He paused and opened his mouth as if to speak, and then closed it again.

"Yes, Forrest?" I said. "Was there something else?"

"If I may speak candidly, Miss Ava. I almost feel sorry for your brother. That is a powerless, broken man. He didn't even stand up for himself when I confronted him. So, unlike you, miss. I remember the day you arrived in the spring and were determined to speak with Miss Lyons. Even though I told you to leave, you stood your ground. He doesn't have half your courage."

We arrived at Gabrielle's later than planned because of train delays. Declan escorted me to the door and said his goodbyes with a kiss on the cheek as Forrest looked on.

I changed for bed and then peeked into Gabrielle's room and was surprised to find her reclined on the divan, staring into the fire.

"You are home tonight," I said from the doorway.

"Darling, you're back!" she called out and sat up. "Come have a nightcap with me and tell me all that happened. I've been waiting with bated breath."

"I thought you were going out," I said as I took my place beside her.

"I was but plans changed. Here, join me in some whisky—I don't like drinking alone," she said, and put a glass in my hand before I had a chance to resist. "Now, start at the beginning and tell me *everything*."

I told her about the condition of my parents' property, and confronting Rees in the tavern, and how it hadn't gone at all how I'd planned. I ended with telling her about the engagement announcement in the newspaper.

Gabrielle let out a long, annoyed sigh. "Do you recall why Declan returned from Pennsylvania early over Thanksgiving? Because his great-aunt was playing matchmaker! That is not the holiday behavior of a family joyously awaiting the joining of two clans."

"Oh," I said and felt the color rise in my cheeks. "With everything that happened at the séance, and Jack, and all the champagne I drank, I had forgotten that detail."

"Forgotten? My God, Ava! Don't you remember the debutante who yearns to make ballgowns for cats? I spotted a fluffy, white Persian draped on a windowsill earlier today and thought, *I wonder how you'd look in pink taffeta* ... I'll probably never look at cats the same way ever again."

She tossed back another whisky. "This whole inane situation could be resolved with a simple conversation. 'Are you engaged, Declan? *Nope*. Thank you.' End of conversation."

Fixing her gaze on me, she jabbed the air with an immaculately manicured fingernail for emphasis. "The far bigger question is, how do Declan's hypothetical nuptials affect you? If you are to be a courtesan, who he marries is not your concern. It can't be. Or it shouldn't be, if you wish to maintain your sanity and stay out of Bellevue."

"You're correct," I stammered.

"You aren't an imbecile, Ava, so don't start behaving like one."

Gabrielle could be cutting in her remarks, but this was unusually harsh, even for her. As I looked closely, her eyes seemed glazed and unfocused.

"Did something happen today?" I asked. "You seem out of sorts."

"Forgive me for snapping at you, that was uncalled for," she said, and reached over and squeezed my arm. "I'm not myself this evening. My relationship with Alexander ended."

"Gabrielle, I'm sorry," I said and grabbed her hand.

She patted me dismissively and poured herself another drink. "Thank you, but it wasn't unexpected. I told you I knew this was coming. I threw all his love letters in the fire before you arrived, but it's not making me feel better the way it usually does. Thus, I have turned to alcohol."

"I wish I knew what to say."

"There's nothing to say," she said, and sat up straighter. "Someone will come in and take his place. They always do. But tonight, I have allowed myself to wallow."

Seeing Gabrielle like this was unnerving. She always seemed to enjoy the company of her men, but to keep them happily at arm's length. I thought about Declan's kiss in the carriage yesterday. On any other day in the past six months it would have been all I would have been able to think about.

Today it was but a facet of a more complicated picture. The thought of being devoted only to him, of having my heart broken by him, was just too much to bear.

"Both my great-uncle and Declan said some troubling things to me," I said, and swirled the liquid in the glass. I didn't want anything to drink, but I appreciated having something to do with my hands.

"Oh? What did they say?"

"Using very different tactics, they both told me that most women who become courtesans meet unfortunate ends."

"They aren't wrong, but it doesn't have to be that way. Life is made up of seemingly endless choices. Some things are beyond our control, but for the things that we can control, it's my opinion we must try to make the best choices possible."

"What does that mean?" I said, not even trying to hide my impatience.

"Where many courtesans come undone is with money and addictions. That is why I've instructed you to always save half of everything you earn. None of us know what tomorrow may bring. And as for addictions, some people sadly seem to be more predisposed towards them than others. Look at Jack—you saw him battling his demons firsthand the other night, and he's a brilliant musician, not a courtesan. Declan and Mr. Vannoy shouldn't be so quick to cast aspersions—addictions can be found in any profession," Gabrielle said, and put her glass down.

"How is Jack? In all the events of the last two days, I forgot to ask Declan."

"As we speak, Jack is on a train to the New Mexico territory. His uncle runs a hotel there and has been trying to get Jack to come work for him for years. He's never really gotten over his breakup with Marguerite and this change will be good for him."

"Were Marguerite and Jack together a long time?" I asked.

"About two years. I suspect they would have stayed together were it not for Jack's drug use. Then she met Gérôme, who is wonderful. And stable. Marguerite made a choice: the better one for her." Gabrielle shook her head sadly. "If I've learned nothing else, it's that relationships rarely end because of lack of love."

"I have this money now," I said. "Declan told me I no longer need to pursue the courtesan's path."

"He doesn't have the right to make that choice for you. Nor do I. Nor does anyone else for that matter. If you wish to continue, I see no reason why you shouldn't," Gabrielle said while she stared into the fire.

She was right: Declan didn't get to make that choice for me. I was embarrassed by my stupidity over believing he was engaged, but I knew it was only a matter of time before there would be another Flora Cavendish. What then? Would it be months from now, or years? Rees's words haunted me. I shuddered to think what my future could evolve into if I didn't take action now.

"Gabrielle, I've made a decision."

"Yes?" she said, focusing her green eyes on my face.

"I'd like to participate in your gala. I want to continue my education from you."

Her eyebrows raised. "I confess, I did not expect that ... especially not now."

"I have some money now, but I don't want to make any rash decisions. I know all too well that things can change at a moment's notice, and I'd like to continue as we planned."

"I understand. We'll discuss more as it gets closer." She stood, pulling me up with her and hugged me. "You'll always have a home with me: I hope you know that. That's something you can depend on. Now get to bed. We have an appointment with my lawyer, who is now your lawyer, in the morning."

We said our goodnights and I walked to my bedroom. I had so much to be grateful for. Almost too much, really.

Meeting my great-uncle and seeing his pale eyes crinkle with joy at the knowledge of my mere existence.

The look of longing in Declan's eyes as he reached for me, and the surprising softness of his lips.

I tried to push the horror of Rees far from my thoughts.

Climbing into bed, I curled my legs up to my chest like a child, wrapping my arms around my knees, and fell into a dreamless sleep.

CHAPTER 11

The following morning, Gabrielle and I visited the offices of Bainbridge & Bainbridge and after little ceremony I was Oliver Hastings Vannoy's heir. Once all the papers were signed, I sent Uncle Oliver a telegram, thanking him again and asking to call on Christmas.

To Declan, my monthly stipend was a modest amount, but to me it was more than I had ever had before in my life. More than anything, I wanted to be conscientious and not do anything rash with my income. On the carriage ride back to Gabrielle's house she and I discussed my options and I was, as always, grateful for her council.

It was a welcome relief from my somber thoughts when we arrived home to a deluge of flowers and gift deliveries unlike anything I'd ever seen. Word had spread overnight that Gabrielle and Alexander were no more, and would-be benefactors had begun their wooing.

"My stars!" Gabrielle said, stifling a laugh.

We stood in the drawing room where all the gifts had been placed. Or rather, tried to find room to stand: it looked as though the annual flower show was being held inside her home. There were so many lilies, roses, gardenias, tuberose and other heavily scented flowers crowded around us that it felt claustrophobic.

"I never thought I'd say this, but the smell of the flowers is overwhelming," I said.

"I know what you mean," Gabrielle said, turning around slowly to take it all in. "I've never seen anything quite like this before."

"What are you going to do with all of them?" I asked. Gabrielle loved flowers, but this was excessive even by her standards.

"I'll keep a few arrangements and have the rest delivered to the Women and Children's Hospital downtown."

The doorbell chimed and soon Janie appeared in the doorway, an unusually bemused expression on her face. "Miss Lyons, there is another delivery for you. The courier insists it must be given to you personally, and I am inclined to agree."

Gabrielle's eyes lit up. "You've piqued my curiosity, Janie. Come, let's abandon this hothouse."

We returned to the foyer and discovered a young man costumed as an eighteenth-century courtier, complete with a white wig and satin knee breeches. He carried a large, golden damask box with a floppy pale pink bow on top.

"What is this?" Gabrielle said as she approached the courtier. "Is the court of Versailles in session?"

Even beneath his white makeup and rouge, I could see his cheeks redden.

"Miss Lyons, Mr. Randolph sends you his fondest regards," he said, and attempted a courtly bow. He handed Gabrielle a cream envelope with a wax seal, which she opened and read.

Her eyebrows raised sharply, and she looked up. "What on earth," she said. She reached over to the golden box, ripping off its top with uncharacteristic speed and flinging it to the ground.

Then suddenly she was lifting the funniest looking dog I had ever seen out of the box, to the delight of everyone present, most of all Gabrielle. The dog was red in color, with large, butterfly-like ears on a rotund little body, with white markings on its paws and on its face that made it appear to have eyebrows. It couldn't have weighed more than ten pounds and looked out at the world from a startlingly intelligent face.

"Oh, you precious thing!" Gabrielle said as she cuddled it against her neck. "It's my Dandelion! I don't know how he did it, but Jonathan managed to find a dog who looks just like my Dandelion did!"

The whole staff crowded around her to meet the newest household member.

Gabrielle held the dog up to look into its face. "I know I said I wouldn't have a pet in this house, but I think I can make an exception for you!"

"You have to keep him, Miss Lyons!" Cordelia squeaked. She looked almost paralyzed with joy at the prospect of a dog in the house. "I'll take care of him when you're busy. I'm very good with dogs. They like me!"

Gabrielle smiled at Cordelia with affection. "I think that's an excellent plan, Cordelia. Would you like to hold him? Actually, is he a him?"

We laughed again as Gabrielle handed the little dog, who was a he, over to Cordelia. He wagged his tail as she cooed and fussed over him.

In all the commotion, the courier-courtier had been forgotten. I glanced over to him and noticed he was beginning to sweat under all the face paint.

Gabrielle remembered him at the same moment, too.

"Please thank Mr. Randolph. I will be sending him my own message privately." Janie saw him out.

"Do you remember Dandelion?" Gabrielle said, and wrapped her arm around my waist.

"Faintly," I said. "I was so young."

She nodded and smiled. "I don't know how Jonathan did it. It's like he's resurrected a ghost. The resemblance is startling. Except of course, Dandelion was female."

At that moment the usually taciturn Forrest had picked up the dog and began talking to him in a high pitched, singsong voice.

"Well, I see a dog is exactly what this house needed," Gabrielle said. She let go of my waist and walked over to join the crowd. "Now we just need to name him."

"Miss Lyons, I thought his name was Dandelion," Cordelia said.

"No, no," Gabrielle replied, and took her dog from Forrest. "That was my dog from childhood. Every living creature should have its own name. Now what is yours?" She held the dog up until they looked each other in the eyes. He wagged his tail and Gabrielle exclaimed, "Fergus! His name is Fergus."

"Fergus?" I burst out laughing. "Really?"

"Yes. It's Fergus. And you haven't held him, yet," she said.

I smiled and willingly took the warm bundle of red fur from her outstretched arms. He was adorable and even smelled good. (Had Jonathan had him perfumed?) The little dog wagged his tail as I cuddled him. "Pleased to meet you, Master Fergus Dandelion," I said.

Gabrielle kissed me on the cheek. "I am going to go and do something I almost never do: make a telephone call."

"I take it Jonathan likes the telephone," I said.

Gabrielle winked and began to make her way up the staircase.

I looked down at Fergus and thought of all the men who sent the flowers, candy, and jewelry, who never stood a chance. Finding this wonderful little dog was a stroke of genius.

"Not chocolate!" I called after her.

She paused on the landing before slipping through the doorway. "Definitely not chocolate."

The night of Marguerite's much-anticipated performance arrived. Given Alexander's departure earlier in the week, there was some confusion surrounding Gabrielle's escort, so at the last minute it was decided that Declan would accompany both of us to the theatre.

I dreamed of wearing red to my first opera, and when we planned our ensembles, Gabrielle finally relented. My gown was ruby-colored velvet, embroidered with roses in a darker shade of red that reminded me of garnets. The only jewelry I wore was Declan's compass necklace.

As I walked into the great Madison Square Garden on the arm of Declan Aldridge, I felt like I had entered a fairy tale. We climbed the gilded marble stairs to the concert hall on the second floor; a palace of white and gold. Declan had arranged for a private box in the first balcony and we were soon greeted by George, Charlotte, and Leopold, who were already seated. Gabrielle's newest benefactor, Jonathan, arrived moments after us. He was the man with the Van Dyke beard who had given me champagne on the night of the unveiling of George's painting.

Declan helped me to my seat in the front row as he took his own beside me. "You are stunning, Ava. Red suits you; I will remember that. Your neck should be adorned with rubies," he said, and leaned towards me to whisper in my ear.

"It should be adorned with other things as well, but we are in public, so I will have to be content to admire it with only my eyes." His lips brushed against my earlobe before he leaned back in his seat.

I smiled coyly as I felt a blush spread down from my ear across my décolletage; I suspected my skin matched the shade of my dress. "You look very handsome yourself this evening," I said, and held his gaze. I was the first to look away, and turned to take in the details of the theatre. "How grand this is! How many seats are there?"

"Over a thousand."

"Really?" I said and craned my neck to look up into the second balcony. "I've never seen anything like this before."

He chuckled. "The performance hasn't even begun yet. But you're right, I take this for granted."

To my left, Gabrielle and her friends were laughing over some bit of gossip. To my right, Declan continued to study me with his irresistible intensity. I glanced up just as a fuchsia feather, undoubtedly a remnant from another woman's gown, fluttered down from the second balcony, and the anticipation of hearing Marguerite sing again, combined with all the beauty of my surroundings, struck me. *This is a perfect night*, I thought.

I glanced down at my program and the wording seemed odd. "*A Concert of Selections from La Traviata*," I read aloud. "I thought we were seeing an opera."

"We should be, but Marguerite has been unable to find a theatre in the city willing to host an opera with artists of color. They are willing to host a concert, however."

"That doesn't make any sense."

"No, it doesn't. It's absurd. And appalling," he said, and gestured towards the velvet-draped stage. "But, Marguerite, in her infinite cleverness, has found a loophole. She has staged the opera as a concert, and removed a few of the pieces she deems less crowd-pleasing."

"Gabrielle said Marguerite's company is unorthodox. Is that what she meant?"

"I suspect what Gabrielle meant is that Marguerite's company is mixed race. The only other company like hers that I know of is Sissieretta Jones," Declan said. "There are many reasons Marguerite has chosen to live in France. She has a kind of freedom there that she does not have here."

The lights began to flicker, signifying the performance was to begin. I looked back at my program and read the synopsis of *La Traviata*: to my horror, it was the story of a courtesan dying. I gasped. If this hadn't been a role Marguerite was known for, I might have assumed Declan had orchestrated this coincidence.

"Is something wrong?" Declan whispered. He reached over and took my hand.

"No, no. Everything is fine," I whispered back.

He nodded and tightened his grip.

The lights went down, and the performance began. Marguerite's company consisted of an orchestra along with thirteen singers, including herself. Everyone who took the stage was talented, but none like Marguerite. She was the reason more than a thousand people came out into the cold December night. The clarity of her voice was unearthly: like hearing an angel sing. When she, as the courtesan Violetta, sang the final aria of her death scene it affected me in a way that all of Declan's warnings and my great-uncle's menacing paintings had not: I felt it. For the first time, I wondered if I might not be making a mistake if I continued on the path I had chosen.

I glanced at Gabrielle and saw tears streaming down her face, as she delicately dabbed at her eyes with a lace handkerchief. Anyone with a soul would have been moved by

Marguerite's performance, but I wondered if this particular piece struck a chord with Gabrielle about her own life.

At that moment, she noticed me looking at her. "Marguerite is breathtaking, isn't she? Just when I think she can't get any better," she whispered, and a fresh flood of tears came.

I kissed her cheek and returned my attention to the stage.

The performance ended after six curtain calls and a five-minute standing ovation. Declan ushered Gabrielle and me through the crowds outside into his waiting carriage. I assumed everyone who had been in the box would meet up again at a party afterwards to celebrate Marguerite's triumphant performance.

"Jonathan received a telegram during intermission, so it seems my evening is ending early," Gabrielle said, as we set off uptown. "I can't say that I'm sorry. I'm looking forward to getting home to Fergus."

"That's understandable." I smiled into the dark at her admission. "Although I thought there would be a party for Marguerite after her performance."

"There is," Declan said. "Across the street at The Fifth Avenue Hotel."

"Yes, there is. Declan was kind enough to offer to see me home. But you and Declan would be most welcome to attend, of that I'm certain," Gabrielle added.

Her response seemed weighted. "You wouldn't be?" I asked. "Marguerite is one of your closest friends."

"Yes, she is, and she has worked very, very hard to reach the level of success she has attained," Gabrielle said, and her voice took on a strained gravity. "I would not do anything that might tarnish that. Given my profession, no, I will not attend her party. This is not something she and I have ever discussed, nor will we ever. I have already sent her flowers along with a note saying that I have taken ill and will not be able to attend her party. Tomorrow morning, I will receive a note from her saying that she will come for tea before she returns to France. We've done this little dance for years."

"Oh," I said, sorry that I had asked.

We passed the next few minutes in silence; the occasional streetlight cast its subdued glow into the interior of the carriage as we drove on. I felt Declan's knees brush against mine as the carriage swerved. In the darkness, his desire for me felt almost palpable; it nearly matched my desire for him. I temporarily forgot Gabrielle was sitting next to me and I so wished we were alone. For the first time she felt like an unwelcome chaperone.

"Ava, why don't you and I head back downtown to the party after we drop Gabrielle off?" Declan said, as if hearing my thoughts.

I hesitated. I wanted desperately to shout *YES!* but felt disloyal to leave Gabrielle.

"Please go," Gabrielle said. "I insist. You both look particularly glorious this evening and I won't have you wasting all this beauty on my account."

"Are you sure?" I said.

"To lie in bed tonight, reading a novel, with my precious dog by my side sounds like utter heaven. At this point I'm going to be annoyed if you *don't* go."

We pulled up to Gabrielle's house and Forrest appeared at the door of the carriage to help her down.

Declan took her place in the seat next to me.

"Have a wonderful time!" she said, and was about to turn away when she quickly stuck her head back in the carriage. "Declan, I keep forgetting to ask you: will you be attending my gala this year? I need to let Janie know as we make the final arrangements."

I felt Declan's whole body stiffen beside me. "Gabrielle, I only attended your gala once. Many years ago."

"Yes, I know, but I thought perhaps you might this year ... given the circumstances."

"What circumstances are you speaking of?" Declan said.

I felt a prickly heat begin to spread over the back of my neck.

In the darkness I couldn't see Gabrielle's face, but she cocked her head to the side. "I may have just bungled things. Ava, have you told Declan of your decision?"

I felt something catch in the back of my throat and coughed. "No, I hadn't yet mentioned it to him."

"What on earth are you two talking about?" he said.

Gabrielle laughed airily. "Oh, dear. Well, there's no time like the present! After all, tonight is a night of celebration!"

I could not believe she was being so flippant.

"Go on, Ava: tell him!" she said.

"Yes, Ava," Declan said. "Tell me."

My breathing had become shallow and I felt a wave of nausea rising. "After much consideration, I've decided to participate in Gabrielle's upcoming gala."

Gabrielle squealed. "Ava is taking the next step in becoming a courtesan. You know how important this party is: I couldn't be prouder."

"You must be joking. Have you completely taken leave of your senses?" Declan said. Fury snaked through the timbre of his voice and I wasn't sure who he was addressing.

"Declan, who are you speaking to? I can't see your face in the dark," Gabrielle said, her own voice taking on an angry pitch.

"Honestly, both of you. Ava, I tried to help you, to save you from yourself, and now you're just going to throw it all away." I felt as though he'd slapped me, but he wasn't done yet. "And Gabrielle, Ava is twenty years old and has been in the city for just over six months. She has no experience whatsoever entertaining the men in your social circle."

"Yes, Declan, Ava is twenty. Three years older than I was when I began."

Declan snorted. "You were incredibly sophisticated, far more than Ava. Why would you have her at the party? Those men are coming to be with you, with a woman of your echelon. What on earth could she possibly offer? Maybe in the future, perhaps. If she survives that long."

"Declan!" Gabrielle roared. "What has come over you to speak like this? You owe both of us an apology."

I was glad we were in the dark, and that no one could see how my cheeks burned with shame. My eyes were quickly filling with tears and I feared I would soon begin sniffling, or worse, openly sobbing.

"I will do no such thing," he said. "I speak the truth, and you know it as well as I do."

"Let me out. I'm not going anywhere with you," I said to Declan. "You say these insulting things about me and judge my choices—yet you have never known what real hardship is. The one time in your life you were a *starving artist* it was an act! And I don't need a savior: put all that effort into your own life, Declan. No, take your hands off of me. Forrest will help me down."

Once on the sidewalk, I reached underneath my cloak until I found his necklace and yanked, breaking the clasp.

"Take your necklace. Give it to your next *Flora Cavendish*," I said, and threw it at him.

Gathering my skirts, I ran past Gabrielle, up the walkway and through the front door where Janie stood waiting for our arrival.

"Miss Ava!" I heard her call after me. "Let me take your cloak!"

But I was not stopping. I raced to my room where I locked the door, and sank to my knees just as the hot tears flowed out of me. Eventually I stripped myself out of my beautiful gown, tearing it as I did, and put myself to bed. Gabrielle came to the door repeatedly, asking to be let in, as did Cordelia, but I pretended to be asleep. I had no intention of leaving my room.

The next morning, I sent my French tutor away. I couldn't keep my own thoughts straight, let alone conjugate verbs. Gabrielle was undoubtedly still asleep, and I sought out the peace of the drawing room. No one would be in there during the day.

I walked over to the side window that looked out onto Fifth Avenue, and Central Park beyond. My favorite piece of furniture stood proudly in front: a small, ebony cabinet with a woman carved across the surface of the doors. I loved tracing my fingers over the undulating curls of her long hair. The top of the cabinet was a slab of dark marble, and displayed Gabrielle's collection of erotic figurines. At first, I had thought they were brightly colored sculptures of fruit or birds, to echo the wallpaper in the room. But as I looked closely, I saw that they were men and women doing everything to each other sexually that one could possibly think to do. Gabrielle told me they were called *shunga netsuke* and had been amassed by Albert over the years on trips to Japan. I picked up a couple carved in coral. Staring into their radiant little faces filled me with despair.

"Those figurines can teach you more about human relations than most people, I assure you," a voice said from behind me, followed by the familiar scent of jasmine.

I glanced over my shoulder as Gabrielle approached. "I'm not sure human relations is a topic worth studying," I said, focusing my gaze on the trees across the street. "I thought you'd still be asleep."

"How could I possibly sleep when I was so worried about you?"

I turned and looked at her sadly, and then returned my attention to the carvings before me.

"Declan has feelings for you, Ava. Don't you realize that?" Gabrielle said.

I shook my head. "Feelings! He certainly had an abundance of cruel words for me last night, but no 'feelings' that I could tell."

Gabrielle rested her hand on my shoulder. "Declan is in love with you, but he is fighting it. To acknowledge his feelings for you would mean that he has to rearrange his life and his perception of himself."

I scrunched up my face.

She chuckled softly. "Declan has built a reputation of being the consummate bachelor: beholden to no one, save himself. Doesn't that sound familiar?" she said, quoting the phrase she had first used months earlier when she'd explained her profession to me.

"He's a male courtesan?" I asked, suddenly more confused than ever.

"No, no, no. He's a rake. One reason he and I understood each other, and became fast friends, is that we both conducted our lives so similarly—but for different reasons. More importantly, unlike me, Declan had never been in love, until he met you."

"That's not true. Declan told me of his first love in Paris. The one who left him disfigured."

Gabrielle rolled her eyes. "That wasn't love. That was lust, or youthful obsession. It wasn't a true relationship. But what he feels for you is real love. Heavens, Ava, the man hired a detective to find your long-lost great-uncle!"

"You speak of love? Gabrielle, he attacked me last night! I heard no love in his words."

"I am not condoning his behavior last night: it was appalling. And the only person who should feel shame is Declan for speaking to you in such a manner. But what I am saying is that what men say, and what they truly feel, can be completely opposite at times. As one who has known him for almost a decade, I assure you, his outburst last night was a declaration of love for you."

But Declan's cruel words had hit a nerve, and I feared there may have been some truth to them.

"Maybe I'm not meant to be a courtesan," I said and fought back tears. I'd cried so much the night before, I didn't think I had any tears left.

Gabrielle moved her hand to caress my face and lifted my chin. "Look at me. If this is something you truly want, then I have no doubt that you will become the most sought-after courtesan New York has ever known. You will eclipse me!"

She said this with such certainty that it made me laugh. "I don't think anyone could eclipse you."

We both turned and looked at her portrait, holding court from its position over the fireplace.

She smiled at the face staring back at her from the painting. "I've had a marvelous time, and no one has surpassed me, yet. But being a courtesan is a young woman's profession, and the day will undoubtedly come when I am no longer sought after. If I were to choose who takes my place when that time comes, I would choose you."

CHAPTER 12

Rebecca returned sometime over the weekend. When I passed her in the hallways, I intentionally stared into her eyes, willing her to say something that would incite me. After the pain from Declan, I was looking for an excuse to lash out at someone else.

But whether Rebecca had gained newfound wisdom over her break, or I looked so utterly pathetic as to illicit her pity rather than wrath, she gave me space and never took my bait.

For the next two weeks I moved through the house like a ghost. I didn't bother with my studies; my mind was too adrift to focus. At night, I struggled to sleep, and during the day all I wanted to do was nap. Food didn't interest me, but Mrs. Kreisler never backed down from a challenge and an endless parade of soups, roasts, terrines and the most beautiful baked goods I'd ever seen found their way onto trays in my room.

Even with Gabrielle's encouragement, what happened in the carriage after Marguerite's performance had left me wounded. Worst of all, I wavered between hating Declan and missing him terribly. Part of me hoped I would hear from him and receive an apology, but it never came. The only things that brought me joy were walking Fergus in the afternoon with Cordelia and reading novels: through other people's lives I could forget my own.

One of my sleepless nights I conceded defeat and went down to the kitchen to make myself a cup of tea. As soon as I entered, I heard a soft rustling from somewhere within the house—I wasn't the only one who couldn't sleep. I raised my lantern to look at the clock: three a.m. Gabrielle was gone for the night, so her staff should have been fast asleep. I was about to search out a teacup when I heard the sound again.

"Hello?" I stage-whispered. No response came, but the rustling continued, accompanied by a soft thud.

Taking a deep breath, I gathered whatever courage I had to push through the kitchen doors into the main hall. I was treading softly through the foyer, towards the drawing room, when I heard the sound again, louder this time, and saw a shadow shuffling back and forth near the entrance to the private wing.

I gasped as the shadow hurtled towards me. "Fergus!" I said, as I put the lantern down and knelt to scoop him into my arms. "What on earth are you doing down here?"

Fergus's squat little body wriggled with joy, and I was quickly rewarded with kisses on my cheek.

"Were you making all that noise? Let's get you back upstairs. I don't know how you got away from Cordelia, but we'll sort that out in the morning."

It was as though Fergus understood everything I said because at the mention of going upstairs he began whimpering and trying to shimmy out of my arms.

"Fergus! Stop it! You could fall and hurt yourself," I said as

I struggled to hold on to him. The normally docile sausage had turned into a snarling hellcat and clawed at me until I dropped him. He fell to the ground and took off running towards the door to the private wing, which I'd failed to notice was ajar.

"No, Fergus! No!" I hissed. I swept up the lantern and took off after him through the doorway.

Once in the hallway he beelined straight to the spiritualist room's door and stood as though he were waiting for me. Something truly was amiss, and I felt all the hairs on my arms stand on end. I quieted my footsteps until I made no more sound than a cat's paw and lowered the light on my lantern until it was nearly extinguished.

As I approached, I knelt down and picked up Fergus again. To my shock, he allowed me without uttering a peep. I could feel his heart pounding in his chest.

The door was unlatched, and a figure stood by the cabinet where Leopold had examined gemstones on Thanksgiving night. A lantern sat on the cabinet's main shelf providing a dim light. I stepped closer and as my eyes tried to make sense of what I was seeing, I realized the figure was Rebecca.

I pushed open the door and stepped into the room. "Put back the star ruby, Rebecca. You're making a mistake you'll regret."

Rebecca spun around, truly red-handed: the now familiar ruby was clutched in her fist.

"Get out of here, Ava. You have no idea what you're seeing."

I tightened my arms around Fergus, as I could feel a low growl building in his little body. "Yes, I do. You're about to steal a very valuable gemstone from Gabrielle."

She snorted and crossed her arms, still holding the ruby. "What little you know. This ruby is a gift from Gabrielle to me—"

I wouldn't let her finish the sentence. "Right. That's why you're retrieving your 'gift' at three a.m. on a night when you know Gabrielle is away."

Rebecca's face reminded me of a sculpture: it betrayed no emotion whatsoever. "Go back to bed and take that wretched mutt with you. This situation does not concern you," she said.

"But it does concern me. I am not going to allow you to steal from my friend," I said. "Especially not one as kind and generous as Gabrielle."

Rebecca rolled her eyes. "I thought after a few months of living here you might lose your virginal taint and actually become remotely interesting, but apparently not. You're as bland as ever. God only knows what Declan sees in you."

Hearing Declan's name stung, but not as much as I expected. I knew Rebecca was trying to divert my attention by humiliating me, but it wasn't going to work. "How could you steal from someone who loves you? And I know Gabrielle loves you. If you need money, all you'd have to do is ask her. I'm certain she'd help you."

My response was not the one Rebecca had hoped for and a new, particularly cruel glint came into her eyes. She smiled, opening her mouth for her next volley, and took a step towards me.

It was that step that alerted the tiny warrior I held in my arms, and before I could stop him, Fergus's body propelled though the air, accompanied by a piercing bark-howl that I didn't know his vocal cords were capable of. He landed midway on Rebecca's skirt, where her knees would be, biting down on the fabric, and wouldn't let go.

Rebecca screamed and let loose a stream of expletives, as she began frantically spinning around, trying to swat Fergus off of her without letting go of the ruby. I lunged at her to protect him from her blows, causing Rebecca to lose balance.

We both tumbled onto the floor and I saw the ruby roll off into a dark corner. Then total chaos ensued.

When Forrest came rushing in a few minutes later, he found Rebecca lying on her back with a self-inflicted bloody nose, her hands clutching at my hair as I kneeled on her chest. Fergus sat panting a few feet away, completely unscathed. Janie and Cordelia soon followed, and everyone who stood in the doorway had the same expression of shocked bewilderment on their faces.

"Thank goodness! You've arrived just in time!" I said, as I climbed off of Rebecca. "I came down to have a cup of tea and discovered her having some kind of fit."

Janie and I made eye contact and she quickly sprang into action. "Forrest, get Rebecca to her room and send for the doctor. Cordelia, collect Fergus: we'll discuss why he is down here later. I'll see to Miss Ava."

I gratefully accepted Janie's hand as she helped me to my feet. We walked silently back to my room. Once we were inside, Janie shut the door and turned to me. "Please tell me what really happened."

Gabrielle arrived home the next evening to discover that Rebecca had slipped out sometime before breakfast, taking most of her worldly possessions with her, and a few of Gabrielle's for good measure, leaving behind a letter.

"The letter says that she's stolen all the jade bottles off of the mantle in the drawing room and a few of Albert's netsuke," Gabrielle said, lowering the note to reach over and scratch Fergus's neck. She sat propped up at the head of her bed while Fergus lay next to her, contentedly chewing on a soup bone. "She's an honest thief; I'll give her that. She told me what she stole. And apparently she's been stealing from me for years."

Janie's head snapped up at Gabrielle's last sentence. She was sitting in a chair at the foot of the bed taking notes. "Miss Lyons, that can't be! I would have noticed if she'd stolen from you."

Gabrielle turned back to the letter. "I would check the silver, Janie. She says she was very discreet and took the occasional fork or candlestick, things like that. Items she knew could easily go missing after a party."

Janie's brow furrowed, and she resumed taking notes. I had been leaning against Gabrielle's dressing table and moved over to perch on the edge of her bed. Fergus wagged his tail at my approach.

"Why would she tell you what she stole?" I asked. "That doesn't make sense to me."

"She said she intends to pay me back for all of it one day."

"Do you think you should contact the police?"

"And tell them what exactly, Ava? That one prostitute has stolen another's candlesticks?" Gabrielle snapped.

"I'm sorry, Gabrielle," I said. "I wasn't thinking."

"No, I owe you the apology. I shouldn't take out my anger on you. This is just unreal." She slapped the letter down on her coverlet and crossed her arms over her waist. "If she was going to leave, couldn't she have waited until *after* the gala? It's only two days away."

"Miss Lyons, we don't need to contact the police, but we could contact the detective who has helped us in the past," Janie said. "He's very discreet."

Gabrielle waved her hand dismissively. "No, it's not worth it. Rebecca is long gone. She said she is leaving the city to head west and she'd been planning this for some time," she said and shook her head. "I truly thought I could trust her, and sadly, I think I was right. But something very bad has happened that caused her to betray me. I can feel it. I wish she'd come to me—she didn't need to resort to any of this."

Fergus had stopped chewing and nosed at Gabrielle's hand, encouraging her to resume scratching his neck.

She smiled and did what he wanted. "And I understand my sweet Fergus is a hero."

"He is indeed," I said. "As long as I live, I will never forget his chunky little body flying through the air to attack Rebecca. Or the warrior cry he let out as he did."

The three of us began laughing at this image, but none so hard as me. After weeks of such emotional pain it was good to feel this kind of joy.

Gabrielle reached over and took my hand. "I'm glad to hear you laugh."

"Fergus got rid of Rebecca, saved you from losing a valuable ruby, and made me laugh again. He really is a hero," I said giggling once more.

"I understand why Rebecca was not a favorite of yours, but she has left me in something of a bind."

"With all due respect, Miss Lyons," Janie said, "that's not necessarily the case. I have already been in communication with Mrs. Wood's establishment as well as others. We have increased the number of young women coming tomorrow morning for rehearsal from twenty to thirty. That's what we did a few years ago when Rebecca took ill, so I saw this particular dilemma as no different. You have worked with almost all of them at one time or another, so they will know what to do."

Gabrielle jumped up and hugged Janie, nearly knocking her off of her chair. "You angel! What would I do without you?"

Janie flushed with pleasure. "When I explained what had happened, Mrs. Woods said 'we always look out for our own'."

"That's very true. We do," Gabrielle said and raised her hand to brush back a tendril of hair from my cheek. "You should get a good night's sleep tonight, love. You have two long days ahead of you. And we'll start early tomorrow."

When Gabrielle showed everyone gathered before her what our "costume" would be, I was horrified.

"It's nothing but paint and a few leaves," I said.

"And jewels!" chimed a high-spirited redhead standing behind me. "Don't forget the jewels."

Gabrielle appeared exasperated. "We are creating fantasy and illusion, Ava. The leaves and jewels will cover the necessities, as it were. And yes, the rest of your body will be covered in makeup. But I haven't shown you the best part: the headdresses. Janie?"

Janie reached into a hat box and pulled out an elaborate crown of golden leaves woven with sparkling gemstones, that stood almost a foot tall by a foot wide. It was dazzling, and I had to concede that an army of thirty-one young women of all shapes and sizes wearing massive metal headdresses, and very little else, would be a memorable sight.

"We have them in all different colors, so if you are painted to look like a sapphire tomorrow night, your headdress will match," Gabrielle said.

Murmurs of appreciation passed through the group.

"You never disappoint, Gabrielle," said an extremely tall woman with frizzy brown hair tied back with a rose.

"Nor do you, Valentina." Gabrielle replied with a wink, which brought a round of laughter. "All right then, back to business. Arrive by seven tomorrow night. Please use the side entrance that you used this evening. Make sure that you are freshly bathed and free of all cosmetics. Now, if you will please follow Janie, she will show you the rest."

We were standing in the banquet hall-sized dining room of the private wing. Tomorrow night the space would be transformed into Gabrielle's wonderland. I started to file out with everyone else when she stopped me.

"Ava, I'd like to speak with you."

I knew those words all too well and my stomach dropped. "Yes, Gabrielle."

She waited until the rest of the women had left the room and closed the door behind them. "You are very special to me, Ava, but I will not cater to you here. You will not be special tomorrow night. Do you understand? You will be one of many."

"Yes," I stammered.

"Good," she said. "Then kindly keep your criticisms of *my* party to yourself."

"I'm sorry, Gabrielle. I meant no disrespect."

"I'm sure you didn't," she said and rested her hand on my elbow. "But I feel I should remind you that you do not have to participate tomorrow night. No one is forcing you to attend."

"I want to attend!"

She raised her brow and tilted her head to the side. "Are you sure? Your reaction to your costume would suggest otherwise."

"I was taken by surprise," I said, aware that my voice had risen to a girlish pitch. "I've never been in a group setting with so little clothing on."

Her eyes narrowed. "If you are to be a courtesan, Ava, then you must be comfortable in your own skin, at all times."

It was a test. She was still not certain that I would be able to follow in her path. I was determined to prove her wrong.

"Once again, Gabrielle, I apologize for speaking out of

turn. Should I ever have concerns again in the future, I will speak to you privately."

Her face softened. "I'm glad we spoke. Tomorrow promises to be a very special night. Now go catch up with the group. I told Valentina to keep an eye out for you. She's a dear friend."

I nodded and saw myself out.

۞

A bedroom in the private suite had been converted into a dressing room for those of us participating in the gala. When I arrived the following night, Janie handed me a hat box with my name written on it. Inside was the beautiful headdress, and sparkling lace-up ankle boots in my size. The color, or theme, selected for me was "opal."

When my turn came to get dressed, I balked. I hadn't realized I would be bare breasted.

"Technically, you aren't," Valentina said as she helped apply a shimmering opal dust to my body. "The gemstones are covering your nipples."

She and Cordelia glued a small scattering of jewels over each breast with a large stone in my navel. I didn't think they were real, but given Gabrielle's extravagant budget, it wouldn't have surprised me if they had been.

Valentina moved on to help others as Cordelia and I put the finishing touches on my ensemble.

I stood in front of the full-length mirror while Cordelia tucked my hair up under the headdress, as per Gabrielle's wishes. With my crown of platinum leaves and rainbow stones, from the neck up I reminded myself of a fairy queen. It was from the neck down that caused me distress.

The body makeup for those of us given the opal head-dresses was not as opaque as the other colors. I was told this was infinitely more comfortable on the skin, but as I looked in the mirror, I realized it also meant that I didn't look nearly as transformed, or covered, as many of the other women present. Essentially, I would be wandering around nude with a crown and a fig leaf, wearing ankle boots. Gabrielle undoubtedly chose this for me intentionally. Yet another test.

"Miss Ava, you are all ready," Cordelia said, as she appraised my reflection one last time.

"Thank you, Cordelia," I said, as I met her eyes in the mirror. "Do you have any words of wisdom for me tonight?"

I turned to face her as she took my hand. "Yes. If the party starts and something doesn't feel right to you, right here," she said and pounded the base of her stomach for emphasis, "just slip out the door and run away." Her expression had the earnestness of a saint.

"Cordelia, sometimes I could just hug you," I said. "I won't, because I don't want to get this blasted paint on you, but I want to."

She blushed. "I mean it, Miss Ava. There are so many girls here, I doubt anyone will notice your absence. If anything makes you uncomfortable, leave straight away and come upstairs. Fergus and I will be waiting."

I said goodbye to her and spent the remaining time helping others get ready. I gleaned that this night was one of the most sought-after opportunities for women who worked in the pleasure houses. If I heard correctly, they would make in a few hours what it normally took them a month to earn. Gabrielle was renowned for looking out for her own.

"You're the one who lives here, aren't you?" asked a woman who went by the name Jezebel, who was in the final stages of being painted emerald green.

"I am," I said.

"She's the one, Diana!" Jezebel cried out across the room to the high-spirited redhead from the day before.

Diana, clad head to toe in gold, soon joined us. "Then you would know. Is it really true: is Rebecca gone for good?"

"It looks that way," I said.

"Good riddance!" Diana said and took a swig from a flask that seemed to appear out of nowhere.

"Say, I'll drink to that! Hand it over," Jezebel said and took a drink. "She was such a chore, always putting on airs. Especially at Gabrielle's Gala. This year really is a celebration!" The two women laughed. "Oh, but that was insensitive of me. She might have been a friend of yours."

I had to keep from snickering. "No. Rebecca and I were not friends."

Jezebel laughed. "Any not-friend of Rebecca's is a friend of mine! Would you like a drink?"

"No thank you," I said, warmly. I had promised myself that if I were to participate in the gala, I would do it clear-eyed with all my faculties intact.

"Are you sure?" Diana asked. "We know this is your first time doing this. It might take the edge off. I remember how nervous I was the first time I worked one of Gabrielle's parties."

"Ava will be fine. She has all of us looking out for her," Valentina said, as she joined our corner of the room. She too was painted gold. "If I'm not mistaken, I think everyone is ready. Are you three?"

We nodded.

"Janie," Valentina called out. "Everyone is ready."

The time had come. Quietly we followed Janie into the dining room; overnight it had been transformed into Wonderland.

The oversize dining room table still stood in the center surrounded by six chairs. The electric lights were turned off, and gilt candelabra lay scattered throughout the room, casting a romantic glow. Vast swathes of gossamer veiling arced across the ceiling, shot through with shimmering stars. A mermaid ice sculpture spouted champagne next to towering urns overflowing with trails of roses that puddled onto the floor. There were representations of mythological creatures in all sorts of colors and textures, giant arrangements of bejeweled flowers interspersed with the real thing, and peacock feathers seemingly everywhere. Pillows and cushions in luxurious fabrics were discreetly tucked into the dark corners amongst all the ornamentation. Gabrielle's concept of "Wonderland" had been intentionally broad and encompassed anything she found beautiful and magical.

We stumbled into this space, agog. And then the music began. In an alcove off of the dining room a small chamber orchestra would play throughout the party. We could hear them, but they could not see us.

"All right, girls," Janie said. "Time to take your places. Dinner is finishing, and the gentlemen will be arriving here soon."

There was a flurry of movement as everyone rushed to find their place. I found my spot in a shadowy corner near the door. Janie approached and handed me two large peacock feathers.

"Do you have everything you need?" she whispered

"Yes," I said.

She nodded and moved on to the next person.

Having done her rounds, she took her leave.

I stood clutching the peacock feathers and looked around the room. Directly across from me I could see Jezebel holding a pose as if she were pouring a jug of water over her head. Next to her was a woman named Daphne, painted in purple, who also held peacock feathers but in a far more coquettish manner than I did. I loosened my grip and tried to relax.

On the other side of Daphne was a strikingly beautiful

woman whom everyone called The Countess. She appeared to be posing with a jeweled hedgehog. I quickly looked away. In my nervous state, I feared that if I started giggling, I wouldn't be able to stop.

The doors to the dining room swung open and I heard Janie's voice. "Welcome to Wonderland, gentlemen."

The men had been mid-conversation when they entered, but soon stalled to a halt at the beauty of the room. Six women, all those painted in gold, appeared and escorted them to their chairs.

I realized there was a hierarchy in the colors: the golden women held the highest rank below Gabrielle.

Valentina helped Jonathan to his seat and stood directly behind him. I searched the faces of the rest of the men and only recognized one from the party I had attended.

A trumpet sounded in the doorway, startling everyone. Four waiters dressed in white carried in a massive, sterling silver domed platter on their shoulders. They placed the platter on the table in front of the guests and then on Valentina's cue, removed the dome and quickly exited the dining room.

The great reveal was Gabrielle. She lay on a gigantic lace doily and was completely nude save for some artfully arranged swirls of whipped cream and a few clusters of fruit.

"Gentlemen, *bon appétit*!" Gabrielle cried.

The room was stunned silent for a moment, and then the men erupted into laughter and applause.

Gabrielle joined in the laughter, as she held court from her platter, speaking to each of her guests in turn as they crowded around her. Her hair was swept up away from her face and arranged into swirls that echoed the cream decorating her skin.

No one made a move until at last she plucked a grape from the bunch lying on her stomach.

"Come now Jonathan, I know how you love grapes," she said, and placed it over her breast.

I watched as he leaned over to take the grape from her fingers and some of the swirl of cream that lay beneath.

Gabrielle let out a squeal. She then did the same thing with each man until they all swarmed around her, licking the cream off of her skin.

The mood of the room began to shift. What had started out as alcohol-induced hijinks turned to something more focused as everyone became increasingly aroused. I watched Gabrielle in awe. While the men used their mouths, she moaned and sighed. A bright flush had crept over her chest and I could tell that what she exhibited was not a performance.

All the while, the orchestra played on. I had no idea what I should be doing; then, as if by some unspoken cue, everyone but me descended on the table and began to break off together into smaller groups. Gabrielle left her platter, and I could see her at the far end of the room with Jonathan, another guest, and a few other women near the urns with the trailing roses. To my right, Jezebel feverishly kissed a dark-haired man, his pale skin streaked with the green paint from her body, as her headdress lay at their feet.

Hiding in my dark corner, I stood with my back pressed against the wall and peacock feathers clutched like weapons over my chest. A familiar ache had begun between my thighs and my heart raced. I realized I'd begun perspiring and looked down to see a thin rivulet of sweat begin its descent from between my breasts, taking some of the glittery dust with it.

From my vantage point, I could see the full sweep of the room's tableau. A shriek sounded to my left, followed by a cascade of laughter. I turned to see a pile of bodies on the floor, pawing at each other. Next to them, one of Gabrielle's benefactors lay on top of The Countess, his hips thrusting with the evenness of a metronome. I watched mesmerized for a moment. The hedonism of it all was dizzying; the liquid sounds of mouths and moaning combined with the music from the chamber orchestra.

It was a strange sensation to be both aroused and terrified. I felt something fall to the ground and realized that in my panicked state, I had begun sweating so profusely that the glue affixing the gemstones to my body was dissolving. I looked down to see the large opal from my navel lying at my feet. It was at that moment that all my desires to become a courtesan vanished. I realized I'd been fooling myself: I was not a libertine like Gabrielle, and I could never abandon myself this way in a group.

Cordelia's words from earlier in the evening came back to me. Excluding me, there were already thirty women in the room besides Gabrielle. I doubted anyone would miss me; none of the men had even noticed me standing in the corner. I started to inch backwards slowly towards the door, waiting for a swell in the music or some other sign that I could safely slip out without attracting attention.

The flames in the candelabra nearest me blew out. I felt a light breeze across the backs of my thighs and thought I heard the doors open. I turned my head towards the sound, when suddenly there was a hand clamped over my mouth, as well as an arm wrapped around my waist.

My fingers dug into the skin of my assailant as I was pulled out of the room into the dark hallway. As he pulled me away, the doors to the dining room became smaller and a dry terror formed in my throat. Tears filled my eyes, and then I smelled something familiar. The scent of the forest, with something smoky and sweet. Declan's cologne.

At last we stopped; the hand was removed from my

mouth and the arm from my waist as I spun around to face Declan.

"I couldn't stand the thought of you with anyone else," he said, and grabbed me once again and planted his lips on mine.

I did not fight him, but yielded fully into his embrace. Initial relief washed over me, and then I remembered the awful carriage ride. I pulled away, shoving him from me. "The last time I saw you, you had nothing but cruel words for me, and now you come swooping in?"

Declan looked stricken and tried to take my hand.

"No," I said. "Answer me. How could you say such horrific things to me?" My voice cracked on the last sentence.

"I could not bear that you would choose another man over me. That you would still pursue this kind of life after all the time we'd spent together." He shook his head. "I've never felt for anyone what I feel for you. I've never been in this position before, and I wanted you to feel the kind of pain that I did. I wanted to wound you."

My eyes filled with tears. "You succeeded."

"I have replayed that awful night a million times over in my head, wishing I could take back all that I said to you."

"You have no idea how you hurt me," I said. "In the last year I have been betrayed by my brother, my father, and then you turned on me."

Standing in the dark corridor, Declan's usual self-confidence seemed diminished. It was unsettling to see him this way.

"The main reason I decided to go ahead with the gala was because I couldn't bear the thought of having my heart broken by you—"

"What—?" he said, interrupting me as he reached out to take my hand.

I didn't push him away this time. "Let me finish. I also felt something for you I'd never felt before, but I'm well aware of your reputation. If I fall in love with you, how long before you grow tired of me and discard me for another? No," I said, shaking my head. "I couldn't stand the thought of that. I've had too much loss in too short a time already. I can't stand anymore. And you said it yourself: I've only been in the city for seven months and wouldn't begin to know how to satisfy a man of your *echelon*."

Declan hung his head for a moment before he looked at me. "I've said many idiotic things in my lifetime and that is one of the worst. It isn't true at all, Ava. I am sorry for what I said and for the pain I caused you. I'll understand if you want nothing more to do with me, but I hope you won't. I hope you'll forgive me."

He placed his hands on my arms. "You're cold," he said, and removed his jacket to wrap around me.

I had been so focused on our words that I temporarily forgot I was standing before him essentially nude.

"I love you," he said, and stared intently into my eyes. "These last two weeks made me realize how much I would lose if I lost you, and I don't want to lose you."

In that moment, all the shards of glass I felt pricking around my heart began to dissolve. "I love you, too, Declan. Part of the reason the last two weeks were so painful was that I alternated between hating you and missing you."

He laughed softly and wrapped his arms around me. "Does this mean you forgive me?"

I nodded. "I do." He started to kiss me again, but I stopped him. "Let's leave the hallway and find somewhere more private." Reaching over to take his hand, I led him to the Aphrodite Room.

The stained-glass window was illuminated even after dark. Serene shades of blue, green and gold rippled in the low light of the room, lending a hallucinatory quality to a night that already felt like a dream.

As I closed the door behind us, Declan turned and looked at me. I yearned for him to touch me again.

"I've thought about you every night," he said, and caressed my cheek, allowing his fingers to trail across my lower lip. He looked up for a moment, his eyes searching the room, until his focus rested again on my face. "Admittedly, my fantasies did not contain this kind of lighting. Or you covered in sparkles."

I smiled. "I can take a quick bath."

"No," he said, and bent down to kiss me once more. "I like it. It adds to the otherworldly feeling of it all."

As he pulled away, to my embarrassment, I realized that my skin was starting to have a reaction to the opal powder and told him so.

"Come over here," he said and led me to the marble fountain that sat in the far corner of the bedroom.

He removed his jacket from my shoulders and flung it away. "Are you warm enough?"

I nodded.

He took out his handkerchief and dipped it in the fountain. Then kneeling before me he slowly began to wipe away the paint and glue from my skin.

"Are you uncomfortable?" he said.

"No, just vaguely humiliated."

"How so?" he said and reached down to untie my ankle boots.

"I realized you were right. I'm not cut out to be a courtesan."

I expected Declan to respond with some kind of acknowledgment of triumph at my statement, but he didn't. He looked up from where he'd just lifted my left foot out of my boot.

"But why are you humiliated?" he said.

"Look at me! Look at what I'm wearing! I've embarrassed myself."

He removed my other foot from the boot and picked up his handkerchief, dipping it in the fountain again. He resumed wiping away the makeup, working his way up my leg until he reached the cluster of leaves.

"May I remove these, too?" he said.

I stared down at him kneeling in front of me and felt my mouth go dry. "Yes," I whispered.

He helped me step out of the leaves and then I was completely nude. He gazed up at me with appreciation.

"I see nothing here for you to be embarrassed about," he said, pressing his cheek against me.

He began a trail of kisses up my body until he reached my mouth. I felt as though my legs would buckle.

Declan reached up and removed the headdress I still wore. I lifted my hands to begin removing the pins that kept my hair coiled tight underneath the crown.

"No, let me," he said. Gently he unwound my hair until it cascaded over my shoulders.

"I've never seen your hair down before," he said. "It's even more beautiful than I imagined."

He kissed me again and then picked me up, carrying me to the bed.

I rejoiced to finally feel the weight of his body on top of my own, and the broad expanse of his chest pressed against me. While he caressed me, my hands did their own exploring. I touched him gently at first and then with each kiss, my timidity began to fall away. I traced the outline of the scar that ran down his cheek, first with my fingers and then with my tongue; the exclamation point to my desire.

"Are you a virgin, Ava?" Declan asked.

"No," I said. "Just very inexperienced."

A slow smile spread across his face. "Then we will make up for lost time."

How different this was from my one experience behind the woodshed. That boy seemed only interested in one specific area, whereas Declan took his time, exploring all of me. He started at the tips of my toes and used his mouth and fingers with exquisite slowness, working his way the full length of my body until I thought I'd lose my mind. My need for him by this point was almost too much to endure.

His breathing changed, becoming more ragged, as I wrapped my legs around him; I didn't ever want to let him go. The scent of his cologne, the glorious combination of sandalwood and smoke engulfed me, mixing with something earthier and more primal. The smell of him. I heard a low moaning and realized it was coming from me. My hands gripped the tangled sheets and then his hands, as we joined each other in our shared rhythm. I looked up into his face, silhouetted against the stained glass, outlined in shades of gold.

⊗⊱⊗

"How did you know where to find me?" I asked, rolling onto my side so that I could look at Declan.

"I knew the gala was tonight. Forrest had just let me into the foyer when I encountered Cordelia about to take Gabrielle's dog for a walk. She became frantic when she saw me, saying something about you, and body paint, and perverted old men who were going to lead you into a life of turpitude. And that I must go save you. I told her that I was there to talk to you, and she began yelling 'Go!'"

"No!" I laughed.

"It's true. I feared she had begun hyperventilating. I

stopped to make sure she wasn't ill, and she yelled at me that I hadn't the time to waste."

I buried my face in the pillow and laughed until my shoulders shook. "Too bad you didn't arrive earlier and save me from the body paint," I said, and reached over to caress his face.

He kissed the palm of my hand. "I have to ask: how did you know about my ex-fiancée, Flora Cavendish?"

I groaned. "When we went to Langley Falls, I discovered that my brother had hired a private detective to find out who had made his inheritance disappear. He confronted me with your engagement notice from a Philadelphia newspaper."

"Ah. Then you should know that Flora is an old friend and our families had been trying to pair us since childhood. We were going to relent, but neither of us could go through with it—it wasn't a love match. And we both wanted to marry for love. I am happy to report that Flora *is* marrying for love, and when I take you to England, we will visit the soon-to-be Lady Flora in her castle."

"You're taking me to England?" I said.

"Ava, I'm going to take you everywhere—you are an adventurer, are you not? Then let's have the biggest adventure of them all. Would you say yes if I asked you to marry me?"

"Are you asking?" I said with a wink. "You shouldn't make jokes like that. After a night like tonight, I might actually say yes."

He leaned away from me and I admired the sculpted muscles of his back as he reached to pull something out of his jacket that lay on the floor.

"I had planned to do this earlier. When we had more clothes on," he said, with a mischievous grin. He held a small, black leather jeweler's box, from which he produced a ring. As he leaned up on his elbow, he reached out for my hand.

"Miss Ava Vannoy Richards. Would you do me the honor of saving me from a life of turpitude and become my wife?"

I stared down at the ring on my finger. It was an unusual piece of jewelry: two outer, yellow gold bands wrought with an ornate floral pattern flanked an inner band of white gold that was largely a series of holes. It appeared to be a ring that was unfinished.

He took my hand and ran his finger over the ring. "Leo made this for us: it is a band with twenty settings for stones of which only one is filled. I picked out an orange sapphire because the shade reminds me of your eyes, and that maple leaf that fell into the carriage the day I realized I was in love with you. A year from now, we'll pick out another stone together and have the next setting filled. And then another the next year. What you see are twenty years' worth of adventures waiting to be had together."

It was the most perfect ring I had ever seen. "What happens after twenty years when all the settings are full?"

"We'll decide that when the time comes. We get to make the rules."

I leaned down and kissed him, breathing him into me. "We may grow tired of each other after twenty years."

"I thought we'd already been through this in the hallway. That won't happen. Besides, I have a ten-year head start on you in life experiences. You are far more likely to grow tired of me than I am of you. I love you, Ava. I don't want to lose you."

"I love, too. I don't want to lose you, either."

"Then what is this hesitation?" he asked.

I couldn't even answer that. It was my own fear from the last year rising up to strangle me.

"Declan, I don't want you to grow to resent me. I doubt I will ever be welcomed into Mrs. Astor's Four Hundred."

His eyebrows raised in shock. "Who on earth would want

to be part of the Four Hundred? Ava, I told you I moved to Paris specifically to get away from those people."

"I know, but—"

"You have more innate grace in your little finger than all of the willing victims Mrs. Astor stuffs into her ballroom. And if we're being technical, may I remind you that you are a Vannoy! That is a name that still commands respect. Hold your head high, Ava, always. You're going to have try much harder if you want to get rid of me."

His echoing of my mother's phrase from childhood caused all the hairs on the back of my neck to stand. I felt as though I was receiving her blessing.

"This is what I propose," he said. "You don't have to answer me now. Wear my ring and answer me in twenty days."

"In twenty days?" I said. "You don't mind waiting that long for my answer?"

"It will be torturous, but I want you to be sure. You will know the answer in twenty days," he said, and stretched out his arms. "Or twenty hours."

I wrapped my arms around his chest.

"Or twenty minutes," he said.

"Twenty days," I said. "And I will wear your ring."

I pressed my cheek against his chest, listening as his breathing evened out into sleep. I knew I didn't need to wait twenty days. I wondered what time it was; it was no use looking for a clock as I wouldn't find one in Gabrielle's fantasy suite. Perhaps I would say yes at twenty minutes after the hour later this afternoon. I'd think of a clever way to give him my answer.

The sound of Declan's heartbeat lulled me to sleep. The sound of my heart's home.

EPILOGUE

I tiptoed down the hallway, quietly opening doors as I searched for Ava and Declan.

The Aphrodite Room, I thought at last. Of course. That had been Ava's favorite part of the private suite. I made my way to the large, arched door, decorated with whiplash designs, and gently turned the handle and peeked in.

As my eyes adjusted to the low, multicolored light that streamed in through the stained-glass window, I saw two figures lying in the bed. Declan lay on his back with his head turned away from the door. Ava rested on his chest, her beautiful face at peace while she slept. Both of them held the other in their arms.

My heart nearly burst with joy at this sight. AT LAST! I thought with triumph.

The reason I have succeeded as a courtesan, where so many others have failed, lies in my ability to know what others want and need long before they do. The day Ava appeared at my door and pleaded her case, I knew she had no business following in my footsteps: she is not the peacock that I am. She was destined for a different life.

I decided that I would give her an education until I figured out what path she should follow, or she discovered it on her own. When

Declan came for lunch that September afternoon, I knew they were destined for one another. Then my real challenge began: to buy enough time for them to realize they were meant for one another, and not do anything that might alter their happy ending.

Many have confused my optimism with naïveté over the years, but I have proved them all wrong. I learned early on that maintaining joy and hope in the face of life's numerous disappointments is a daily discipline. But it is a worthwhile pursuit, as the end result is the creation of my own reality. To my detractors I say: if this is a dream world, then let me never wake.

Watching the two of them sleep, illuminated by the otherworldly light from the Tiffany window, it really did seem as though I'd stepped into a dreamland. Gently I closed the door, ensuring I didn't startle them.

Let the dreamers dream.

AUTHOR'S NOTE AND SELECT
BIBLIOGRAPHY

On October 16, 2016 I took a walk with my beloved dog around our neighborhood in Manhattan. I had just read an article about the famous French courtesan Cora Pearl and I was contemplating her life story as we walked along. The sun was setting over the Hudson River and the light illuminated a floral motif carved into the awning of a building. I realized all the buildings surrounding me were from the late 1800s and suddenly a question arose: *did New York ever have a courtesan during the Gilded Age to rival the Parisians?*

In my research I've come upon famous mistresses and a multitude of women who worked in the high-end brothels in the West 20s (Kate Woods' famous Hotel de Wood was located on West 25th Street and her even more opulent House of All Nations was on West 27th Street), but I've never been able to find a woman who was operating as a courtesan in the French tradition. Ultimately, this story came rushing in as an answer.

Students, fans and historians of the Gilded Age will note that I have taken some intentional (and undoubtedly unintentional) liberties with this story.

Ava and Declan live in my heart and imagination, but some of their friends are inspired by real people from history.

Gabriella Lyons is inspired by the famous French courtesans of the mid to late nineteenth century in general, and by two in particular: Cora Pearl (1835-1886) and Celeste Mogador (1824-1909). Technically not French, Cora Pearl was born in Plymouth, England but went on to become a famous member of the Paris demi-monde. She was renowned for her love of opulence, and lavish entertainment and quickly became a minor celebrity. An anecdote that is told about Cora concerns a dinner party she threw at her chateau in 1864. As the final course, she had herself presented on a giant silver platter wearing nothing but a few sprigs of parsley. Celeste Mogodor came from a painful and impoverished background, as so many of the courtesans did. She eventually became a dancer and soon attracted the attention of many wealthy and well-connected men (there is a rumor that the main character in Bizet's opera *Carmen* was inspired by her). Her story ends very differently than most of the other courtesans. She married a French count and went on to become a writer, publishing her memoirs as well as eight novels and a number of plays. After her husband's death, she started a charity to look after wounded soldiers, and children orphaned during the Franco-Prussian War.

Further reading:

Pearl, Cora. *The Memoirs of Cora Pearl: The English Beauty of the French Empire*. General Books LLC, Memphis. 2012. (There is another book that is supposed to be her memoirs but it is fiction: it was written by a man in the 1970s)

Griffin, Susan. *The Book of the Courtesans: A Catalogue of Their Virtues*. Broadway Books New York. 2002.

Mogador, Celeste. *Memoirs of a Courtesan in Nineteenth-Century Paris*. University of Nebraska Press. 2001.

George Montgomery Tilton is inspired by William Merritt Chase (1849-1916). He was an American artist who studied in Europe and maintained a studio at 51 West Tenth Street in New York City. Renowned for his personal flamboyance and love of eclecticism, his studio overflowed with lavish and unusual objects he collected on his travels. This was intentional: his studio became a destination for New York's elite, fashionable crowd. Consequently, American artists began to be taken as seriously as their French counterparts. He went on to found The Chase School which would later become Parsons School of Design. William Merritt Chase's paintings can be found in most major American art museums.

Further reading:

Pisano, Ronald G. *A Leading Spirit in American Art: William Merritt Chase, 1849-1916*. Exhibition catalogue. Seattle: Henry Art Gallery, 1983

Marguerite Wallingford Légère is inspired by two women: Sissieretta Jones (1868-1933) and Aida Overton Walker (1880-1914). Sissieretta was a conservatory-trained, American soprano and said to have one of the most beautiful voices in the world. Sadly, no recordings of her voice have been found as of this writing. She performed in the White House for President Harrison, as well as for the British royal family. She toured internationally to tremendous success yet was not allowed to perform at New York's Metropolitan Opera because of her race. She founded the Black Patti Troubadours, a musical and acrobatic company made up of forty dancers, comedians and forty trained singers. It was a variety act of minstrel songs and dances, but always ended with her performance of operatic selections. The Black Patti Troubadors was one of the most popular acts on the American stage at the time. Aida Overton Walker was a chorus member of the Troubadors but went on to find great success on her own as a dancer and choreographer. She toured throughout the United States and Europe and was renowned for her dance of *Salome*.

Further reading:

Lee, Maureen D. *Sissieretta Jones: "The Greatest Singer of Her Race" 1868-1933*. The University of South Carolina Press.2012.

Further reading about New York City during the Gilded Age:

Falino, Jeannine, and Donald Albrecht. *Gilded New York: Design, Fashion, and Society*. Museum of the City of New York and The Monacelli Press. 2013.

Crain, Esther. *The Gilded Age in New York: 1879-1910*. Black Dog & Leventhal Publishers. 2016.

Gilfoyle, Timothy J. *City of Eros: New York City, Prostitution, and the Commercialization of Sex, 1790-1920*. W.W. Norton & Company. 1994.

Cockerell, Dale. *Everybody's Doin' It: Sex, Music, and Dance in New York, 1840-1917*. W.W. Norton & Company. 2019.

ACKNOWLEDGMENTS

First and foremost, I must thank Angeliki Ebbesen: my first reader and *Gilded Dreams'* fairy godmother. Thank you for your friendship, your extraordinary insight into the human condition, and your ability to tell me a scene wasn't quite working in such a way that it made me laugh until I couldn't breathe.

Thank you to Laura Livoy for your unwavering loyalty and support from the very beginning, for talking me down from the proverbial ledge on multiple occasions and always making me laugh when I needed it most. To Allison Van Etten for being my cheerleader and encouraging me to ditch the pen name. Weatherly Emans for also encouraging me to stick with my own name and for blazing the trail! Alex Gray for sending a very funny text years ago that helped inspire a pivotal aspect of this story. To all my Baldwin Girls: the close female friendships in this story are a direct result of your template! I treasure you. To Charles Heil, thank you for being such a great sounding board! And for braving tropical cocktails in diners and holing up with me in a dark pub in the dead of summer to talk character development. Thank you to Amy Carlson Dearn for your generosity and vision: you've helped me far more than you know.

Thank you to Bev Katz Rosenbaum, editrix extraordinaire, the story is so much better and stronger because of you. The magnificent Monique Conrod for copy editing and fact-checking: you've made *Gilded Dreams* sparkle and shine- and kept me from embarrassing myself in myriad ways. To the amazing Casey Harris-Parks: you distilled the story down to its essence and gave me the confidence to persevere (Gabrielle would applaud your intuition and perfect timing). Thank you to Beverly Jenkins for your wisdom, exceptional advice and many kindnesses. That I am writing this to you is proof that wishes come true! Thank you to Nancy Napier for listening and being one of my most important teachers. I know this book would not exist without you. To Raven Keyes: in your teachings about spirits, you also taught me about characters- when either start speaking, I listen. Thank you for all your incredible support and love.

To Paul Caravetta: there is a reason this book is dedicated to you. Thank you for encouraging me to write in the first place and being my champion- and for listening to endless minutiae about life in the 1890s over the past three years. To my parents, Robert and Barbara Steer: thank you for raising me in a house overflowing with books, surrounded by adults who loved to read. Thank you for your enthusiasm about this story: your open-mindedness speaks volumes about who you both are and I'm so lucky to be your daughter. Due to some scenes I may never be able to make full eye contact with you ever again, but we'll have decades of eye contact to look back on fondly. I love you both.

And finally, to Phoebe. You were with me on that first walk when all the characters came rushing in. You were the quiet heartbeat at my feet or across my lap the many hours I spent writing this book. Now that the time has come to write the acknowledgements, it seems inconceivable that you are gone. You will live in my heart forever.

THANK YOU

Thank you for reading *Gilded Dreams*! This is my first novel, and I hope you've enjoyed reading it even half as much as I enjoyed writing it. If you did, please consider leaving a review with your online retailer of choice or mentioning it to others- all word of mouth is deeply appreciated.

And I'd love to hear from you! Please visit me at www. MeganSteer.com or on Instagram at www.Instagram.com/ lurajewelry and on Twitter at www.Twitter.com/lurajewelry

ABOUT THE AUTHOR

When Megan Steer was born her father had her birth chart cast. It foresaw a career in visual art that eventually led to writing and publishing books. So far, this has all panned out. When not writing, Megan can be found carving wax and wrestling metal into form- she is a jewelry designer. She divides her time between New York City and Wayne, Pennsylvania.